# Paper or Plastic

written by

## VERA LINTON

BY VERA LINTON

THE MAGGIE BLOOM SERIES:
FULFILL A PROMISE
(Book Two)
IN FULL BLOOM
(Book Three)

Dancing On The Water's Edge

When Granny Came To Quiggley
(Chapter book for children) by V.K. Linton

*Paper or Plastic* is a work of fiction. Names, characters, places, and incidents are the product of the author's imagination or are used fictitiously. Any resemblance to actual events, locales, or persons, living or dead, is entirely coincidental.

Printed in the United States of America
First Printing, 2014

# DEDICATION

This book is dedicated to *Nyura*, my mother. She lived her life with love, hope, courage, and strength and met life's challenges with grace. Thank you for teaching me, *"If life brings you rain, learn to dance in it."* I love you always.

# THANK YOU

I am grateful to be surrounded by extraordinary people in my life. I would like to thank my husband, for his encouragement and patience. My son, who seems to believe that I can do anything. My sisters, who are my safety net. And a huge THANK YOU to Brittany who edited this book and encouraged me along the way.

All of your support has been invaluable.

# Chapter 1.

Well, it's official. I finally got that dreaded piece of mail in my mailbox from the AARP. I am now old enough to receive discounts on my bacon and eggs from Denny's, AND I can go to the movie theater for almost nothing. I know it's a cliche, but where does the time go?

My name is Maggie Bloom, and I'm a senior citizen. I turned fifty a few months ago, and suddenly my mail has disoriented me. It appears it is now essential for me to know a funeral costs almost as much as a compact car and I can receive life insurance for less than a dollar a day, WITH the bonus of NO medical exam.

My life is now complete. To add insult to injury, I am one of the oldest employees at my current job, and I'm surrounded on a daily basis by co-workers I could have birthed. They refer to me as their Market Mom.

Could it only have been one short year ago my life completely changed? My husband of twenty-five years up and died on me. He left me with a house I couldn't afford and bills I didn't know existed. Most importantly, he left me alone. Well, not entirely alone. We had two magnificent children, a son named Henry and a daughter named Isabella. Her father affectionately called her Izzy. I most often call her Bell.

Henry and Bell are technically all grown up. Henry is finishing up his Master's degree in Business at UC San Diego, and Bell is a sophomore at Chico State studying marketing, making my home an empty one.

Henry and I are very close, and we text on a daily basis. Isabella, however, is not returning my calls or my texts. Always her daddy's little girl, Bell is angry with me for selling our family home and moving into a 1,400 square foot condo with much-needed repairs. She accuses me of wanting to forget about my life with her father and moving on too soon. But that's another story.

Regretfully, I sold our home to cover outstanding bills and to pay off a line of credit Edward had taken out on the house. Finances were Edward's department and something he had always taken care of, while the children's needs rested primarily on me. Apparently, times were more desperate than they seemed. When all was said and done, the sale of our home left me a down payment on a new place to live and a trust fund to help the children finish their education.

So to summarize my year so far; I became a widow, bought a new home and moved, found my first job in twenty-three years (outside of raising a family), and qualified for AARP. I'm pretty sure I'll be 107 years old before I retire. But things could be worse, right?

Starting over has never been more difficult. Turning fifty is a big deal all on its own. My life as I knew it was over. The only choice before me was to move on.

There is only one thing I'm sure of in this world. The longer I live, the more I know nothing about life. When I was younger, I was so sure about everything. That's no longer true.

It seems the death of a loved one should at worst kill you where you stand, or at best stop the world from spinning on its axis, if for only a moment. Death leaves no visible scars, but an x-ray of your heart should find it riddled with a million tiny holes. When I look in the mirror these days, I only vaguely recognize myself. The holes have aged me. The woman's reflection is a stranger who gradually began to vanish over twenty years ago. I see qualities that disappoint me, qualities that pleasantly surprise me and conditions I am learning to embrace. The question I now ask myself is, "Who are you, Maggie Bloom?" The challenge is to begin and eventually find out.

I am five-feet-eight-inches tall, a middle-aged brunette, and currently employed as a cashier at Bay Fresh Market. My beautiful curly brown hair, which I blow dry straight, comes out of a bottle, my eyes are green, and I have a slim nose with a great sense of smell. I have a great appreciation for good food, and I am currently closer to my wedding weight now than a year ago with twelve more pounds to go.

As I awakened from my musing, I was startled to see a line three customers deep at my register, all waiting for some sign I was open for business. It was a bustling day at the market, but I was having a hard time staying focused.

"Maggie, can you hear me?" cried Mrs. McGee.

"I am so sorry, Mrs. McGee, I was lost in thought and forgot where I was."

"Well, hello, Maggie dear, and welcome back to earth."

"Hello, Mrs. McGee. How are you today?"

"I'm still vertical, Maggie. This ol' Irish girl is still breathing."

"That's a great start, Mrs. McGee. A great way to start the day. Plastic as usual?"

"You know I love those bags as liners for my wastebasket."

"Good for you. The great state of California thanks you for recycling. Have a wonderful day, Mrs. McGee, and Jacob will help you to your car today. See you next time."

"I hope so, Maggie. God willing, goodbye dear."

I checked my last customer through and decided this would be a good time for some caffeine. As I sipped my hot coffee, I fell in and out of meditation over my life.

Losing Edward was one of the hardest things I had ever survived. Since I watched him take his last breath, I drank too much and cried too often. I am confident there is little in life we can control. But I can control me. Right now, today. My thirty-something unhappy pasta pounds are slowly melting away. And a year later, I don't cry as often anymore. On bad days, I've substituted popcorn for cookie dough. Ok, I still have a little cookie dough now and then, but I'm careful to balance it with a healthy portion of protein.

Since my recent influx of senior junk mail, I exercise most days and try to treat myself to a small, new experience every payday. I am ever so grateful my condo came with a little abandoned outdoor patio-garden area. Gardening has saved me. My garden has given me a space that transcends time. It wraps three-quarters around the perimeter of my condo. I have divided my garden into three different garden rooms. The first, a sitting area located right outside the French doors of the living room. So far, my favorite place to be. The other two are far from finished and are mostly a dream on paper.

My garden is where all things in the past leave my mind as my hands' toil. The present is where the soil matters. It is part of the life force. It's a place I can shape and change at any time without judgment. A victory garden, where the words of Eleanor Roosevelt give me courage: "Where flowers bloom, so does hope." My garden reminds me hope is within my reach, a day at a time.

# Chapter 2.

Bay Fresh Market has always been my favorite place to shop. Because of the distant drive from what was once our home, I didn't buy there on a regular basis, only about two or three times a month. Their fresh local produce is the best in town. One reason is it's in the number one ranking county in California, known for growing fresh produce.

At Bay's you can find "Food TV" gourmet products, and the products Grandma used to use. Now that I live just around the corner, it seemed like a logical place to begin looking for work.

I had been a stay-at-home mom and chief activity director for over twenty years. During that period I took part in many local charity functions, organized fundraisers at my daughter's school, and worked hard to be the trophy wife a good executive husband needed. I knew I could do at least three things: I made great baked goods, could make change for a twenty, and I could charm at least a hundred bucks out of anyone for a worthy cause.

In college, I had been a journalism major but long since given up the dream of becoming Diane Sawyer. I needed to start somewhere, and somewhere familiar seemed easier until I figured out the next chapter of my life. So Bay Fresh Market it was.

Going on a job interview is the most terrifying, sucky (as my young co-workers would say) thing imaginable for someone with a concise resume. But I soon realized I was up against eighteen-year-old youngsters with no resumes. How hard could it be to get a job at a market? They could use a bit of maturity around Bay Fresh anyway. I assumed I wouldn't be considered for a managerial position (they wear the blue shirts) with a lacking resume. Although I believed my skill sets were sufficient for management, I was determined to do my best, as usual, wherever I started.

I walked into Bay's on a late summer day, wearing a summer skirt, cotton blouse, medium heeled sandals, and a smile that was sure to get me, at the very least, an interview. Our hottest days in the valley were behind us now, but if you still wanted to make a fresh impression, you had to do it in the morning. I carried two copies of my resume and a contact list tucked into a manila folder and approached the counter of the courtesy booth. Before me sat a thin young lady straddling a bar stool, staring at a computer screen.

"Excuse me," I said. "I don't have an appointment, but I was wondering if I could drop off a resume and possibly fill out an application for employment? Do you know if you are currently hiring?"

"Yeah, hold on let me get a manager for you. He's right over there. Manager to the courtesy booth, please," her young voice boomed across the P.A. system, interrupting the lyrics of someone I recognized from the radio, but whose name I couldn't place. "It'll be just a minute," she concluded setting her eyes back onto the computer screen.

My palms began to sweat a tiny bit, and my heart pounded a split second faster. I told myself how great I was and if I was just "myself" I was sure to get a job. After all, I would hire me.

I saw a clean looking gentleman, about twelve years my senior and about six feet tall, making his way over to me. As he approached, he asked if he could help me.

"Yes, I hope so. My name is Margaret Bloom, and I was wondering if you are accepting applications for hire," I said extending my hand.

He reached over and shook my hand and introduced himself as

George Smith, the General Manager. For some odd reason, that made me smile inside. It happened when I got nervous; the smallest things become comical to me.

He told me they were accepting applications for various positions. He walked himself around to the entrance of the courtesy booth and searched under the counter for an application for me to complete. He asked me if there was a particular position I was interested in (inside smile again) to which I responded: "I'm not exactly sure."

George then led me to the café sitting area next to the bakery. He asked me to complete the application. When I finished, I sat in my seat and stole glances around the store, wondering if I could do the job.

George came back fifteen minutes later and looked over my resume and application. He sat down in the seat across from me and didn't seem to be in a hurry to send me away, so I took that as a good sign. George offered me a brief history of Bay Fresh Market and its standards. He scanned my resume again and asked me a few questions.

"I haven't had many official jobs in the past few years," I found myself explaining. "I discovered early on that raising two little ones is a full-time job."

"That it is," George laughed, then his expression grew serious. "Honestly, Maggie, you have had excellent experience working with people, official jobs or not. After talking with you today, I think you would thrive as a checker. We need someone with your people skills."

My racing pulse suddenly relaxed, and I felt happy I had met George. The next step for me was to come back on Friday morning at nine and meet with Dean Phillips, the Store Manager. Just like that, I got myself a second interview. I couldn't help but wear a happy grin on my drive home.

The grocery business is an exciting industry. I learned in my interview that the name "Bay" came from the herb from a laurel tree, not the bay where sailboats dock. We live nowhere near the water, so that made sense. In fact, we are in the Central Valley in California.

The Central Valley is an easy driving distance to the Sierra mountains, the Central Coast, and two large metropolitan cities. We are only hours from some of the most beautiful places in the world and only in our summers do I wish I were anywhere else but here.

The intense heat we experience is essential, given we are the largest producers of food in our nation. And our visitors from the east remind us at least we have a "dry" heat. One hundred and eight degrees was just too freaking hot, wet or dry.

I also learned the grocery industry has one of the highest divorce rates in any industry. Long work hours that lead to affairs perhaps? The prospect of working for Bay's was becoming more interesting.

Friday morning came quickly, and I arrived at Bay Fresh Market at eight-forty-five. I was a bit excited and a bit early. I sat in my car telling myself how much potential I had while I executed the "fresh breath" test on the palm of my hand at least three times.

At eight-fifty-five I entered the market, adrenalin pumping on all cylinders. I walked straight to the courtesy booth and announced my arrival to a handsome man in a blue shirt who stood behind the counter.

"Oh, hello, Margaret. I'm Dean Phillips," he said, reaching out to shake my hand. "Your interview is with me this morning." I swallowed hard. "However, I need just a few minutes, so if you wouldn't mind waiting for me in the café, I will be with you shortly?"

"Certainly. I can do that," I said removing my hand from our handshake.

OK, he looked harmless enough, I told myself. I created a brief checklist in my head: intimidating good looks, amazing blue eyes, possible future boss, and a wedding ring on his left ring finger. OK, good. Deep breath and you'll be fine.

Our interview was brief, repeating some of the same answers I gave to George in my previous interview. He commented on the familiarity of my face.

"Well, I have occasionally shopped here over the years," I offered. "I have always loved this store, and recently, I moved into the neighborhood. I do patronize the other stores in this shopping center as well."

"That might be it, but I feel like we've met somewhere before. Oh well, I'll think of it eventually. I usually do," Dean smiled.

Our interview concluded with a handshake, and Dean told me he would be in touch after speaking with George. I thanked him for his time and said I hoped to hear from him soon.

By the end of the workday, Dean called me to tell me Bay Fresh Market would like to make me an offer. He asked, "Are you available Saturday morning?"

"Yes," I replied. "I looked forward to it. As I ended the call, I set my phone on the counter very carefully. I couldn't help but hop right into my very own special victory dance and yell "Yes...Yes, Yes," with so much enthusiasm, I thought dirty old man Tucker from next door would think I was having more fun than I was.

Bay Fresh Market hired me Saturday morning. Dean offered me a decent hourly wage, and I was to report to work Monday morning at nine.

I had a restless sleep Sunday night, anticipating my first day of work come Monday morning. I kept checking the time to make sure I didn't oversleep. When I did sleep, I had one of those dreams where I was in high school, but I couldn't remember where or what my next class was. I just stood there in the middle of campus, lost and frightened.

Needless to say, I was a little sleep deprived on Monday, but it was nothing I hadn't experienced before while raising two children.

When I arrived at work, we went over policy, insurance, dress code and the like. Dean handed me a black apron. He walked me over to the front office and introduced me to Stephanie of Human Resources.

"Stephanie, this is Margaret."

"Actually, most people call me Maggie," I said to her.

"Nice to meet you, Margaret," Stephanie replied.

"Maggie will be starting today as our new cashier. Please page me and I'll come up when you're done with her. Thanks, Stephanie. Maggie, I'll see you soon, but for now you are in Stephanie's very capable hands," Dean said, smiling reassuringly at me as he left the office.

Stephanie was a no-nonsense kind of gal tightly packed into a five foot frame. She explained pay periods and house rules, W2s and other logistics pragmatically and to the point. If I had any questions I was to come and see her directly. She then paged Dean Phillips to retrieve me in a most time-efficient sort of no-fuss way. Note to self: Don't mess with Stephanie.

I was handed back to Dean who gave me the Bay Market tour and introduced me to other team members along the way. Last but not least, we headed back to Dean's office where he placed a name badge in my hand with my name "Maggie" neatly typed under the words "Bay Fresh Market." Dean also handed me a card with a magnetic strip, much like a hotel room key card, so I could clock in and out of work. The time key card had my full name typed neatly on it, Margaret Bloom. It was official. I was now a Bay Fresh Market team member and a full-time paid employee. It had been over twenty years since my last full-time paid job.

With my first day of training behind me, I walked away with a little more confidence then I had arrived. There were many codes to memorize, but I came up with a system. I unlocked the door to my Mini Cooper with great satisfaction and opened up the sunroof above me. I let out a sigh and looked at myself in the rearview mirror. I told myself I was one step closer, closer to what was uncertain.

I started up the engine and turned up the radio. With conviction in my voice, I promised Tina Turner from now on I would dance like nobody was watching.

This was a big step in my new state of independence. I could now bring home the bacon and possibly be a part of something bigger than myself. Now, I belonged somewhere forty hours a week, and I had a name badge and a time key card to prove it.

# Chapter 3.

"Manager to checkstand three, please," I called for the third time today.

Dean entered my cubicle, "What's up?"

"I'm sorry, I entered the wrong item code and need it voided."

"No problem," he replied. "You're due for a break after this customer. Come over and see me after."

I nodded and took in a deep breath, noticing the proximity one shares in a checkstand cubicle.

My break seemed to be on fast forward and was over before it started. I stopped by the front desk to have a word with Dean as instructed.

"You wanted to speak with me?"

"Hi, Maggie. I feel like you're stressing over the codes, and I don't want you to. They will automatically come to you the more you use them. When it's slow, I want you to familiarize yourself with the produce department. Notice the differences between the organic and the regular produce. The organic has a rubber band. Also, the produce sometimes changes daily so give yourself time before your shift to walk through the department. You can find the product codes on the bottom left of the display tags. I sense you learn visually, so get yourself over there while it's quiet. And Maggie?"

"Yes."

"Cut yourself some slack. It's only been a week," he concluded, winking at me.

I managed to complete my shift with only one more call to

management. I clocked out and walked back into the warehouse to retrieve my belongings from my locker. I grabbed my purse and headed out to the parking lot where I fell into step with Dean who was also on his way home.

"Long day?" he asked.

"On the contrary. I've just concluded my first week on the job, and it's flown by."

"So I won't see you tomorrow?"

"I'm afraid not. Off for the next two days."

"You're doing great, Maggie. You fit right in. I still haven't figured out where I know you from, but it'll come to me. Good night."

"Good night, Dean." He passed me, making his way to his truck. As I opened the driver's side and slid in behind the wheel, I found myself smiling not for just a job well done, but also for the compliment.

I parked my car in the garage and closed the door behind me. I let myself in through the connecting door to the laundry room and plopped my things down on top of the dryer. I turned on the lights as I made my way through the condo into my bedroom. They made me feel less alone.

After freshening up, I changed into yoga pants and a tee shirt. Walking back to the kitchen, I stopped to turn on the television for some company. I noticed being around people all day, made me feel even more alone at home.

I retrieved my phone and typed out a message to my kids: First week on the new job complete and still employed : ) xoxo Mom, and then hit send. I placed the phone on the counter hoping for a response as I made a chicken salad for dinner. My cellphone binged, and I hurried over to see who had responded.

It was Henry: Never doubted for a minute.

I smiled and continued to stare at the phone waiting for Bell to reply. After a minute, my smile faded, and I placed the phone back on the counter. Her silence was deafening. Something she picked up from her father.

I plated my salad and added fresh curls of parmesan cheese to the top. After pouring myself a tall glass of water, I added a lemon slice to it. Picking up both the water and the salad, I walked to the den to eat my dinner and watch some television. Placing the items on the coffee table, I sat on the couch and pulled up my legs sitting cross-legged. After a minute of channel surfing, I decided on HGTV. After I counseled a couple to sell their home and said a few words of thanks, I reached for my salad and dug in.

It was eleven at night as I stared up at the ceiling from my bed, wishing my days off would go quickly. Was I pathetic? Most people could hardly wait for their weekend. I wasn't sure I was most people. I wasn't sure about a lot of things.

"Gosh it's quiet," I whispered out loud.

Our anniversary was coming up. Was that the cloud I felt over me today? Sometimes, I would observe Edward as he watched television. We would sit without conversation for hours. Me in my world, Edward in his. Where did the part of our lives we shared together go?

"What?"

"Nothing."

"I can feel you staring at me."

"I'm not staring at you, Edward."

"Is there something on your mind?"

"Everything and nothing."

"Well, that narrows it down. If you don't tell me what's on your mind, I can't fix it can I?"

"No, I guess you can't."

I reached over for my phone and pushed the sleep machine app button. The sound of small waves and wind chimes filled the quiet space around me. Long after the light from my phone dissipated into darkness, the comforting sounds began to lull me to sleep. Before I surrendered, I reassured myself tomorrow brought a new opportunity to recreate my life.

# Chapter 4.

Bay Fresh Market recently celebrated its fortieth anniversary. It's founder, Thomas Warner, decided that it was time to retire and step away from the day-to-day operations of running the store. However, the problem he faced was who would take over.

As the story around the market goes, Mr. Warner had two sons, Benjamin, and Michael. His wife was deceased. Michael, I knew well enough from working together in the store. All I knew about Benjamin Warner is what my friend and co-worker Bobbie had told me. Bobbie was going on twenty-two years with Bay Fresh Market and the go-to-person when it came to vital information.

Benjamin, now forty-nine, had worked in the store as a young boy and throughout high school. He moved to Southern California for college, and he graduated with honors from the School of Engineering and Architecture. Upon graduation, he began an internship with one of the most formidable companies on the west coast. He was quickly hired at Hansen and Lynch Associates and eventually made partner. Benjamin traveled the world studying and designing beautiful buildings and complexes. His work took on the influences of traditional European architecture but with a modern approach. Ben took a short leave of absence to help Michael and his father remodel the store a few years ago before I had come aboard.

Michael Warner is Ben's younger brother by nearly ten years. Michael, from what I've heard, is Ben's opposite in almost every way. Ben resembles his father in the dark, rugged good looks and stature, whereas Michael Warner, although also attractive, has lighter features, a much smaller frame, and very little scruples.

Michael, who is now thirty-nine going on eighteen, began degrees in art, business, and engineering. After years of high tuition and uncompleted coursework, Michael finally received a degree in philanthropy. Unfortunately, his charity extended only to beautiful women in varying degrees of marriage. His latest sidekicks were mysterious gypsy types, and my guess was they were not law-abiding citizens.

I met Benjamin Warner quite by accident. I decided to come to work early for a bagel and coffee before my shift. With just five minutes to spare, I ran upstairs to use the restroom near the executive offices. I washed my hands and checked my teeth, for any lingering bits of bagel, before popping a mint into my mouth. Throwing my handbag over my shoulder, I rushed out of the restroom and bolted down the stairway. As I approached the bottom stair, I missed it entirely and found myself traveling in slow motion. My head-butted into a set of hard abs as a pair of muscular arms grabbed me keeping me from hitting the floor. Suspended in the air, almost upside down, I felt as if I were stuck halfway through a gymnastics move. That's when my mint popped out of my mouth and landed on the floor below me. At least I didn't choke on it, I thought.

It took a few seconds before my brain caught up with my reality. As I turned right side up again, I slowly lifted my chin, to see who saved me. A tall, dark, handsome stranger with a concerned look on his face peered down at me.

With only inches between us, and his hands holding me steady, the man said, "Are you alright?"

Staring back at him, I finally managed, "I think so."

"Is your neck ok? Can you move your head back and forth?"

I mimicked his question by moving my head around. "Yes, my head's fine, but I'm not so sure about the rest of me."

His smile broadened across his face, exposing straight white teeth. "Hello. I'm Ben Warner."

"Maggie Bloom and I am late to work," I replied.

He looked down at my name tag and said, "Don't worry about that Maggie. Are you sure you're alright?"

"Yes, I am. Thank you for saving my life. I wish you could do the same for my pride."

Ben laughed, "I hardly saved your life. But I'm glad I was here to help."

I smiled back and gingerly inched around him. I walked deliberately toward the warehouse, to put my handbag away. I desperately wanted to escape. I could feel the heat on my face as I scolded myself. As I hurried past the front desk, I spotted Dean in my peripheral vision.

I could hear the smile in his voice as he said, "I see you met the new boss."

I waved him away, mumbling, "Yeah, yeah, yeah..."

# Chapter 5.

The first time I met Dean's wife, Carolyn, was on my day off. Isabella was coming for a visit, so I went to the store early to do some shopping. I was picking out apples for a tart when I noticed Dean quietly talking to a beautiful woman with long auburn hair. As I came closer, I saw she had small features, milky white skin, and stunning hazel eyes.

"Look out, here comes Bloom. Be careful! She might accidentally take you out with her cart," Dean joked.

"Ha, ha, ha," I mocked, as I pulled up to the couple.

"Carolyn, this is Maggie Bloom. She's one of our checkers," he introduced me with some pride.

"Hi, Maggie," she shook my hand. "It's so nice to finally meet you. Dean has mentioned you several times. You must know when he teases, it's because he likes you."

"Well, that's comforting to know. I thought he just enjoyed tormenting me."

"Oh, no, no," she laughed. "It's his special way." I took note of how she touched him and played with the back of his hair, protectively. "He's told me how dependable you are and how hard you work," Carolyn continued. "So don't let his sarcasm fool you."

"Good to know, Carolyn. At least now, I might have a little ammunition."

"Don't believe anything she says," Dean joked. "She's just trying to make you feel better."

"Is he always like this?" I asked.

"He grows on you."

"Aah," I pulled my cart away. "It was very nice to meet you,

Carolyn. I have company coming, so I better scoot."

"Nice to meet you too. Enjoy your visit."

I was standing in line to check out when I noticed Ben coming toward me. Was I starting to sweat a little... really Bloom? Good grief, he was cute.

"Hi, Maggie.

"Hello, Ben."

"Doing a little shopping I see."

"My daughter is coming down from Chico for a visit this weekend ... grabbing a few of her favorites."

"Nice. Enjoy your visit."

"Thanks," I replied as he continued past me. Do I dare, nonchalantly, turn to watch him walk away? I slowly looked over my shoulder and snapped my head back as I noticed that he had too.

"Uh, Maggie? What's the matter? Are you having a hot flash? Aaron, help her get her groceries on the belt please," Roberta said.

"Oh yeah, sorry," I said, quickly pulling my groceries out of the cart.

"I saw you checking him out," Roberta said under her breath.

"Everyone has been checking him out, even you Bobbie," I was quick to remind her.

"Yeah, but it's fun watching you do it. Besides, I check all the good looking men out. That man, however, is fine, fine, fine..."

Why was I still blushing, I thought, as I carried my bags to the car? Ben was just a man, wasn't he?

My ploy to get Isabella home had worked. I told her if she wanted her next semester's tuition money, she would have to come home and get it in person. Peeking through the window, I saw her pull her car into a parking space next to the house. I closed the gap between the blinds so she wouldn't catch me waiting for her. Despite the tension between us, I was pleased to see her.

"Isabella," I called out to her from the front door. "Can I help you with your bag?"

"Don't bother."

I stepped toward her as she made her way closer to the front door. I put my arms around her and invited her in.

"Wow, Mom you've done a lot to this place."

"Yes, I have. I can't wait to show you my garden. Put your things in the guest room."

Just like my sweet Nonnina taught me, I had refreshments and snacks ready for my guest in the kitchen.

"Come on over and sit at the bar. I made some of your favorites."

"You didn't have to go through the trouble."

"Nonsense. Cooking for my daughter is never any trouble. You look good, Bell. You lightened your hair. I like it."

Isabella shrugged.

"Have you spoken to Henry lately? He's swamped writing papers."

"We text."

"Good, I'm glad," I encouraged.

"He's got a girlfriend."

"He does? He hasn't mentioned it. How on earth does he find the time?"

"She's a book nerd too."

"How are your classes coming? Grades?"

"Fine. Everything is fine. What is this talk you wanted to have with me?" she said abrasively.

I hesitated and then said, "Well, first of all, I don't understand why you've been so angry with me, Isabella. It's time we discussed it and cleared the air between us."

"Whatever."

"No. Not whatever. You are my daughter, and you treat me like a stranger. I love you, Isabella. We are a family. I want things to be right between us. You haven't been the same toward me since I moved."

"Exactly. Since you couldn't wait to start a new life and leave Daddy's memories behind."

"Surely, you must understand there was no possible way I could have afforded to stay in our old house. There were bills to pay, and I couldn't afford the mortgage without a job. And the power bills and upkeep of that place alone was more than I could handle." My heart willed her to look at me.

"I can't believe Daddy didn't take care of all that for you. He wasn't like that. How are you affording tuition? I don't believe you couldn't afford the house. I use to hear the two of you argue. You couldn't wait to be out of that place and away from anything that reminded you of Daddy." Isabella's fingers clenched and unclenched in and out of fists.

"No Isabella, you're wrong. I don't know what you thought we argued over. Couples argue about a lot of things, but that doesn't mean they don't love each other. Couples go through tough times together. You'll find that out someday. Having disagreements is natural." I reached out and touched her fingers. "Just because you are married to someone doesn't mean you agree with everything that person says and does."

She twitched and pulled her hand away. "You used to laugh together and dance in the kitchen. I remember those times. You used to go out on dates together. Then it stopped. What happened? Daddy loved you with all his heart, and you acted like you didn't care anymore."

"Isabella…I loved your father. I did. I can't tell you what happened between us because I'm not sure myself. Sometimes people change. But you must know, if I could have, I would have stayed in our home. That is where I brought you and Henry home from the hospital when you were born. But you and Henry were on your own when your father died. Have you ever thought for one second what it was like for me sitting in that big house all by myself? Memories don't keep you warm at night, and things aren't always as they seem."

Isabella sat quietly for a few minutes. I saw tears form in her eyes and roll down her face. Walking around the counter, I sat next to her at the breakfast bar. I reached up to touch her hair, and I saw her tense.

"Can I go for a walk now?" she asked.

I placed my hand on my lap and bit my lip. "Sure."

After Isabella came back from her walk, I had dinner ready.

"Mom, I decided not to stay. I need to get back."

"Do you want to talk about this some more? I made dinner; I thought we could at least share a meal together. You can leave in the morning if you want to."

"No, Mom, please. I need to get back. Can I have my check for school?"

"Isabella, you can't run away from your problems. Let's talk about this," I pleaded.

"I understand that you couldn't afford to stay in the house," she waved her hand around my living room. "But look around. Where are all of our things, our memories? You hardly have anything around here to remind you of Dad except a couple of photos."

"Don't judge me, Bell." Tears filled my eyes. "People grieve in different ways. Do you want to see his clothes in my dresser drawers? Would it help you to know I sleep in his tee shirt every night? Is that what you want to hear? I have a garage full of boxes I can't seem to bring myself to look through. I've had to make new friends because I'm not a couple anymore. My life as it was doesn't exist anymore."

I felt my voice raise an octave against my will. She needed to understand. "I have had no choice but to make a new life. I hope this is something you will never have to learn first hand. Our time is short on this earth – don't take too long to forgive me, Bell."

Isabella was stunned. She stood still and just stared at the floor. I walked into the bedroom and picked up the check I had written to her and brought it back with me into the living room. I held it out to her. She slowly removed it from my fingertips.

"I'll always love you, Isabella, no matter what. Drive back carefully and please text me when you get home."

She retrieved her small bag, and I met her at the front door.

"Please stay, Bell," my words softly called my daughter back to me.

"Next time," was all she could manage before leaving me standing at the front door.

# Chapter 6

It was hard to believe this was my second holiday season with Bay Fresh Market. As I watched a vibrant winter sunrise on the horizon, I found myself anticipating the week ahead. I sipped hot coffee while I stared out the French doors to the patio garden. Thanksgiving week brought anxious shoppers who gathered food like chipmunks storing up for the winter.

Steam rose from the adjoining fence separating me and my nosey neighbor, Mrs. Fisk. I always loved mornings like this. Stepping out onto my patio, I closed my eyes against the morning sun. I soaked up the sun's rays on my face as the colors beneath my eyelids went from bright red to orange and then to a warm yellow hue.

We had a good rainstorm yesterday that lasted through the night. The sky was clear now, the ground no longer thirsty and the birds were out to celebrate early this morning. I opened my eyes to take in the private concert from a small brown bird, who sat on the edge of the fence, joyfully rehearsing for me.

"Bravo, little bird," I assured him. "She would be crazy not to fall for you after that sonata." I shrugged my shoulders up and down attempting to loosen my tense neck. Over the past seasons, I have learned being a grocery checker isn't as easy as it looks, at least not for a fifty-something-year-old. At the end of my day, my back aches, my hips are sore, and I can hardly wait to come home and plop down into my favorite chair.

It occurred to me at one point being a grocery checker is much like being a rock star. The call of my name thrills me, as it is announced over the intercom, "Maggie, customer service please, Maggie." That's when the curtain rises and the lights will flair. They will illuminate my way from the paper goods section on aisle thirteen to checkstand number five. As I begin my ascension, the crowd of eager shoppers, my groupies, look my way with awe and anticipation. They wonder at which checkstand I will be performing so they can quickly make their way to the front of my line.

Out of the corner of my eye, I see a courtesy clerk approach the next customer in line. He points in my direction. Smiling, I take my position behind the counter, flicking on my light switch to illuminate checkstand five. The courtesy clerk, who now stands next to me, awaits my signal. He stands ready to receive and bag the groceries I will send his way. It's show time. I turn to him and say, "Let's do this; rock 'n roll!" Let's face it, sometimes you need a little bit of an imagination to get through your day.

I laughed at myself as I rinsed my coffee cup and placed it in the dishwasher, making a mental note of the time. I had approximately ten minutes to brush my teeth, pull on my shoes, and point the Mini toward Bay Fresh Market. Traffic was light and I made it to work with five minutes to spare.

The market's exterior has a beautiful appeal as you approach its front doors. The main body of the building is painted a muted Kelly green with dark weathered brown trim, almost black. Large tile mosaics on either side of the store's entrances greet you with a modern graphic of a giant, happy sunflower on one side and an abundance of fruit and vegetables on the other. The large front panes are etched with bay laurel leaves that run along the bottom of the windows. The large sign that welcomes you to Bay Fresh Market sits high on the roof line. The sign exhibits another bay laurel leaf, accenting the word *Bay*.

Garden pots line the pillars along the front of the store with seasonal blooms spilling out of the tops of each one. I took note of the recently potted red Cyclamen and Ornamental Kale which strategically hid the dwindling blooms of the geraniums and roses on the verge of dormancy.

The interior of the market welcomes you with walls painted in nature's colors of greens, gray-blues and chocolate browns. The ceiling is a midnight blue that mysteriously suspends lighting far below it, creating a feeling of infinite space above you. The floors are polished concrete. Live plants, trees, and umbrellas divide the different areas throughout the store. In some sections, false ceilings are used to create more intimate spaces. Two inch wide maple wood strips, constructed into fourteen inch squares, hang like patio lattices suspended above the dining area and service deli. I thought to myself how beautifully designed it was.

My favorite part of walking into the west entrance of the market is the way my senses are struck by the exquisite scent of baked chocolaty goods and freshly baked breads. If you entered the store through the east entrance, you were welcomed by the soups of the day and crispy roasted chickens spinning inside the rotisserie.

Today, the smell of fresh coffee seduced me into one more cup, as I made my way through the store toward the time clock. I made my ritual salutations and waved to the butchers through the glass windows. I couldn't help but feel melancholy today. Thanksgiving was only days away, and as usual, I missed my daughter. Isabella only spoke to me when she had to. I had high hopes she would spend Thanksgiving with me this year. As it turned out, Henry wasn't coming home this

Thanksgiving either. He was up to his elbows in writing papers for finals. I thought for the hundredth time that living alone was a daily adjustment. I shook my head to empty my sad thoughts and re-focused on the moment. My shift was eight-to-five today, and it promised to be a busy one.

"Morning, Dean, where am I today?" I asked.

"Hey, Maggie, let me see here," he replied, looking at the day's schedule. "You're on lucky number seven," his lips formed a smile, but I noticed he still hadn't looked up at me.

"Thanks. Are you ok this morning?"

"Yeah. Busy."

Hmmm, I thought and shrugged my shoulders as I walked to my checkstand.

"Good morning, everyone. Let's kick some booty today," I said to no one in particular as I made my way down to lucky number seven. I keyed in my code and removed my CLOSED sign at the end of the register. It was Thanksgiving week, and I was now open for business.

Our in-store phone system lines are designated by colors and hold four lines. For example, you can speak with someone anywhere in the store on the red line, green line, orange line, or yellow line. My closest friend at the store and the one closest to my age is Roberta. We call her Bobbie. Sometimes I call her Boobie because she has a great set and doesn't mind showing the girls off.

I removed the phone from its cradle and called across the checkstands, "Bobbie, red line, please."

Bobbie was two registers down from me today. Accused of having too much fun when we shared registers back to back, she picked up her phone.

"So, did you do anything I wouldn't do last night?"

"Being you would do just about anything, doesn't leave me with much to choose from," I smirked.

"It doesn't sound like you've had your coffee yet, beautiful."

"You know I love you. Has Martha been in this morning?" I asked.

"I swear, if her boobs get any larger she's likely to float away."

"You're so bad," I laughed into the receiver. "Honestly, I'm a little worried about her. She hasn't been in for three days, and the last time we spoke there was a lot of drama," I explained.

"Darlin', she's nothing but drama," Bobbie chuckled. "Hey, don't look now, but here they come."

"Play nice. Let me know if you see her, OK?"

"Gottcha. Bye," she quickly ended our call.

I wasn't open for more than ten minutes when they began to swarm like bees to every available register. Customers with carts filled to the brim; canned items, frozen items, breakfast items, and for-the-day-after items. Shopping carts filled with ingredients for desserts, stuffing, you must have soda and don't forget the liquor. Some came with turkeys and others with prime rib. It was a food fest in carts a mile long, all connected like a freight train.

Business was good during the holidays, but of course, that meant customers. Lots and lots of customers. From all walks of life. Some were our favorites and some we wished upon other checkers. They came in various shapes, sizes, and ages. But on busy days like today, all you hoped for were smooth transactions because those still waiting in line would turn on you. Rumored to eat their young if the wait was too long, I hoped it was only a rumor.

If today were a movie, this would be the part when the camera would move in tight on the protagonist; that would be me. That spooky music would be playing in the background like in a horror movie. The kind you hear just before psycho slashes through the shower curtain at Jamie Lee Curtis' mom--eeek, eeek, eeek, eeek! Customers are now five deep in my lane, and my current customer was at about $350 when she realized she had forgotten something. Before I could tell her I would send a courtesy clerk after the item, she walked away. And not at a very fast pace because like most of our customers, she's a senior woman.

I scanned her last item. She wasn't back yet. I could sense the crowd starting to get ugly. Ever notice how people are always in a hurry to go nowhere? They stamp and snort and can't wait a minute longer just to get home and do nothing.

Calmly, I stated to the maddening crowd, "I'm sorry, it'll be just a minute. She forgot something. I'm sure she'll be right back."

The extended wait spurred those in line to look at each other. They mumbled under their breath. I turned around to find the kind old lady walking back at a snail's pace, apologizing for the delay.

"Oh, and by the way, I have coupons," she said. "Hold on a second, and I'll get them out of my handbag. I think they're right here in my checkbook. Can I write a check and make it over the amount by $50?" she rambled. "The grandkids are coming for the holidays. Oh, and I'll need fives and ones. It looks like a lot of money. Thank you, Honey, I'll get my wallet out now."

Eeek, eeek, eeek, eeek! This is when you tell yourself not to make eye contact with the people waiting in line. They will eat you alive.

Every clerk had their favorite customers. My favorites were Elizabeth and Joe. Elizabeth and Joe were sweethearts for forty-five years. They know what the other is thinking and what they're about to say. They even help each other finish a sentence when the other is stuck.

Elizabeth had been going through severe health issues in the past year. She had cancer removed from her left breast and the lymph nodes from under her arm. If that wasn't enough, during the process, she incurred a damaged blood vessel somewhere in her arm. She wore a tight elastic sleeve, because of the painful swelling. Her local doctors couldn't find the source of the problem and referred her to U.C. Berkeley.

I spotted Elizabeth and Joe walking through the west entrance and waved. They waved back with a smile. I was due for a break, so after Dean gave me the go ahead, I put up my CLOSED sign and walked toward my friends.

"My two favorite people in the whole world," I said as I reached over and gave them both a hug.

"Hello, Maggie. Are you on break?" Elizabeth asked.

"I am."

"Joe get three combos. Maggie and I are going to sit down for a chat."

"Yes, ma'am!" Joe replied.

"Make that two combos, Joe. I've got a yogurt waiting for me," I explained.

"Nonsense child, you need a raisin snail. I can tell. Now get over here and sit down next to me." I've learned not to argue with Elizabeth.

"What's up, Elizabeth? How are you doing?"

"Damn these docs. How can none of them know what's wrong with me? Joe made me an appointment with a specialist in the Bay Area. I told him I was fine, but you know how men are. We leave tomorrow morning, so I told my boyfriend we should make a weekend of it. I haven't been to the city in a long time."

"Boyfriend?…does Joe know about him?" I grinned.

"We've been dating for forty-five years, so he should know about him."

"Elizabeth, you're my hero. I hope I grow up to be more like you someday."

"Honey, a man is waiting for you. I know it. You have much too big of a heart to keep it all to yourself. You just haven't met him yet...or have you?" she asked, peering at me with a twinkle in her eye.

"If I have, I sure don't know about it. I don't need a man anyway; I have my kids."

"Hogwash! Your kids are fine and making their own lives." Elizabeth waved her hand at me. "That's why we give birth to them after all. We try to raise productive citizens and give them wings. We embrace them, but try not to hold on too tightly. Then with a kiss on the forehead, we hope we haven't screwed them up too much before we open up our arms and let them fly. Now it's your turn, Honey. Make your own happy. You've been alone long enough, haven't you?"

"Elizabeth, you shock me and make me laugh all at the same time." I smiled at her and tucked her words away for later thought.

"Hey, here comes a cutie with three combos," Elizabeth said. "Shall we ask him to join us?" We laughed and helped Joe with the combos and quickly settled in for a ten-minute visit.

Since I've worked in this market, people never ceased to amaze me. There are those who will go out of their way to make your day miserable and those, like Elizabeth and Joe, who will embrace a stranger and make them a friend.

Later, when Joe and Elizabeth checked out through my line, I made Joe promise to update me, and I wished Elizabeth luck in the city.

"Maggie, green line," Bobbie called.

"Yeeeesss."

"Miss Martha just walked down aisle seven for her daily chocolate fix. Over and out."

At least I now knew she was alive. The girl was always in an impossible situation. Martha was a lovely woman with absolutely no clue of who she was and what she needed. The first time I met Martha, she was a tall, thin, red-head, tiny-breasted woman wearing a very short skirt. Cute, I thought, with the saddest brown eyes I had ever seen. Like a lost puppy. She's the kind of person who had you rescuing her when you knew you shouldn't.

She met a man while waitressing at a breakfast house. A month later, she was married to her third husband. Martha was now blond with huge breasts. Her clothes, still worn tight and short, accentuated her new breasts that were more prominent than I could imagine humanly possible.

I noticed Martha was not herself. Something was wrong. When I had a reprieve from customers, I put up my CLOSED sign and walked over to see her on aisle seven.

"Hey, Martha," I said.

"Hi, Maggie," she replied without looking up at me.

"How's it going today?"

"OK…you?" Her head remained down.

"Fine. Are you OK?"

She slowly looked up at me with those "help me" eyes. Oh no, here we go. Martha was not wearing makeup, which was highly unusual. Her eyes were puffy from either crying or lack of sleep, or both.

"Martha, what's going on with you?" I demanded to know.

"I've been sick, that's all. Flu I think. I'm better today though,"

Martha explained.

I looked at her curiously. I didn't believe her. Dean called my name over the sound system.

"Ok. Take care of yourself," I offered. "I have to get back to work."

Bobbie was right. Martha was all about drama. As I hurried back, I found Ben Warner waiting in line.

"Hello, Ben, sorry to keep you waiting," I apologized.

"Hi Maggie, not at all. Just thirsty," he responded as he handed me a cold water bottle. "How are you surviving our holiday shoppers today?"

"A girl's gotta do what a girl has to do," I smiled.

"I've noticed all the extra care you seem to take with our customers, especially our seniors. It hasn't gone unnoticed, and I want you to know we appreciate you."

"Thank you, but I'm just doing my job," I felt my face flush at his compliment.

"It's more than that. I just wanted you to know I've noticed. See you later, Maggie," he said.

I quickly went over our conversation in my mind just to be sure I responded in English. The man made me nervous. Not just because he's the boss, but because he was…beautiful. I'm confident his brown eyes shot lasers because if you stared at them too long, they cut right through you. His hair was dark with a bit of a natural wave and a dusting of gray near his sideburns.

I turned around to look at Bobbie over my shoulder. She shook her left hand signifying "hot." I rolled my eyes, and we both tried to contain our laughter. I continued to smile long after Ben walked away.

# Chapter 7.

Dean Phillips and I began to forge a working friendship almost immediately after I started work at Bay's. Carolyn and I often chatted whenever she came into the store to shop. We both shared an interest in gardening. She was in the process of taking classes toward becoming a Master Gardener.

On one of Carolyn's more recent trips to the market, she asked me a curious question. She wanted to know how I managed the first year after my husband's death. Carolyn called me brave. I wasn't so sure about that.

It came as a horrifying shock when I discovered that not long after our conversation, Carolyn became ill. Diagnosed with uterine cancer, she died three months later. Her passing shook the market. The outpouring of affection toward Dean, from staff and customers, was heartwarming. Dean had been in the grocery business for many years and knew quite a few people in the community.

It was through Carolyn's sad passing; I realized I had developed close bonds with my co-workers. Most of the young employees came and went with the change of their college class schedules. But the rest of the established team members stuck around and became friends.

Occasionally, we met for drinks after work. We became a platoon of soldiers, and when one of us was down, the rest came to the aid.

The service deli team members prepared trays of food for Dean's family and friends, many of whom traveled in from other states and stayed at his home. Other departments pitched in cash for any other incidents he might need. The store owners, Thomas, Ben, and Michael respectfully represented the market at the private services for Carolyn

Phillips.

I sent a card of condolence along with others from the store. Instead of flowers, monetary gifts, in Carolyn's name, went to a foundation for cancer research.

Dean took nearly two months off of work during the latter part of Carolyn's life and subsequently following her death. He came into the store on brief occasions to touch base, answer questions, or pick up a few grocery items. It was on one of these occasions I had a chance to speak to him briefly. I was at my locker in the warehouse when he unexpectedly came through the double doors.

"Hey!" I said, surprised.

"Hey, Maggie," there was little of the jovial Dean, I remembered, in his voice.

"You're probably tired of answering this question, but how are you doing?"

"Getting ready to come back to work."

"It helps to stay busy," I knew this all too well. "Friends and family still coming by?"

"Not as much."

"It'll get quiet soon. Too quiet. There's no remedy, you know. It takes time."

"You've been there - done that?"

"Yes, I have," I began to move away, giving him space. "Take care, Dean. It'll be great having you back."

"Thanks."

I left the warehouse to clock back into work, remembering it wasn't too long ago, I had walked in his shoes. My heart ached for him.

About a week later, I had finished my yoga routine and went into the kitchen for a glass of cold water. As my body cooled down, I decided a hot chai latte would be perfect to drink out on the patio. It was a recipe I saw Bobby Flay make on the cooking channel once and became hooked.

I brought water to a boil and decided on English Breakfast tea. Opening the cupboard, I reached inside for my grandmother's teapot.

My Nonna spent endless hours with me in her garden, teaching me all about growing flowers. Each rose bush had its personality, and every variety in her garden had its own needs. We would end each lesson with hot tea that we sipped in the garden. Her particular teapot, painted in pink roses, had a handle shaped like a branch from a rose bush. A small pink rosebud topped the lid. I thought of Nonna every time I used it. I was in the garden with her every time I made tea.

I poured almond milk into a pan and brought it to a boil. Then, I whisked it into a frothy foam. I added a teaspoon of orange honey into a tall glass mug and poured the hot tea over it. After stirring it, I added the warm milk and topped it off with the frothy foam. I began to shake freshly ground cinnamon onto the top of the foam when the doorbell rang. The sound transported me back to my kitchen from somewhere in my Nonna's garden.

The time on my microwave flashed seven-thirty. I wasn't expecting anyone. Curious, I looked out of the peephole, I was shocked to see Dean standing at my door. Wearing a puzzled look on my face, a midriff support tank top, and yoga pants, I unlocked the front door.

"Hi. What are you doing here?" I asked Dean.

"I'm sorry I didn't call first," he apologized. "I was out driving around and somehow ended up at your front door."

"That's ok," I hastened to reassure him. "I'm just surprised.

Come on in."

"I'm not interrupting anything, am I? No gentleman caller?" he teased.

"I'm afraid you just missed him. My yoga instructor," I led him inside. "Are you ok, Dean? Come in, sit down. I was making a tea latte. Would you care for one?" I offered.

"Don't you ever have a nice cold Coke once in a while?"

"Never. You look awful by the way," I walked into the kitchen to retrieve my tea latte. "Can I get you anything else? Whiskey?"

"You don't have whiskey...do you? I figured you for a Limoncello kind of gal or Crème de Cocoa," he smiled, teasing me.

"How do you know that? See, that bugs me that you would know that."

Dean chuckled low to himself as he sat down on one of the barstools that faced into the kitchen. Dean and I have a strange relationship. We knew things about one another, yet we didn't know each other at all.

"Nice place you have here, Bloom. It's a lot like I expected," Dean's head turned as he surveyed my little home. "Contemporary furniture with the occasional sentimental antique piece. The Asian accents are a bit of a surprise. And of course botanical prints for the love of gardening," he observed.

"Ah, but you have yet to see the piece de resistance!"

"What?"

I enthusiastically walked over to the French doors and threw them open to the garden patio. I leaned over and flipped on the lights that illuminated my garden. Hundreds of twinkling lights lit up the archway and garden shrubs. Dragonflies came to life and danced across the roof line. Simultaneously, the big red and gold ceramic fish fountain spilled water from its gaping mouth into a large round bowl beneath it. I turned on my toes to face Dean with a big smile on my face. "Isn't it lovely?" I said, proudly.

He tilted his head, looking at me and smiling like he remembered something sweet.

"It's my favorite part of my home," I affirmed.

Dean walked through the French doors out onto the patio to have a closer look.

"I'm working on a succulent living wall on the north side of the garden. That's going to take me awhile," I said to us both.

Dean sat in one of the two chairs at the bistro table near the door and looked up at me. It was then I realized how exhausted he looked and wondered again why he was here.

Dean reached up and grabbed my waistline with both hands and pulled me closer to him. He laid his forehead against my exposed stomach and sighed heavily.

I didn't know what to think. My mind raced. I was sure if I spoke, I would babble. There was something vulnerable happening. As I began to breathe again, I kept my arms bent at the elbow wondering where my hands should go. The moment felt sad and sweet, but at the same time very sensual. What was I feeling, I could hardly know? I reminded myself he was only a friend as I reached for the top of his head and lightly stroked his straight blond hair. Gently, I laid my left palm against his back. He was here for comfort. He needed someone who knew.

Dean quietly began to explain. "I can't sleep. I try to sleep in our bed, in our house, but I just can't sleep. I walk around the house late at night, and sometimes I fall asleep on the couch watching T.V. or upright in my chair…the one she picked out. She's everywhere in that house, Maggie." His voice broke. "In our house, she's everywhere, and yet she's nowhere.

Family and friends come and go and although they mean well… sometimes it feels smothering. Maggie, I'm so tired," I could barely hear him speak.

My heartfelt his sadness and his despair. I understood what he was feeling. "Dean…there isn't anything anyone can say to make this better. It is something we survive. You get through it, not over it. I promise you one day it will hurt less. You will come to accept and live with it," I slid my hands down to meet his and pulled him up to his feet.

"She said you would understand… Carolyn. She said I should talk to you."

"Come on. You can sleep here tonight. You can take a nice hot shower if you'd like, and I'll make you something warm to drink."

I led him to the bathroom and handed him a clean white towel. Slipping out of my condo, I walked across the way to Mrs. Brewers. When she answered my knock, I asked her if I could borrow some brandy. I told her I would gladly buy her a replacement, next time I was at work.

I returned home with the drink, stopping just inside the door to hear if the shower was still running. It was, so I proceeded toward the kitchen to make Dean a hot toddy, to guarantee a good night's rest.

I brought enough hot water to a boil to make three-quarters of a cup. I added one tablespoon of raw honey, two shots of brandy, and a slice of lemon. Edward loved to have a hot toddy every now and then before bed. Edward, I sighed, remembering.

I made my way toward the guest bathroom to retrieve an unopened toothbrush. In the guest bedroom, I opened the dresser drawer and pulled out a clean tee shirt my husband used to wear. I placed the items on my bed in the master bedroom. I set the toddy on a coaster next to the bed.

As I turned to leave the room, Dean opened the bathroom door and stepped out wearing only his boxer briefs.

"Ahh, uhh, I, uh, I made you a hot toddy. I didn't mean to walk in on...well; you should drink that," I motioned toward the drink and walked out of the room. I hurried back into the kitchen and stood in front of the sink. I reminded myself a friend needed me and although this turned out to be a bizarre night, I needed to get a grip.

Dean followed me into the kitchen carrying the hot drink. "Is it ok that I'm here?" he asked.

I turned around to face him and found he was wearing Edward's tee shirt. Although I knew I had just left the shirt on the bed for him, it took me back to see Edward's shirt come to life on Dean's body.

"Yes, of course it is."

The dark circles under his eyes were evident in the kitchen light. His wet, blond, messed-up-Gordon-Ramsey hair endeared him to me. He drank down the Toddy, grimaced, handed me the empty glass and disappeared toward my bedroom. I stood in the middle of the kitchen for a moment and then checked the time on the microwave. It was after nine.

I decided to get my things out of my room so that I could stay in the guest room for the night. I entered the room to turn down the bed and saw Dean brushing his teeth in the bathroom through the open doorway. Quickly, I gathered my things and turned to leave again. Dean's hand reached for me just as I passed the bathroom.

"Please...is it too much to ask of you to stay with me?" he said.

"No...it's not too much," I answered after a pause. If that was what he needed, I thought.

I took my things into the bathroom and closed the door behind me. I stood still looking at myself in the mirror before I turned on the water to warm. Slowly, I washed my face and brushed my teeth and changed into my comfy dog print pajama bottoms and my white cotton camisole. The camisole had a built-in bra, and tonight I was glad of the extra support. After running a brush through my hair, I took a deep breath and opened the door to my bedroom. I found Dean sitting at the edge of my bed with his head in his hands.

"I sleep on the right side of the bed," I announced.

"Looks like we were about the same size," Dean said, looking down at the shirt he wore.

"Sometimes I wear it when I'm missing him," I offered. "Would you like the television on?"

"No, thanks."

We climbed into bed and slipped under the covers. I reached behind me and turned off the lamp on my bedside table. I had just settled into a comfortable position on my back when I felt Dean's arm slip around my waist. He pulled me closer to him. I held my breath for a minute as he left his arm laying across my stomach. Then he let out a slow, exhausted sigh as he slowly fell off to sleep.

As I listened to his slow, even breathing, I thought about how long it had been since I shared my bed with anyone. I wondered if I ever would again. As much as I would never have expected to see Dean, of all people at my doorstep, something about this scenario felt familiar and comforting. Willing myself not to move and wake him, the tense muscles in my body soon gave way to the hypnotic breathing resonating next to me. Slowly and rhythmically, I soon found myself drifting off to sleep.

I awoke just as the morning light crept through my bedroom window. From his rhythmic breathing, I knew Dean was still asleep. Carefully, I turned to look at him and discovered his back was toward me. He exhaled deeply, and I was glad he had been able to sleep. Turning to check the time, I was thrown into a mild panic seeing it was eight-thirteen.

Darn, I'll be late for work, I thought until I realized it was Thursday, and I was scheduled off. I breathed a sigh of relief and slowly lifted the covers and slipped out of bed.

I crept out of my room, slipping my robe off the back of the door while closing it behind me. I walked into the kitchen and shook my head in disbelief. Was my boss really asleep in my bed in the other room... really?

I picked up my cell phone and texted Isabella, just like I did every morning.

Good morning Bell, hope you have a great day. Thinking of you always : ) Love you - Mom.

Maybe today, she'll text me back, I thought. I blinked back the tears that pushed at my eyes as I refused to give up hope. A mother never gives up.

Vacantly, I stared out my kitchen window toward the side garden for a minute and then decided to make coffee.

"Good morning," a groggy voice croaked from behind me. I turned to see Dean standing in the doorway of my kitchen.

"Good morning. Did I wake you?" I replied.

"No, no, not at all. I'm in the grocery business; I'm usually up by four-thirty. What time is it anyway?"

"Around eight-thirty. Do you drink coffee?"

"Yes, please, one cup. Eight-thirty? I guess I slept in this morning." He shook his head and scratched his temple. "Better yet, I guess I slept. Did you drug that toddy, Bloom?"

"It was the magic spell I cast into it."

He smiled. He hesitated for a moment. "Was this too weird for you last night?"

"Very weird, but it's ok," I offered with a shrug. Yeah, it was weird. I couldn't deny that.

"Well, first of all, thank you for opening the door last night," he chuckled. "I was driving around aimlessly and remembered the time I dropped you off in front of the complex. When your car was at the dealership," he replied to my puzzled look. "So, I parked my car on the street and looked you up on the phone listing outside the gate. I know it was bold of me to drop in as I did. But thanks," Dean shrugged. "I guess I needed to be with someone who didn't have to take my temperature every half hour."

I waved away any explanation because it wasn't necessary. I honestly understood but curiously asked, "How did you get through the gate?"

"The pedestrian gate was unlocked."

"Hmm. Do you eat breakfast?"

"Yeah...yes, I eat breakfast. Sometimes anyway."

"Good," I clapped my hands together once. "You look like you could use some breakfast and lucky for you, I love to cook. The coffee is almost ready, and the paper should be on the front doorstep if you care to read it. I'm going to make breakfast just after I freshen up." I turned and hurried back to my bedroom.

I wanted him to know I understood he had been to hell and back in the last couple of months. He didn't have to explain any of it to me. Last night and this morning were neutral territories, no questions asked.

I brushed my teeth and pulled a brush through my hair while giving myself the once over. I nodded. Ok, you don't look too terrible, I thought. Reappearing in the kitchen, I found Dean sitting on a barstool sipping coffee and reading the paper.

"I hope you don't mind, but I helped myself to milk. Well, almond milk. Bloom,... really?"

"It's not too bad. Real milk doesn't always like me," I explained.

A few minutes later, the olive oil I had drizzled in the skillet was hot. I chopped potatoes and sweet onions and tossed them into the skillet and listened for the sizzle. As I seasoned the mix, I heard Nonna remind me to add a bit of chopped garlic. The aroma quickly filled the kitchen. I loved to cook, especially for someone else.

After cracking open a few eggs, I whisked them briskly until they were frothy. After seasoning the eggs, I let them stand while I washed and sliced yellow squash and rinsed fresh spinach.

A smaller skillet joined the other on the stove. Adding a touch of olive oil inside, I tossed in the squash. While the squash sizzled, I dashed outside to the window box to snip some fresh dill for the eggs and cilantro for the potatoes. While out, I took a moment to inhale the crisp morning air that promised a beautiful day.

Returning to the kitchen, the heavenly aroma of an excellent breakfast attacked my senses, and my stomach growled in anticipation. I pulled two slices of cinnamon raisin bread out of the fridge and placed them in the toaster oven. I added the spinach and fresh mushrooms to the gorgeous squash along with a pat of butter. A few minutes later it was time for the eggs to join the vegetable medley. But first, I added a splash of cream and a tablespoon of fresh chopped dill.

I turned down the heat, and while the eggs cooked to perfection, I retrieved a block of cheddar cheese out of the fridge along with more butter. Happily lost in my world, it surprised me to find Dean watching me.

"Wow, you know your way around a kitchen, Bloom."

I smiled back at him, "Just wait until you taste it."

I flipped the potatoes and topped the eggs with cheddar cheese. Pulling the eggs off the heat, I turned the oven to broil and popped the pan into the oven to melt the cheese. In went diced cilantro into the potato mix, and they received a final stir. The bread was buttered and placed on two white plates.

Suddenly inspired, I rinsed fresh blueberries and sliced an orange and a banana. I filled two glass parfait bowls with the delicious fresh fruit and added a dollop of honey Greek yogurt. The orange zest sprinkled onto the yogurt added a dash of brightness. I plated the rest of the breakfast and smiled to myself in approval.

"Voila!" I announced. "Breakfast is served."

I placed the bowl of fruit and the plate of food in front of Dean and watched his eyes light up. All I needed now was to hear him moan in culinary delight and make me a very happy cook.

"Wow, you outdid yourself. I was expecting buttered toast with my coffee. Delicious coffee by the way," Dean rubbed his hands together. "I don't know where to start," he exclaimed. "It all looks and smells delicious. You're a woman of hidden talents, Bloom. Do you always eat this much?" he asked, eying me skeptically.

"I'm especially hungry this morning," I explained. "What did happened last night after I fell asleep?" I said mischievously.

I didn't expect Dean to choke on his coffee. Sputtering, he managed to say, "Don't worry, if something happened last night, you would have remembered it." We laughed, and then the kitchen fell silent as we sampled our breakfast feast.

"Bloom, you've always been a bit of a mystery to me," Dean spoke breaking the silence. "And now I see a whole different side of you. This meal is amazing."

"When I was married, we did a lot of entertaining," I replied. "In time, I became a pretty good cook. Now, with the help of my friends on the Food Channel Network, I've learned to love cooking. But it's the fresh produce...that's what does it for me."

We both chuckled, and he nodded in agreement.

"When are you thinking about coming back to work, Dean?" I inquired gingerly a few minutes later.

"I have a few issues to attend to regarding, Carolyn. I'm thinking in about a week or so."

"Well, we've certainly missed you around the store. It hasn't been the same. No one at work gives me as much grief as you do."

"I appreciate that. Maybe going back to work is what I need at this point," he stated, more to himself than to me.

"A sharp razor is what you need," I teased. "You're sporting quite the caveman look these days."

"I can always count on you to be straight with me."

We ate comfortably in silence for a while as we read and exchanged parts of the newspaper.

"So, I'm going to leave," Dean rose from his seat. "Thank you for a very delicious breakfast and for allowing me to invade your personal space last night."

"Don't mention it," I stood to join him. "Thank you for letting me cook for you."

I walked Dean to the front door. Just outside the doorway he paused and looked back into my eyes.

"Thanks," he said. I nodded.

I must have stood looking at the back of my door for at least five minutes. A whirlwind of conflicting thoughts ran through my head.

Finally, I turned and walked toward my bedroom. The bed was messy, but I decided to leave it for now. Slipping out of my clothes, I headed into the shower. As hot water ran through my hair and down my body, tears began to fill my eyes. They spilled onto my face. As I wept, the shower washed my tears away. I didn't know for whom or what I was crying. I just stood and sobbed.

# Chapter 8.

There is a process one goes through after they have lost a significant person in their lives to death. There comes a shock, disbelief of sorts, the surreal concept that you will never see that person alive again. It is an abstract truth our minds struggle to understand.

One minute you are arguing about something as insignificant as which restaurant serves the best sushi. Later that same night, you are just begging for a chance to say, "Ok, you were right. Sakamoto's does have the best sushi. Do you hear me...you were right!" For me, that day had come a few years ago.

It was early fall, and I had just run upstairs to change my clothes and freshen up for dinner. Edward had been in meetings all day, so I hadn't heard from him since morning. In our last conversation, we had agreed he would pick me up at the house around seven. Our excellent friends, Tom and Emily, were to meet us at Ono's Seafood and Sushi. I had won that argument.

I pulled myself together. I had lost track of time while planning a local charity event. Isabella had just begun her first year at Chico State, and Henry was in his senior year at UCLA. We were empty-nesters now. Our home was noticeably quiet.

Edward's adjustment proved to be the hardest. With all the traveling he had done over the years for business, he always believed he would still have time for the kids. He missed them now. Sometimes, I caught him crying over Hallmark commercials...but who doesn't really?

I came downstairs about five after seven and peered out onto the driveway. There was no sign of Edward yet. Relieved, I took a deep breath, flopped down onto my favorite chair and flipped the pages of a new food magazine I hadn't had a chance to look through. I looked up at the clock and noted it was now ten minutes after seven. I thought I would give Edward five more minutes before I texted him. I was beginning to wonder if something happened since Edward was always punctual.

I finally texted. Are you on the way? No answer.

Hello, anybody there? Still nothing.

I decided to call Tom and Emily to see if they had heard from Edward. "Hello," Tom answered.

"Tom, hi, this is Maggie. Have you heard from Edward by chance?"

"No Maggie, I haven't. What's up?"

"Well I'm not sure but Edward was supposed to pick me up at seven, and I haven't heard from him yet," I explained. "You know what a stickler he is about time." I heard a noise outside. "Oh hey, I hear a car in the driveway, I bet it's him. See you soon," I said, ending the call.

I grabbed my wrap and headed out the door. I locked the door behind me, and without looking up, I headed down the driveway. Then I realized the car on the path was not Edward's but a police car.

Two officers had gotten out of their vehicle and approached me on the sidewalk. What is going on, I thought; suddenly, my hands began to sweat.

"Can I help you, officers?" I asked.

"Evening Ma'am. I'm Officer Atkins, and this is my partner Officer Jones. Are you here by yourself tonight?"

"I'm waiting for my husband to get home. He should be here any minute. What is this all about?" My shaky voice reflected my growing inner panic.

"Do you have a neighbor or a relative nearby you can call to come over?" asked Officer Atkins.

"Tell me what this is all about, please," I responded. I was about ready to lose it.

"I'm sorry to have to tell you this, but your husband has been in a car accident," he said slowly.

"Is he alright?" I demanded.

"Well Ma'am, he's unconscious and on his way to the hospital. Is there someone you can call to go over to the hospital with you?" Officer Atkins asked.

"What do you mean? I can drive myself over," I replied firmly.

"I think we should go in and call someone," Atkins replied.

I turned abruptly on my heels and walked back toward the house. I unlocked the door and called my sister Elizabeth.

"Hi, Sweetie, I thought you were going to dinner tonight," she said.

"Lizzy, thank goodness you're home," I was close to tears. "Something has happened, and I need you to come over. There are police officers here, and they told me to call you. Can you come, please? I don't know what's going on," I tried to explain calmly.

"I'll be right there," she said.

The officers explained to me the accident had been minor, but Edward had been found unconscious, by the other driver. The driver had called 911 when Edward didn't respond. The police and ambulance responded quickly. He was at Leland General Hospital. They found Edward's wallet in his briefcase and sent the two officers to the address on his driver's license.

With car tires squealing, Elizabeth pulled up to the curb in front of my house. I rushed toward her saying, "Lizzy, thank you for coming.

I'll explain everything in the car."

The police officers had escorted us to the hospital and left us at the entrance. I rushed to the front desk and asked for directions to the ICU. The ICU took me to Edward's bedside. The nurse told me she would page the doctor and he would be in shortly, to tell me what they knew.

I found Edward on a ventilator. He looked ghostly white. The heart monitor assured me it was still beating. Suddenly, my knees buckled, and I sank into the chair at his side. I was in a state of shock.

Immediately, I took his hand in mine and began to pray. Elizabeth came into the room and stood next to me.

After some time had passed, a doctor entered the room and introduced himself as Dr. Nickles. He proceeded to explain Edward's condition. Dr. Nickles discovered Edward had an embolism in his brain. The doctor couldn't say how long it had been there or what may have caused it. However, it had apparently ruptured, causing him to lose consciousness. The accident was a consequence of the rupture.

The doctor asked me if Edward had complained of headaches or had any recent health problems. I replied that he traveled a lot and had been quite tired.

It was just like Edward not to say anything to me regarding health issues. I asked the doctor what the prognosis was for Edward. And his words pierced my soul.

"I'm sorry to have to tell you this, but we believe your husband is brain dead. He is not responding…lab results in …scans."

Nothing the doctor said to me made any sense. I realized at that moment, my life as I knew it would never be the same. Elizabeth asked him a multitude of questions. I couldn't respond from inside the tunnel in my mind. I could only see my husband's face. Eyes taped shut so that they wouldn't dry out. I was oblivious to anything said. I sat lifeless staring at him.

"Maggie…Maggie…Maggie, can you hear me?" Elizabeth shook me as she called my name.

"I'm sorry, what?" I replied. Tears streamed down my face.

"You need to call the kids, Maggie. They should see Edward as soon as possible. They are giving you time to get the children here before they take him off the ventilator," she explained.

I nodded, but I had no idea where to begin. It was close to nine and probably a good time to reach Bell and Henry. I made the calls. Strangely enough, when it comes to your children, you become a pillar of strength. I calmly explained the situation and made arrangements for travel. Henry would fly standby tonight. Bell had a friend to drive her. Elizabeth would meet them at home. I would remain at the hospital, just in case something were to change.

The next few hours Edward and I talked. Well, I guess I spoke and he, I hoped, was listening. We talked about the kids, the house, and vacations we went on together. I reminded him of the first time I saw him and how we first met. I also told him I could have been a better wife. I was sorry the last few years weren't as good as they could have been. I was sad we had stopped talking lately and had nothing much to say to one another.

"I always thought we would have time to fix it, Edward. The kids grew up so fast and then they were gone. You traveled, and I had to try to find new meaning in my days. I got fat and became lost because I thought I no longer had a purpose. But I always thought that tomorrow things would be different. We would figure it out, tomorrow. Reinvent our relationship, tomorrow. Make love again, tomorrow. I guess our time finally ran out," I explained.

Bell, I knew, would have the hardest time losing her father. She was Daddy's little girl, and Edward spoiled her. Although I had to remind Edward to tell him, he was as proud of Henry. He wanted more for Henry, and he was undeniably hard on him. Henry didn't always understand it was out of love. Yes, this would change us all.

# Chapter 9.

I decided to join a gym. Those last fifteen pounds were killing me. I couldn't seem to yoga or walk them off. The young ladies, at the market, talked about their exercise classes and workout programs. Most of them worked out at the same gym. A social thing I guessed. Apparently, Zumba was all the rage.

Thursday was my day off. I woke up with a single thought: No more excuses. An hour later, I stood in front of my neighborhood gym. Bravely, I pulled open the glass door and walked up to the counter.

A pair of adorable young ladies greeted me; their long ponytails swung cheerily. I was pretty sure I caught one of them snacking on cookies. In my head, I rolled my eyes as one of the darlings walked me over to a salesman.

The gym salesman was a buff and manly version of the darling girls behind the counter. I asked him about the advertised offer I had heard on the radio. He filled in the blanks. I also inquired about a trainer. I would get three free days of training along with my new membership. The offer was sounding good, I thought. I found myself getting a little excited about this new adventure and pulled out my checkbook.

The salesman assigned me a membership number and took my photo. It was one of those weird photos they make with a computer camera. My image came out distorted but to my benefit. If I looked like the photo in person, I wouldn't need the membership.

It would be two weeks before my membership was activated. Along with my appointment with my trainer. Two weeks! It had taken me two months to decide to sign up for the gym. Now, I had to wait two more weeks. It was possible I could change my mind again waiting for the activation.

Two weeks later, I found myself outside of the gym once again and fifteen minutes early for my appointment with my trainer. My early arrival would give me time to warm up, I thought.

Please don't let him be one of those guys, I thought. You know the one? The adorable one, fit, big muscles, and tight pants. I wondered if they had a scrawny, ugly guy who could train me. Suddenly, I felt vulnerable and a little self-conscious.

I showed my membership card to the cute receptionist and walked over to the treadmills. The treadmill looked complicated, and I wasn't sure how to start it up. Note to self: Next time, stand on the side rails before starting the treadmill. Do the same when shutting it down.

Fifteen minutes later, I made my way back to the front of the gym to meet my trainer. My trainer's name was Brock, and he looked just like his name. I guess they didn't have scrawny, ugly guys at this gym.

Brock showed me around, and I got the lay of the land. He wrote my name on a workout schedule and led me to the first piece of equipment. Today, we were covering the upper body and the lower body on my next appointment.

I listened to his presentation while I scanned the equipment I was to learn to use. I wondered how I would ever tell them apart. Most of the equipment looked like something you could launch into space.

I spotted a few much older ladies, and they seemed to be managing well on their own. I used their example as my pep talk. If they could do it, you can do it too, I told myself.

Brock strapped me into a pulling machine after he demonstrated how to use it. Once I was securely in the seat, Brock stood behind me.

His hands guided me so that I wouldn't injure myself. I had to give him props because he managed to teach me while returning the "hellos" from a menagerie of flirting women. And so it began, for the next half an hour and two additional appointments later. Brock was extremely popular.

I found myself thinking the gym was a funny place. It was a world all unto its own. Its members flocked there for various reasons. All in different stages in their lives. Some working hard for healthier bodies while others strived for perfection. There are those coming back from injury, while the old and frail are looking for strength. Last, the young, awkward females and males working to gain confidence.

There are those members, I am sure, I will never become. The perfect women in designer outfits, wearing the right shoes with the best accessories. Those who perform every move with confidence and seem to know every staff member on a first name basis. Their bodies tight and muscular, running with poise and grace. I confess to having girl crushes on a number of them. While I admire their dedication, I knew in my heart of hearts that perfection doesn't exist. Quite frankly, I am way too lazy to attempt the goal.

I do my best. I try to show up every other day with my headphones on. I mind my own business. Or at least, until Miss Wong appears. The woman must be seen to believe that she exists.

Miss Wong is an eighty-year-old Asian woman who probably weighs all of eighty-five pounds wet. But her presence is enormous. Most recently, she had a boob job that was way too big for her petite frame. Her hair is dyed jet black and stacked on top of her head. She always wears white midriff yoga tops with matching bottoms. On the treadmill, she can walk faster and longer than I can. Sometimes, I think her little bones are going to snap, but she keeps on going. She's terrific,

and I think she thinks so too. And that's probably my favorite thing about
her.

# Chapter 10.

I enjoyed the days I worked from seven to four, provided I didn't have the closing shift the night before. Prior to Edward's death, the early mornings were our best time together. Early in our marriage, we got up while it was still dark outside and took in a run. The race led to sharing a shower, which led to making love, which led to a very happy breakfast together. I missed those mornings.

Our happy relationship had come to a screeching halt after the children were born. The morning runs ceased for me. Edward ran on his own, while I stayed behind with the kids. And as in most marriages, the shared showers became less frequent too. As the demands of life increased, it became a delicate balancing act to keep up the romance in our marriage.

Those early mornings were on my mind as I parked my Mini Cooper in my usual spot. I noticed Ben's car was already there. In my somber mood, it was a happy thought that I might see him.

Before store hours, there was only one set of doors unlocked. One must push it open with some force, like a massive sliding glass door. I forced the door open and walked inside. My brain perked up from the strong aroma of freshly brewed coffee from inside the bakery department.

Lucky for me, I arrived early. I eagerly followed the tip of my nose to the bakery, for my morning cup of joe.

"Good morning, Lisa. I would love a cup of coffee, please," I nearly begged the woman behind the counter.

"You bet, Maggie" she replied.

"Good morning, Maggie," a robust masculine voice came from

behind me. My smile broadened as I recognized the familiar voice.

"Hi, Ben. You're here early today," I replied.

"You know," he shrugged. "It's the early bird thing. You have the early shift too, huh?"

"Yes, I do," I replied. "I love it. I'm an early riser anyway and then at the end of the workday; you still have some daylight left to enjoy," I said, appreciating Ben's eyes as they met mine.

"Listen," Ben said. "I would like to talk to you when you have a chance. Is that possible this morning?" he asked, lowering his voice.

"Well, yes," I nodded. "Although, I am the only checker until about nine-thirty."

"I'll speak to Dean about covering you around that time. Just let him know that you're coming up to the office."

"I'll do that," I answered. I paid Lisa for my coffee and walked toward the warehouse to put my things in my locker. I waved to the guys in the butchery, as I passed by their window.

I wondered why Ben wanted to talk to me. My mind searched for any actions at work that might be in question. I couldn't think of anything that could get me in trouble, so I decided to focus on morning tasks instead.

I clocked in with only a minute to spare. The call sheet hung on the wall, and I looked it over. Lucky number seven again. I hurried toward my register when I caught Dean in my peripheral vision.

"Good morning, Dean," I called out to him.

"Hey, Maggie. How are you today?" he asked.

"It's going to be a great day. Ben should be calling you soon. He needs me in the office around nine-thirty."

"What did you do now, I wonder," Dean teased.

"Well actually, I'll have you know I am a significant person with essential things to do." I turned on my heels with my nose in the air.

Two and half hours flew by, as I rang up bakery Early Bird Specials. The early mornings brought in many of our retired male customers. They met to discuss politics, sports, and the escalating price of goods.

Dean covered my register while I ran upstairs to meet with Ben. I knocked on his office door, and he beckoned me inside through the window.

"Hey, Ben, you ready to see me?" I asked.

"Maggie, thanks for coming up so promptly. Have a seat." Ben set aside a stack of papers on his desk.

"I've watched you handle yourself around the store," he began, "And I'm impressed with your professionalism. It's evident to me you care about our customers, and they often compliment you."

I found myself blushing at his unexpected words.

"Our managing staff has given you high marks on the review you had last week," Ben picked up a form from his desk and read it. "An area of improvement is assertiveness," he said and smiled. "Frankly, I think you are more than capable of being assertive when you need to be. I've witnessed that quality with a few of our male customers. Do you have anything you would like to add?"

I shifted in my seat and thought quickly about what to say. "Thank you for the update on my review, Ben. I enjoy working here and being a part of the team. I can only say I try to give you my best and try to improve on my weaknesses," I said unsure of what else to say.

"Well, you are doing a great job," Ben said. "Maggie, please look over your evaluation sheet and sign it on the bottom. Effective our next pay period, you have earned an increase," he announced with a grin.

"That's wonderful. Thank you," I said with enthusiasm.

He nodded. "You deserve it. I also would like you to think about joining our Manager's Training Program. I will have Dean talk with you more about that since he is your direct supervisor."

"I had no idea I was a candidate. Thank you very much," I reached over and shook his hand.

"Listen, you earned it," Ben paused for a moment. "There is something else I would like to run past you, but please understand it is sensitive in nature and confidential." Ben's voice lowered. I straightened my posture and leaned in a bit closer.

"Since you know many of our customers, what can you tell me about Paresula Malarsis?"

"Who?" I asked, confused.

"His family has been around this area for generations. Word has it; they are gypsies."

"Oh, you mean Parcey. I've heard they were a gypsy family," I paused for a moment to collect my thoughts. "Well, I can say that he's an interesting man, very polite. His son, Gabriel, comes in with him sometimes."

And they look like characters in a mobster film, I thought. It's strange to listen to Gabriel's voice because of his New Jersey accent. How on earth would he develop a Jersey accent born and raised in Central California? Last week he came in wearing white poly slacks and white patent leather shoes. Gabriel was a man trapped in a time warp from the seventies.

"I've noticed, when Parcey comes into the store, he usually chats with you," Ben's voice pulled me back from inside my head. "Am I on

personal territory here because I don't want to offend you in any way?"
he asked cautiously.

"Not at all," I hastened to assure him. "He mostly tells me stories
about his father and family. I don't know why he goes out of his way to
speak to me. Parcey is never flirty or disrespectful."

"I know why he goes out of his way. He's a guy, and well, you're
you," he said.

Was that a compliment? Was I blushing?

I took in a breath before saying, "I know that he is married," I
offered. "He came in wearing a tux one evening when I worked the night
shift. He was buying champagne to celebrate a wedding anniversary. He
doesn't come in regularly; sometimes only once every few months.
They're a boisterous group, that's for sure. Their voices travel throughout
the store. I can't say I've ever overheard anything sinister. Parcey has
never discussed business with me. I don't even know what he does for a
living. He only shares stories about growing up with his father," I
concluded, inhaling to catch my breath.

"Have you noticed the palm reading storefronts in the strip malls
all over town and off the freeway south of here?" Ben asked.

"Yes, I have," I responded.

"All of those are owned by the Malarsis family. They have made
a fortune in fortune telling, so it appears," Ben chuckled at his pun, then
his face became serious again. "Now, this is the part where it becomes
sensitive, Maggie."

He paused for a moment, calculating whether he should proceed.
I was growing more and more curious about where this conversation was
heading. Our eyes met and held for a few seconds.

"Have you noticed Michael in conversation with Parcey at any time; parking lot, warehouse?"

"Ahh," now I was beginning to see where this was going. "Nothing more than quick exchanges. Maybe some laughing between the two of them. Nothing that sticks out in my mind as being out of the ordinary."

"There are, let's say, occurrences between them I'm trying to figure out. Let me say this for now," Ben waved his hand at me. "I don't want to put you in an awkward position. Feel free to say no, to what I'm about to ask you. Would you be okay with letting me know if you notice anything strange happening on the grocery floor?" He held my eyes for a few seconds.

"I'm okay with that," I said.

"Ok then," Ben said, rising from his seat. I stood up too.

A few moments later, I returned to my station, my mind whirling with everything Ben had said and what he had implied. Dean paged me on the in-store phone.

"What did you do?" he teased.

"Apparently, a lot of things and very well. When do I start the Management Training Program?" I asked.

"Yeah right," he joked. "I'll get back to you about that," I heard him chuckle. "Congratulations, you work hard, Bloom."

"Thanks for the good review."

"It's all you, Bloom; it's all you," he said, disconnecting the line.

# Chapter 11.

Growing up, we all believe our families are "normal". It isn't until later in life when you begin questioning your existence; you realize just how dysfunctional your own family is. Let's face it; we are all a little broken.

My father died young. He had a weak heart due to a childhood illness. I was sixteen when he died. My sister Lizzy was twenty-two. Mom turned forty the week of his death. It's been the three of us, plus Nonna, ever since.

Like most families, Lizzy and I have had a love/hate relationship most of our lives. Mom always had to be the referee. With six years between my sister and I, we were never on the same level playing field until I went to college. Fortunately, time is a great unifier. We are very close now. She is the godmother of my kids.

Lizzy had always been popular. In high school, she was on the cheer squad, she was the student body president, and on the honor roll. If something needed doing, Lizzy would always volunteer to lead it. She could do it all.

My sister had been petite her entire life. Beautiful, with straight, dark brown hair. She had worn it long all through high school, and the boys went nuts over it. Her chocolate brown eyes never gave her away, always confident in anything she tried.

In college, she had never been without a date. She was committed to her education, but struggled to commit to love.

It wasn't until Lizzy was getting her Ph.D. that she finally fell prey to the love bug. The man who won her heart was Dr. Daniel Baxter, and he would not take no for an answer. He merely wore her down until the smarty pants couldn't think of any more reasons not to accept him. She had finally met her match. It had taken a man with high intelligence and patience to win the hand of Elizabeth Morgan.

The two doctors never had children. Their to-do list was long, and they quite frankly didn't want to share each other with anyone else. Since they were both professors at the university, they spent their summers traveling the world and writing papers. I have always looked up to Lizzy.

Sometimes, I find myself looking back many years to a time when Margaret Eleanor (Morgan) Bloom was not the most popular girl in high school. The teaching staff had looked forward to my high school career since I was the sister of Elizabeth Morgan. My very average succession severely dashed their expectations to her glory days.

I had been skinny, but an athletic girl. I was a bit of a tomboy, so cheer hadn't been a good fit. Unlike Lizzy, I had to study hard just to make B's. I never became prom queen; however, I did help lead our volleyball team toward a valley championship.

When I was just a young girl, boys had not called our house looking for me. Nonna would pat my hand and tell me not to worry. As we baked together in her kitchen after school, Nonna taught me the way to a man's heart was through his stomach. And, as she put it, high school boys did not have a discerning palette.

"Hi, Lizzy," I said to my sister when she picked up the phone. "I'm thinking today is a great day for lunch on the patio at Estrada's. I'm picking Mom up at eleven-thirty. You in?"

"Hi, Sis." My sister sounded pleased to hear from me. "That sounds good. Skinny margaritas included?"

"You can go skinny if you wish," I laughed. "I, on the other hand, want it loaded, brain freeze and all."

"You must be off today?" she inquired.

"Yep. And making the most of it. Can't wait to see you, Lizzy. Mom and I will meet you at Estrada's before noon. I hope the Mariachis are there today. Love you," I concluded happily, excited about the opportunity to spend time with these two particular ladies.

I sent a quick text to Bella: Meeting Gran for lunch today. Auntie Liz coming too, yes! ; ) xoxo

I picked up my Mother promptly at eleven-thirty. I jumped out of my Mini and knocked. As she opened the door, the sight of my mother lit up my face. I smiled from ear to ear. She had dressed for a festive occasion. Mom twirled showing off her ensemble. She wore a brightly layered skirt she bought on a Mexican cruise, and red sandals adorned her feet with a silk flower between her toes. A red tee shirt with a crocheted neckline matched her red shoes perfectly. Her toes were painted bright yellow and embellished with tiny pink flowers. As always, my mother looked fabulous.

"Look at you, sexy mama!" I exclaimed.

"Oh, Ellie," she protested. "And I love your fabulous white hat. I must borrow it sometime. A pair of high heels would look much better with your outfit. You would make your mother so happy if you ditched those mules," she teased pointing to my feet.

My mother had called me Ellie ever since I was a baby. Her sister was the original Margaret. Aunt Maggie already had dibs on the name, so I became "Ellie" after my middle name of Eleanor. Daddy and my sister had called me Maggie and when referring to my mother's sister, called her Auntie Em. Mother, however, had never broken her habit of calling me by my nickname.

"Oh Mother, you know my feet have never been the same since I gave birth to your grandchildren." I always laughed at her attempts to improve my fashion sense. "Besides, this turquoise top with these sexy shoulder slits will keep anyone from looking at my feet. Anyway, I think these mules are cute."

"Yes, but much cuter on a mule," she said while she closed her front door with a bang and locked it up.

"I can't wait to ride in the Mini. Can we open the sunroof?" she asked.

"That's why I'm wearing the hat." I helped her into the car. "It's a gorgeous day for margaritas, don't you agree?" And off we zoomed toward Estrada's. O'lay!

Mom and I were happily seated on the patio of Estrada's when I spotted Lizzy looking for us. I waved her over. She looked great as usual in her sleek neutral palette.

"You guys look great. You look like you're on vacation," she said. I stood to give her a hug and kiss her on the cheek.

"I know this was last minute, but I'm so glad you came," I said into her ear.

"So sit and tell me what's going on with you ladies," Lizzy said, wanting to know everything.

Mom told us about her Bridge Club and got us caught up on all the latest gossip. Two of the ladies in the group, Sue and Joan, had a falling out, and things just weren't the same for the group. She and her friend, Lydia, were planning a bus trip to Reno. Mother's hand had been itching lately, which meant good luck at the casinos. She and Lydia had decided to take a two-week respite from Bridge, to give the ladies time to work it out. My mother loved it when she had the undivided attention of her two daughters.

"Well, honestly," she chirped, taking a sip of her drink. "They are just spoiling the fun for the rest of us. Nobody even remembers what the quarrel was about and I doubt very much that they do either."

My mother turned to me and gripped my hand. "So tell me what's new with you at the store, Ellie. And how are my grandchildren I hardly get to see anymore?" she concluded.

"So much to say, so little time" I pondered. "The kids are great. We text every day, practically. Things are so much better between Bella and me. She just needed some time," I explained.

"Such a headstrong girl," Mom said. "I have no idea where she gets it. Although my sister, Maggie, was very headstrong, wasn't she?"

"I didn't want the kids to know about the financial stress I was under. Edward's life insurance policy had lapsed. He was juggling so many accounts; things just slipped for a while. And you know how he was, he wanted to handle everything himself. There was always a plan."

Our conversation drifted to other topics, but my children lingered in the back of my mind.

I had invited the kids to come home next weekend. There were boxes I wanted to go through of Edward's, and I thought it would be a good idea to do it together. I could hardly believe it had been two years since I moved and I still had boxes stacked to the ceiling in the garage. I couldn't even remember what was in them anymore.

"If you remember, Maggie," Lizzy began, "At the time, we packed everything without consideration of what you wanted to keep, toss, or give away. It seemed we were more in a hurry to get you moved. It's probably easier for you to look through things more objectively now, and the kids are helping you. Better, I think. Don't you agree, Mother?"

"Yes. It's better for everyone now," Mother agreed, shaking her head as if to erase a bad memory.

We all fell silent.

"So, what's brewing at the store?" Mother asked after collecting her thoughts.

"Tell us about Dean. How is he getting along these days after his wife's death?" Lizzy asked.

My mind skipped to what had happened between Dean and me when he unexpectedly showed up at my front door. I hadn't told anyone about the incident.

"He has been back for a while now and is doing well, I think," I replied. "His wife was a beautiful woman. She was kind. You could tell by the way she interacted with people. She was quiet and introspective. It was the way she looked at Dean that sometimes stopped me," I concluded, thoughtfully.

"What do you mean, Maggie?" Lizzy asked.

"Like when Daniel looks at you, Lizzy. It's as if he can't get enough of you. It's love at first sight, every time he sees you."

Lizzy tilted her head to try and understand.

"Anyway, Carolyn looked at Dean just like that," I continued, trying to explain what I had observed. "She loved him. I sometimes wonder if she knew she was going to die. I wonder the same thing about Edward. He was in such a rush to get things done. I often wonder if somehow he felt his time was short. Anyway, Dean is finding his sea legs again. I recognize the process."

"He has gorgeous blue eyes. Don't you think so, Ellie? And always so charming when I come into the store to shop," Mom interjected, never one to fail to appreciate a good-looking gentleman.

"Yes he does," I smiled, picturing him at my front door. "But not always that charming, Mom. He can be an arrogant pain in my backside too. Oh, and there is something mysterious happening with ownership," I continued, suddenly remembering my conversation with Ben. "I think Michael is in some trouble. I think it might be drug abuse. His personality has become erratic lately. I've never really liked him much. He's quite impressed with himself, and I can't seem to find any reason why."

"And what about the handsome man with those hypnotic chocolate eyes?" Mom teased.

"Ben? Well, he gave me a raise and suggested I look into the management program at the store. And he asked me to be his amateur sleuth," I jiggled my brows up and down for effect.

"Congratulations! You do work so hard there, Ellie. They are always complimenting me about you...but, sleuth?" I had finally caught her interest. Mom leaned in closer so she wouldn't miss anything.

I quickly perused the restaurant, making sure there was no one I recognized within earshot before I continued.

"Well, Ben did compliment me on my customer service skills. We do have the best customers."

"Ellie!" Mom hurried me along with a wave of her hand.

"Oh, I'm sorry. Ben asked me how well I knew a certain customer named Parcey. He's a gypsy."

"What? Maggie, seriously?" Lizzy doubted me.

"You know all these fortunetelling businesses around town? Well, they're Parcey's family businesses."

The ladies nodded, leaning in closer as I spoke.

"It seems Ben is concerned with Michael's relationship with

Parcey. Personally, I think Parcey is Ok. He tells me stories about his family, especially his father. And you know what? He has never mentioned to me what he does for a living, never. Nice man," I nodded. "His son, on the other hand, Gabriel....it's him I'm not so sure of. He's a deal maker, you know? Talks loud like he wants everybody to hear what a smart guy he is. Personally," I shook my head, "Not so smart. He sounds more like a thug."

"Wait a minute. Go back. What do you mean, amateur sleuth?" Lizzy asked cautiously. "What exactly is Ben asking you to do?"

"Oh, nothing. Just to keep my eyes and ears open and report back to him. It's just that I seem to be the go-to-person in the store. I usually end up knowing just about everything that goes on there. Even things I don't particularly want to know." I gave my head a shake remembering the day I caught the butcher and the married deli manager, inside the meat locker. There are some things in life; you wish you could un-see.

"That's because you are very trusting, Ellie. You're sincere, and you have trusting eyes. But people can take advantage of that trust." My mother held up her index finger to make her point. "You really must be careful dear."

"Thank you, Mother. Anyway, Parcey is a very colorful man. I think you would like him, Mom. He and his son both have a New Jersey accent. I have no idea where it comes from," I shook my head, picturing the pair.

"Maggie, seriously. Are you sure you want to get yourself involved in this?" Lizzy said, turning her head toward our mother to get her support. "Hypnotic chocolate eyes or not, this sounds like it could be dangerous."

74

"I'm not doing anything. In fact, just listening. Don't worry. I would never put myself in a situation I wasn't sure about." I wondered if those would be my famous last words.

# Chapter 12.

A few days after my lunch date with my mother, I woke up early and shot straight up in bed in a moment of panic. I had overslept and was late for work.

"Crap! Wait…no. I'm on vacation," I reminded myself. "It's all right. I'm on vacation for a whole week. Nice."

I stood up in bed and did my victory dance. I twisted my hips and jumped up and down on my bed just like my mother always told me not to do.

My victory song went like this, "I'm on vacation, woo-hoo. I'm on vacation, woo-hoo. I want some Starbucks too; I'm on vacation, woo-hoo!" The hips and the neck bop, happened simultaneously.

The kids were coming in tonight. I jumped off my bed and ran into the living room. There, I performed my encore of the victory dance and jogged into the kitchen. Swinging open the refrigerator door, I began to take stock of the groceries I would need for dinner.

It had been three months since I had both of my children under my roof, at the same time. I was so excited and looked forward to holding Henry and Bell in my arms. I pulled open the kitchen drawer and fished out a pencil and pad and began my shopping list. I was going to cook all of their favorites. Steaks for dinner, whole grain waffles for breakfast and dessert? Dessert had to be limoncello cupcakes, and a plum galette with fresh cinnamon whipped cream.

It was only seven-thirty in the morning when I jumped into the shower. I pulled on my favorite gray Capri sweatsuit, the one with the hot pink strip running down the side. I shook my hair out and lightly painted my face, brushed my teeth, and added a bit of clear lip gloss. Tying my black and lime green jogging shoes to my feet, I skipped into the kitchen to find my car keys.

I backed the Mini out of the garage and turned up the radio to Maroon 5's, Mick Jagger song. I was Starbucks bound for a grande latte. I zoomed in and out of the drive-through and headed toward Bay's Market for a mixed seed bagel with cream cheese, and everything on my shopping list.

I was "walking on sunshine" all the way into the store without feeling the pavement beneath my feet. Today, I was a delighted woman.

As the doors of the market opened, the warm, comforting, smell of freshly baked goods assaulted my senses. I closed my eyes and took in the delicious aroma when suddenly, my face smashed up against Ben's chest.

"Is this becoming a habit with you?" Ben quipped, smiling down at me.

I was embarrassed and slowly raised my eyes to meet his. I tried to respond in a casual manner. "You need to take out accident insurance on this bakery. The smells are hypnotic."

I took a step away from his firm body and could do nothing more than smile.

"I hear you're on vacation," Ben said to me, still smiling.

"Obviously, my mind seems to be elsewhere. My kids are coming to town this evening, so I'm stocking up on all their favorites. I might have to ask you for an advance on my next paycheck," I joked. I glanced over his left shoulder, to find Dean shaking his head at me in bewilderment. Wanting desperately to stick out my tongue at him, I merely returned my gaze to Ben.

"How many kids do you have?" he asked.

"Two, and they're coming home for spring break."

"Ahh. I have a daughter at UC San Diego. She'll be home for the weekend too," he said happily.

"My son is working on his masters there."

"My daughter is in her senior year."

"What is she studying?" I wondered.

"Architecture," he smiled with evident pride.

"The apple doesn't fall far from the tree, I see."

"Not really. My daughter's mother, however, is a little disappointed she isn't studying interior design. One more reason to hate me, I guess," he chuckled.

Ok, so now I'm guessing, divorced. Not that I care...or am ready to care, but an interesting tidbit.

"Were you getting coffee when I tried to take you out?" I asked.

"It's a good thing I wasn't already drinking it. What are you having? My treat, since you're obviously on vacation," he offered.

I raised my container for him to see. "I have some, thank you. I'm here for the best bagels in town."

"The best. Really?"

"Don't you think so? They are hands down the best bagels in town."

"What's your bagel of choice?" Ben walked the few steps over with me to the bakery.

"I would like the mixed seed bagel," I said to Melissa, who stood behind the counter.

"Anything for you, Ben, besides the coffee?" she asked.

Like me, for example, I finished her sentence for her inside my head.

"I'll have the same as Maggie. Thank you, Melissa."

"Toasted or plain?" she directed her question toward Ben, apparently forgetting that it was my idea for the bagel.

"Maggie?"

"Toasted please, with extra cream cheese," I said to Melissa.

"Same for me, thank you," he said. "Can I join you for a bagel or are you eating while you shop?"

Damn, I thought. If I had known Ben was going to join me, I would have ordered a plain bagel to avoid those nasty black seeds getting stuck in my teeth.

"Great," I said. "I don't have to be anywhere. I'm on vacation." I announced, happily. Melissa shot daggers out of her eyes at me as she prepared our bagels.

When they were ready, we carried our bagels over to the seating area. We picked a table rather than the stools that faced out to the walkway. Ben watched me from the corner of his eye as I prepared my bagel.

Carefully, I scooped out the cream cheese and proceeded to spread equal amounts of it on both slices of the bagel. Then, I sandwiched the pieces together and cut the bagel into pieces like a pie making sure each piece would be exactly bite size. This method, I hoped, left little chance for the pesky seeds to lodge themselves between my teeth.

Ben picked up his bagel and remarked, "It's a good thing you're on vacation cause that little science project of yours took some time. You couldn't possibly do that on a ten-minute break."

He sure was cute, when he was sassy, I thought. "You caught

me," I chirped. "I like to play with my food. My mother highly encouraged it when I was growing up."

He chuckled at me. "Tell me about your kids. Do you get to see them much?" he asked, biting into his bagel.

"Not very often. My kids are busy with their lives. They are both intelligent, something they get from their father, but very different from each other." I chewed a delicious bite of my bagel. "You need to promote these bagels more. They are the best bagels in town, hands down."

"Agreed," Ben said.

"Now you," I prompted.

"Grace is my only child. Her mother and I divorced when she was young. I traveled quite a bit during most of that time. I missed a lot of Grace's first few years, and I guess I'm still trying to make it up to her. She came to live with me after the divorce. It's been just her and I ever since until I started to commute here. Well, I guess I live here more than I commute. She stayed in San Diego to finish school."

Ben was paged to pick up line one. "Sounds like your break is over. Thanks for the bagel," I said.

"Darn. Enjoy your time off, Maggie. See you in a week," Ben said with a "no bagel seed" smile.

I cleaned off the table, and we went our separate ways. I began to think about what a great guy he was. As I passed Dean in the produce department, he had that look in his eye, like he just couldn't wait to tease me about something.

As I approached him, I hastened to head him off. "Don't say it, Dean. I know you want to, so very badly. But don't do it. Let me think kindly of you while I'm on vacation."

I strolled past him and heard him call out, "But Bloom, you

make it so easy for me."

In response, I merely raised my hand to silence him, "Don't do it, Phillips."

"I'll miss you," he teased.

"I'm sure you will," I laughed and continued my shopping.

In the course of one's life, there are many people you meet along the way. What you can never know, upon first meeting them, is how long they will be in your life. Are they here for a brief moment or will they be with you for the rest of your life? In the grocery business, you meet a lot of people who share moments with you. Some of those moments will impact you forever.

"Good morning, Dr. Peters," I greeted him, exiting the produce department.

"Well, good morning, Maggie. Are you grateful today?" he asked me as he always did.

"Yes, Dr. Peters, I am grateful this morning," I replied.

"It's the secret of life, my dear. A grateful heart is the secret of life," he said, pushing his cart down the aisle.

I couldn't tell you how often we had that exchange over the last two years. But today, I heard the words differently than any time before. A grateful heart is the secret of life, Maggie, I whispered to myself as I continued my shopping.

# Chapter 13.

I got home with my groceries before it started to rain. April showers bring May flowers. It was hard to tell if this was a bit of a tease for the thirsty bulbs or if we were in for a water table changing event. Having lived in the Central Valley all of my life, it was not unusual for a freak hail storm to develop, even in July. Our climate was similar to the Mediterranean.

I put the cold groceries in the refrigerator and piled up the fruit bowl. I reached for my favorite vase, to fill with sunflowers I purchased from the grocery store. These were Bell's favorites, so I placed them in the spare room for her.

Technically, my small office/den can be used as a third bedroom and in this case, it would be Henry's room for the weekend. I invested in an excellent hideaway mattress for the sofa, for just these occasions.

Mom, Daniel, and Lizzy were scheduled for dinner tomorrow night. I decided to make a fresh plum galette for the occasion. The limoncello cupcakes, the kid's favorite, were next on my list. I retrieved my black recipe box with a white "M" monogrammed on the front of it. Edward had gifted it to me years ago for my birthday. In it, I housed all of my favorite recipes, the ones that were tried and true, especially those from Nonna.

I smiled, remembering how young we were and how excited Edward was to give me the recipe box. I lifted the lid and looked inside for the recipe. Although I have made limoncello cupcakes dozens of times, I still read over the ingredients and place them on the counter in front of me.

"Your cupcakes are orgasmic," Edward would whisper into my ear after sampling a batch. He was never fond of sweets like I was, except for this one. It was my Nonna's cupcakes recipe.

Smiling as I recalled the memory, I reached into the refrigerator door for the bottle of limoncello. It's a lovely treat any time of the year. I often added it to hot tea in the winter and ice tea in the summer with a sprig of fresh mint.

Ahh, the simple things in life. I thought about my dream of living in Italy for a summer. I wanted to stay on a working farm and learn the secrets of Italian cooking from someone else's Nonna.

I cracked, splashed, squeezed, creamed and filled until I finally placed my cupcakes on the middle rack in the oven. I licked the cupcake mix from my pinkie approvingly and closed the oven door to bake. I grated the zest of a medium-sized lemon into a small bowl and set it aside for the frosting.

For the central portion of our dinner, I washed and scrubbed red potatoes, beets, carrots, and towel dried them. Chopping them into large pieces, I dropped them into a large ziplock bag. I added olive oil, salt, pepper, and garlic powder to the bag. I zipped it shut and massaged the vegetables inside the bag, then placed it in the fridge to marinate. I cleaned and washed green beans and asparagus and marinated them the same way as the root vegetables. Our meal was halfway complete.

The aroma of lemon cupcakes filled the kitchen and was ready to be pulled out of the oven. I opened the door and lightly pressed my finger to the top of the cake, testing it. It sprung back, telling me it was ready. I set the cupcake pans on the counter and turned off the oven. I started to mix the limoncello frosting while the cakes cooled.

I washed the cupcake batter out of the mixing bowl and placed it back under the mixer. I creamed together butter, vanilla, powdered sugar, and lemon juice. Next came a touch of milk, lemon zest, and a lot of love. My grandmother always told me that love was the essential ingredient in any recipe. As long as it was sincere, the dish would never fail. So, into the mixer it went, whipping the frosting into a delightful aroma of citrus and love.

A lemon cupcake is not complete without a glazed lemon slice. I sliced two lemons into quarter-inch slices. After removing the seeds, I rolled them in sugar. I coated a skillet with Pam Spray and placed it on the burner to warm. In a single layer, I arranged the lemon slices. Turning them only once, I let them cook about eight minutes, watching that they did not brown. I removed the slices from the skillet and set them onto parchment paper to cool. When the slices were room temperature, I rolled them in sugar again and set them aside.

The clouds began to part, letting in a warm ray of sunshine through my kitchen window. I placed the frosting into the refrigerator and stepped over to the kitchen window to look out. The rain clouds were passing, I thought gratefully, making a safer trip for my children.

What a beautiful day this was turning out to be. I could see a group of small brown birds sitting at the edge of a bird bath I had tucked in between some shrubs, out on the patio. I confessed to them I could hardly wait for Henry and Isabel to arrive.

I decided to run the vacuum across the carpet in each bedroom and over the hardwood floors and area rugs. Turning on the television to the music channel, I noticed for the next hour a tribute was underway for Rod Stewart. I turned up the volume so that I could hear the classics from any room.

Back in the kitchen, I pulled open a drawer and retrieved my pastry bag and a large decorating tip. From the fridge, I took out the lemony frosting and scooped it into the pastry bag. Rolling up the sides, I then twisted the top of the bag. I was ready to decorate the delicious cupcakes.

I squeezed the bag until the frosting gave way to the pressure and began to push through the decorating tip. I traveled around the edge of the cupcake into a center peak. I repeated the process. I walked over to the pantry door and hunted for sugar beads to sprinkle on top of the cupcakes. Gently, I shook the container over the cakes, until the heads glowed in yellow.

I left one cupcake naked. That was my tester. Unwrapping the cupcake, I took a large bite. As my eyes rolled to the back of my head, I moaned in creamy, lemony delight. Edward was right.

# Chapter 14.

I woke up on the couch from a deep, sugar-induced sleep by the ringing of my cell phone. Dazed, I searched for the phone. My heart pounded as I picked it up and saw it was Henry.

"Hello, Henry," I said.

"Yeah, Mom, it's me. We're about an hour away. I just wanted you to know we'll be there soon."

"We, Henry?"

"Yes. I have someone with me I want you to meet. Her father lives in town, so I'll be dropping her off later. If that's ok? Are you ok? You sound like you've been running?"

"I'm good, Henry," I pulled myself together. "Of course that's fine. I'm always happy to meet your friends. See you soon. Love you. Be careful."

"Ok, Mom. Love you too."

Henry was bringing a friend. I wondered what kind. I would see soon. I got up off the couch and decided I needed to freshen up. Rod Stewart had long since finished singing his classics, and Eric Clapton was now singing about a gal named Leila.

I turned down the volume and went to fluff. The hour rushed by quickly. Before I knew it, there was a knock at the door. I looked through the peephole to find my son giving a quick kiss to a small, dark-haired girl. Friend?

I opened the door in jubilation and clapped my hands at the sight of my first born.

"Henry," I said, throwing my arms around him. I had to reach up on tip-toe to kiss his cheek, his height now equaling his father's.

"Hello, Mom," his voice softened, holding me close. "I've missed you."

"You've missed me? I miss you every minute," I said, pushing back tears.

"Mom, I'd like you to meet Samantha. Samantha, this is my mother."

I stepped back to shake the hand of the pretty girl. I took note of her lovely brown eyes.

"How are you, Samantha? Please come in...the both of you."

"Nice to meet you, Mrs. Bloom. Henry has told me a lot about you," Samantha said.

"Come in, come in. Do you need something to drink or a moment to freshen up?" I asked them both.

"I would like to freshen up," Samantha said. I showed her the way to the guest bathroom.

I came back to Henry with quizzical eyes. "So, tell me about your friend. She's a surprise. You didn't mention bringing someone up with you."

"I know, Mom. Sorry about that. Is it ok that she's here?"

"Of course it is. I want to know all about you, and that includes your friends too. She must be special," I queried. "Can she stay and join us for dinner?" I offered.

"I think that will be ok. I'll drop Samantha off at her father's house later. Are you sure you don't mind?"

"Mind? I'll let you know after dinner," I laughed. "It's fine Henry. I'm happy to see you," I said, hugging him again.

Samantha came down the hall shyly. I gave her a tour of the place and showed off the on-going construction outside in my garden.

"Mrs. Bloom, your garden is beautiful. Henry told me you like to cook and garden, but I hadn't imagined a garden like this. It's...magical."

"Thank you, Samantha. Some people go to a psychiatrist. I garden," I explained, laughing at the truth.

We stood outside for a few minutes, getting to know one another. After a while, I excused myself to the kitchen for iced tea and lemonade. I arranged hummus, assorted cheeses, vegetables, and toasted pita bread on a small platter and brought everything out to the patio on a tray. The morning rain made for a crisp, beautiful day.

I placed the snacks on the bistro table out on the patio. "Please help yourself to anything," I told them both. "Can I pour you a glass of tea, or lemonade, or mix them for an Arnold Palmer?" I asked. They both agreed on the mix.

"It's my favorite concoction," I handed them each a glass.

"Who are you trying to fool, Mom? Your favorite includes a shot of limoncello," Henry joked.

"I would, Henry," I teased, "Except the last of it is inside the cupcakes."

"Tell me, Samantha, are you at UC San Diego?" I asked her.

"Yes, I am. I'm in my last year," she added.

"Did the two of you meet on campus?"

Henry replied for the both of them, "Actually, we met at a party."

"And you have family here?" I asked Samantha.

"Yes, my family is originally from here," she said.

"It's a nice area to grow up. Henry, have you heard from, Bell? I wonder what time she left Chico?"

"She told me she was leaving a little later, but would make it by seven."

"Okay. We'll wait for dinner until then if you don't mind. Speaking of which...you two relax, and I'll get dinner started."

"Can I help, Mrs. Bloom?" Samantha asked.

"No, thank you, Samantha. You relax. Most of the works done. I have to put it in the oven. You don't happen to be a vegetarian, are you?"

"No, why?"

"Cause I planned on steaks."

I left the two of them on the patio and went into the kitchen to finish up dinner. I turned on the oven to 400 degrees to roast the vegetables. I set the meat and vegetables on the counter to come to room temperature. After a few minutes, I peeked out onto the patio. They were both talking and laughing. I smiled. Henry certainly had good taste in women. Samantha was beautiful. I found myself wondering just how serious this relationship was. She was the first girl he had ever brought home.

I put the vegetables in the oven but left the green beans and asparagus out until the last five minutes. Those vegetables I enjoyed crisp. I seasoned the steaks and let them sit out on the counter covered in plastic wrap. Washing a head of iceberg lettuce, I cut it in half and left it to drain. It was destined to become a wedge salad with a feta ranch dressing.

The doorbell rang, and I hurried to see who it was. I looked through the peephole, gasped and flung opened the door. Isabella was home.

We exchanged hugs and kisses. I helped Isabella bring in her suitcase and set her up in the guest bedroom.

"Oh, Mom...Sunflowers; my favorite," she purred.

"Yes I know," I put my arm around her waist and squeezed.

"Your brother brought a friend with him," I said, testing the water.

"I met her on Skype once. She seems very nice and pretty," she said.

"Well, freshen up and come on out to the patio," I leaned over and kissed Isabella on the cheek before I left.

I stopped in the doorway and said, "I'm so happy you came, Bell."

Walking out to the patio, I announced Isabella's arrival. I asked Henry to get the barbecue lit and prepped for the steaks. Dinner was almost ready. I introduced Samantha to Isabella when Samantha came in to help me set the table.

Isabella joined us to put the finishing touches on the salad. Our side dishes made it to the dining table at the same time as the steaks. I surveyed the meal and felt pleased with myself. It was a colorful feast for the eyes, and the smells were making my mouth water.

"Henry, you did an amazing job on the steaks. They look perfect," I said.

"Thanks, Mom. Dinner looks delicious," he replied.

"Don't forget to leave room for dessert. I made your favorite, Bell."

"You made lemon cupcakes?" Isabella asked.

"Yep. I'd like to say a prayer before our meal," I paused, looking around the dining table. "We have a lot to be grateful for."

Our family dining table was something I hadn't been able to part with after selling our home. Our history was at this table. This moment, with my children around me, I could not help but "happy cry." Thanking them for coming, I dabbed my eyes with a napkin. With a renewed appetite, the four of us dug into the meal we had prepared together.

# Chapter 15.

After dinner, Henry drove Samantha home. I sent four cupcakes with her to share with her father and grandfather. I decided to wait up for Henry so we could talk a little before he went to bed. Isabella had already wished me a good night.

The Late Show was coming on when I heard the spare key in the door. I sat up, anticipating some answers to my curious questions.

"Hey Mom, you're still up?" Henry asked.

"Well yes....I have a couple of questions for you, Mister. I know you're tired, but I need to have some answers before I can sleep."

"I figured. Go ahead, but I won't answer any questions until I get a cupcake," my son chuckled as he walked over to the kitchen. I heard the refrigerator open.

"Hey, bring me one of those too, while you're in there," I added.

Henry handed me a cupcake on a napkin, and my soul moaned as I took a generous bite.

"These are the best things ever," Henry muttered with a mouth full.

"Hey, no stalling. Spill the beans about Samantha."

"I met her at a New Year's Eve party that one of my college friends hosted. We were outside in the backyard of this huge house, and Samantha walked out onto the patio. I took one look at her and said "wow" to myself. I knew I had to meet her so I asked around for someone who might know her. I made the connection, and we spent the rest of the night talking inside a gazebo. We've been hanging out ever since."

"By hanging out do you mean dating?" I requested clarification.

Henry just smiled.

"So, do you think that you're in love with her?"

"I think you could call it that," Henry suddenly seemed shy. "I've never met anyone like her. She's great. Don't worry; we aren't rushing into anything too heavy. Sam is still deciding whether she is going for her Masters or joining the workforce. I'm deciding on whether I want to stay in San Diego or come back here and start a business with my mother." Henry looked at me to gauge my reaction.

"Huh? Start a business with your mother?" I stared at him in shock.

"This is going to come as a shock to you, but Mom....I've learned something about myself. I'm pretty sure I got it from you. I have a mistress, and her name is cooking. I love to cook. The smells and tastes. I've watched you cook all my life. There you'd be, in the kitchen explaining to me about food and nutrition. You could hardly wait to have us try something new you'd dreamed up, or Nonna had made. I could see what cooking meant to you by the expression on your face, especially when we liked what you created," my son said as he paced across the living room.

"I went to college to learn business because that's what Dad did," Henry continued. "He loved helping people with their businesses, and he talked about me taking over his business someday. But Mom, my dream is to have a food truck. Maybe it can be something you and I create together. I've learned a lot about business, but now I want to take what I've learned and apply it to something I'm passionate about. I want to cook, excellent food for people."

I sat in silence just looking at my son. He had left home a confused kid and returned a grown man with a passion.

"Wow...I had no idea you felt this way."

"Neither did I, Mom, but I've figured it out. Sam has helped me realize what it is I love to do; she's very supportive. I'm good at it. Let me cook for you this weekend."

"I think this is wonderful, Henry," I said, smiling at him. I stood up and touched his cheek with the palm of my hand. "Some people spend their entire lives searching for what they are passionate about, trying to realize their dreams. I believe whatever you decide to put your hands to, with the right effort, you will succeed at it without question. Now, whether or not that includes me is another thing," I concluded.

We were silent for a moment, and then I went on. "I once dreamed of owning a cafe of sorts, and I'm thrilled you would consider me as a business partner. But I'm still trying to figure out what it is I need. I'm getting to know myself all over again, and I need some time to think about the idea."

He nodded, and I went on, "Samantha is lovely by the way. She reminds me of someone, but I can't think of who. I'm so glad to see you happy, Henry. It seems you have found someone special."

"She is special, and I am happy," he said.

"Good."

I headed to bed, but before saying goodnight, I turned to my son and asked, "By the way, what would you call the food truck?" I asked.

"Bloomers," he grinned.

"I like it," I grinned in return and walked down the hall.

"Wow," I said out loud after brushing my teeth. "Henry wants to be a chef. Crazy...wonderful. What a surprise. And Samantha too... he doesn't know this yet, but I'll bet he marries that girl."

I drifted off to sleep thinking all was right with the world. My babies were under my roof, and all seemed well. Except of course there was always the chance Isabella could spring something on me tomorrow.

# Chapter 16.

After breakfast, I took the kids out to the garage to help me with boxes I hadn't gotten to since the move. I unstacked a few until I came to the ones that had their names written on the outside. I instructed them to go through the keepsakes of their childhood, determining what to keep and what to discard.

I reached for another box marked "Edward's Business" and handed it to Henry.

"Henry, your Aunt Lizzie emptied the contents of your father's desk and filing cabinets into a few of these boxes. I know it's a big job, but I was wondering if you can go through them. There are five in all. Please take a look and see what is important to keep and what can be shredded. You can look through them here or take them with you, whichever you prefer. I took care of the receivables after he died and that one is labeled. As for the rest of it, I really couldn't tell you."

Henry decided to go through what he could over the weekend and take the rest of the boxes with him. I could tell both Henry and Isabella enjoyed the walk down memory lane. Each set aside those items they treasured. The rest of the things were up to my discretion. Some of the gently used items would do well in a charity auction.

Suddenly, Henry jumped up after realizing the time. He made a mad dash inside to clean himself up. Henry was off to Samantha's grandfather's house, to meet her father for the first time. Apparently, her father had to warm up to the idea before he agreed to meet Henry.

Isabella and I wished him luck and continued on our journey through the past. Working up an appetite, we had a quick bite to eat and decided a shopping trip was in order. We cleaned up and made our way to the Macy's shopping mall.

After a few hours of shopping, we toted our packages back to the car and made our way home to prepare for the family dinner party. As Isabella and I chopped, peeled, and sauteed it gave us a chance to talk.

"How's everything going at school, Bell?" I began.

"Good Mom. Everything is good. It looks like I'll have a high B average this semester."

"That's great, Honey. Have you decided on a major yet?"

"Not yet. I'm leaning toward Interior Design. My friend Brittany is going that direction, and I think it might be something I could be interested in."

"What are some of your favorite classes?" I asked.

"I have enjoyed the speech class this semester. I feel like I have more confidence in myself. At first, talking in front of the class was difficult, but now I look forward to it."

"That's wonderful. Have you thought about a marketing major?"

"I met with my dean last week, and that was one of the areas he thought I should consider. I'm not sure yet."

"You still have time to decide," I said. "Take more electives in the areas you're considering. You never know what might click."

The door opened and in walked Henry.

"I was supposed to do the cooking tonight," he exclaimed.

"Go for it. We've just been doing some prep work. Do you need help?"

"No thanks, I've got this. Isabella," he waved at his sister, "You may go do what you do best....relax and read a glam magazine," he teased.

"So how did it go with the dad?" I asked.

"Good. He's a nice man. He tried to muscle me a little bit, but Sam knows how to work the poor guy," he said, a faint smile spreading across his face.

"I've seen those beautiful eyes. Dads don't stand a chance with eyes like that."

"Neither do boyfriends," he laughed. "Mom, speaking of boyfriends...have you thought much about dating? You are all alone here. You don't have to get serious with anyone but maybe for some companionship."

"Are you giving me your permission or worried about me?" I tried to gather my thoughts after the quick change in subject.

"You don't need my permission, but I guess I'm doing a little of both. Besides, Samantha thinks you and her dad would have fun together if you were ready to date. I told her to stay out of it," he laughed.

"You are very wise, Son. Very wise indeed," I said reaching up to kiss him on the cheek.

# Chapter 17.

Dinner was a huge success. Henry cooked an outstanding meal. This child had paid attention in the kitchen. I can honestly say he used a few tricks of his own that sent this meal right over the top.

"Well, Chef Henry, this meal was spectacular," mother exclaimed.

"Thank you, Gran," Henry replied humbly.

"So, tell us more about Samantha. Your mother already told us she was beautiful. Where's her family from?" Mother asked.

"Her dad and grandfather are from this area. Her grandfather owned or still owns a local grocery store," Henry replied.

"Oh really? Which one? What's their last name?" Mother asked.

"Warner. Thomas Warner is her grandfather. Do you know them, Gran?" Henry replied.

It was at that very moment when the iced tea I was drinking sprayed out of my nose, mouth, and possibly my ears just like, Old Faithful. The projection even amazed me. Everyone around the dinner table stared at me before breaking out into laughter.

"Nice one, Mom," laughed Isabella.

Gasping for air, I managed to say, "As in Ben Warner...my boss?"

"Oh, Ben? He's Samantha's father?" inquired my mother with a mischievous twinkle in her eyes.

"Mom, are you ok?" Henry asked coming over to pat my back. "The Warner's market is where you work?"

"Yes, but it's called Bay Fresh Market. Now, I know where I've seen her eyes before," I coughed as I wiped myself off and dabbed those in my general vicinity.

"Does Ben know your last name?" I asked Henry.

"He never asked. I just told him I grew up here, and my mom and dad had owned a business consulting firm until my father passed away. He was more interested in my plans with school, my intentions, and eventual employment. Will this be a problem for you, Mom?" Henry asked concerned.

"No, I don't think so unless you break Samantha's heart or something. Then, I'll be out of a job, and you'll need to leave the country. It's just one of life's funny circumstances, that's all. They say it's a small world, but what are the chances of this happening?" I shook my head in astonishment. "You meet a girl in San Diego, and your mother works for her father, in the opposite direction. That's a crazy coincidence."

"Or fate," Mother interjected with a smile.

"Here we go," said Lizzy.

"What?" asked Mother. "You're going to tell me this is all dumb luck? There is no way things happen like this."

"So, you're saying Ben and Maggie are cosmically meant to be together?" Lizzy said shrugging her shoulders.

"I'm just saying this is all very interesting and maybe not just life's practical joke, that's all," Mother crossed her legs and adjusted her napkin.

"Ok, whatever. Change of subject, please," I demanded. "Let's enjoy our dinner and leave room for dessert. We have a plum galette, and Henry made some homemade brandy ice cream to go with it. It's delicious. OK, come on everyone….enjoy."

"Besides, Mom may not even be ready to date. Right, Mom?" Isabella said. She couldn't resist the opportunity, and I chose to busy myself with my plate of food.

# Chapter 18.

My visit with the children flew by quickly. At the end of the weekend, I helped pack each of their cars with luggage and keepsake boxes. The problem with weekend guests is; eventually, everyone goes home.

"Thanks, Mom, for everything. Are you sure there isn't anything else you need?" Henry asked.

"No, thank you. Get through your father's boxes as soon as you can. I have this feeling I may have overlooked something," I said as I wrapped my arms around his waist. "Samantha is wonderful, by the way. Thank you for bringing her. And we'll talk more about your plans very soon. I'm proud of you, Sweetheart," I said and sent him away with a kiss and a hug.

Henry was the first to leave. He was picking up Samantha at her grandfather's house and heading back to San Diego. They had a long trip ahead of them. Samantha was starting an internship with Ben's old architecture firm in the morning.

Isabella chose to stay through the morning to help me with a much-needed make-over. I was ready for a change, and she knew where to send me. Julia, her friend from high school, was working at a new spa that was getting great reviews. They did it all: hair, make-up, pedicures, massages, and the like.

Julia did her old friend a favor and got me in to see Roberto. According to Julia, he was fabulous.

We pulled up to Salon Revive, and I suddenly began to doubt my decision.

"Come on, Mom. Don't be nervous. You're going to look great.

You said yourself you were ready for a change."

I remembered a customer once told me, "When you're ready for a change, the whole world opens up to you." So, I exhaled and followed Isabella.

I smiled at my confident, energetic child. Isabella, who was all about fashion and glamor, was the right person to trust. She had already talked me into a fabulous summer handbag and gorgeous sandals to match.

"Oh, what the hell," I said under my breath.

As we entered the spa, I dare say, it was revitalizing. The sound of running water from a nearby fountain coupled with soothing Zen music was enough to begin to loosen my nervous tension away.

Julia squealed at the sight of Isabella and ran around the counter to hug her. "Izzy, I've missed you."

"Mom, you remember Julia, don't you?"

"Yes, I do. So nice to see you again, Julia. The two of you were inseparable your senior year," I said, reaching around her petite body to hug her. "Thank you so much for squeezing us in this morning."

"Happy to help old friends," Julia replied.

Julia faced Isabella and exclaimed, "So, you have to head back to Chico this afternoon? Too bad we can't hang out a little while."

"I know, Julia. I'm sorry about that, but this weekend was all about family stuff. Hopefully another time."

"Well, no matter," Julia said. "Mrs. Bloom, follow me, and we'll get you set up with Roberto. Izzy, I have you scheduled with Shawna for your pedicure." She gave another little squeal and off she went.

Roberto gasped when he met me. He immediately pushed me down into a chair, twirled me around and began to formulate a plan. I had a feeling this makeover was going to set me back next year's vacation fund. Isabella blew me a kiss, and that was the last I saw of her for the next hour and a half.

It wasn't long before I looked like something from a sci-fi movie-meets-horror film. All I lacked was black circles painted around my eyes. Roberto moved me to another chair, handed me a magazine, and set his timer. There between the pages in the magazine I learned all about what Hollywood was doing. I had not the faintest idea who half of these stars were. The fact they had just broken up with other stars I didn't know, left me cold. I tossed the magazine aside.

After a while, I was back in Roberto's prized chair. He explained to me, "Your natural curls should be celebrated, Mz. Bloom. Do not straighten your hair anymore. It's bad and damaging."

That's when he began to snip. And snip. And snip. Before I lost all consciousness, Roberto whispered something to me about Hallie Berry.

"Mom, you look sooooo great! Roberto, you are as fabulous as Julia said you were," I suddenly regained consciousness to the sound of Isabella's voice squealing at my side.

I examined myself from different angles and decided that Roberto was indeed fabulous. My hair was short and sassy, and my natural curls sat perfectly in all the right places. Roberto sold me a lot of hair products, promising me I could style my hair just as he did. My new hair color was softer and lighter than the bottled hair color I used at home.

"Mzz. Bloom, you are getting older now, yeah?" Roberto kindly reminded me. "Softer colors make our skin look younger, yeah?"

"Yes you're right," I said and promised him I would be back soon to keep up the illusion of a younger me.

Back in my driveway, Isabella said, "I love you, Mom. Thanks for everything. You look pretty. Not that you didn't before, just better. My friends at school always told me what a pretty mom I had, and it's still true."

"I love you too, my darling Bell. Please call me if you need anything," I said. "I'm here for you, alright? And thank you for all of this and for coming home this weekend." I hugged her and held her to me. "Text me when you're home."

I stood in the middle of the driveway watching Isabella drive away. With a little beep, she turned the corner and was out of sight. I took a deep breath and let out a sigh. Children are such a large part of our soul.

I strolled back into my home and looked around to make sure nothing was left behind. There was nothing but the faint smell of Isabella's perfume. I let out a sigh. This visit with her was enjoyable.

Then my phone binged. I saw a text from Henry's phone: Thank you, Mrs. Bloom, for everything. It was a pleasure meeting you :) Sam.

I smiled and sent up a prayer for the protection of my children on their long journey home.

I couldn't resist the urge to walk into my bathroom to check myself out. For years, I had been shocked to see an older version of myself. In my mind, I was still a college girl searching to find my purpose. Today was different. I did a little dance as I sang, "I'm too sexy for my hair, too sexy for my shoes, too sexy for my - new - clothes."

I ran the vacuum, cleaned the bathrooms, and dropped the sheets into the washer. I made my way into the kitchen and opened the refrigerator door to see what surprises lurked inside. There were three cupcakes left. Feeling a little low and alone, in spite of my new look, I debated the number of cakes it would take to make me feel whole again. My phone suddenly binged, saving me from an immediate decision.

The text was from Dean: You said last week you wanted a ride on my Harley sometime. You in for a ride to the old bridge before dusk?

I pondered the invitation and weighed the choice between three cupcakes or my first Harley ride. What could it hurt?

Hell yeah : ) I texted back.

I changed my clothes from a spring skirt to a long pair of jeans and a long sleeve white shirt. Spring evenings could be cold, so I debated bringing a jacket. I wished I had some riding boots, but my Nike running shoes were the best I could do. I wrapped two cupcakes and made a thermos of hot coffee as a treat.

It wasn't long until I heard the engine of a Harley making its way up the driveway. A happy feeling came over me as I anticipated this road trip.

"It's a new life, Bloom. Start living it," I reminded myself.

I ran out the door and approached the beautiful midnight blue Harley with childlike wonder. Dean cut the engine and smiled at me. He wore the whole get-up, and very well I might add. Jeans, leather, and when he pulled off his helmet, I discovered he was even wearing a black Harley bandanna around his dirty blond hair.

"How did you get past the security gate without calling me?"

With a cunning smile, he only replied, "You ready, Bloom? What's in the bag?"

"A treat for the bridge. You got a trunk or something on this thing?"

He laughed, "Something like that."

Dean got off the Harley and opened up a compartment. He stood about five-eleven in his boots. He weighed considerably less now than when I first met him. I knew his countless hours at the gym was less about healthy habits and more about avoiding an empty house. He pulled out a leather jacket and handed it to me.

"This is one of my extra riding jackets. You'll need it for protection, and I also have a helmet in here for you. Hey..." Dean stopped short and stared at me. "You changed your hair. Are those natural curls?" he asked pulling on one.

I felt like the cheerleader in high school, wearing the quarterback's letterman's jacket, as I slipped into the soft leather.

"Yes. I've straightened my hair since college," I replied. "My daughter talked me into a makeover with a stylist named Roberto, and they agreed my hair should go natural."

"I like it. It's a lot shorter, but I like it," he said with an approving nod.

Dean tucked the insulated bag into a compartment and helped me with my helmet. He got onto the Harley and motioned me aboard. I was excited and terrified at the same time. I hopped on and got myself situated. I found my footrests, and I settled back into a comfy seat with back support and everything.

Dean started up the Harley, and all I could think was, "Holy shit!" He backed it up and turned it around. He gave it some gas and my hands flew up to his shoulders, to hang on. My heart was pounding in my chest with a mixture of fear and exhilaration.

We pulled up to the exit gate and waited for it to swing open. I watched it with interest, suddenly seeing it as a striking metaphor for my life. The massive gate slowly swung open to let us out onto the busy street.

Traffic was high, but Dean maneuvered us through it, weaving through cars as if he was one with the road. We made it out to the old highway, and that's where we gained some speed. Unable to hold back my excitement any longer, I let out a loud, "Yahoooo." I could see Dean's face in the rearview mirror, laughing with me.

The fresh spring breeze engulfed us as we took flight. I began to relax, confident in Dean's driving. We left the busy city and the traffic behind us, making our way past the children's hospital and out onto country roads.

Without a care, I marveled as we passed green fields and blossoming fruit trees. As we came closer to the river bend, the air became a little cooler, and the road began to wind. The roads ebbed and flowed as we traveled toward the bridge.

The sky began to turn a golden hue, promising a show for us from the top of the old bridge. Few people came out this far anymore, except for photographers and bird watchers. But on a Monday evening, people were hurrying home to catch the six o'clock news or pick up their kids from soccer practice.

Dean brought the Harley to a stop at the top of the bridge. As we got off the bike, I reminded Dean of the insulated bag. I hurried to the front of the bridge, overlooking the riverbed. I pulled off my helmet and shook out my hair.

"Hey, before I forget," I said, taking my cell phone out of my shirt pocket. "Would you take a picture of me in front of your bike? My kids won't believe I did this."

Dean snapped my photo and handed the phone back to me. We sat down on the edge of the bridge with our feet dangling below us, getting a front row seat to the sunset.

I looked over at him sitting beside me and said, "This is the best thing I've done in a very long time. Thanks."

"You're welcome. So, what did you pack us?" Dean asked.

"Ahh. A delicious treat while we watch the light show." I took out the thermos and filled the lid to the top, leaving an equal amount of coffee inside the thermos. I handed Dean the cup and set the thermos next to me. I reached back into the bag, retrieving the lemon cupcakes. I gave one of the wrapped cakes to Dean, keeping the other for myself.

"Holy cow, Bloom," he exclaimed after his first bite. "I think this is the best cupcake I've ever tasted. This coffee is pretty good too. You could start a business."

"Thanks. I made them for my kids; they're Isabella's favorite." We sat and ate in silence as we watched the sky change and the sun began to set.

"Did Carolyn ride with you?" I asked Dean.

"Only once. She hated it. It scared her to death, and she wasn't interested in getting used to it. I could tell she didn't want me riding either, but she never said anything to me out loud. I think she knew it was my outlet. It's always been my way of getting away from it all. So, I joined this group of guys that I knew, and we started taking short trips together. In fact, I'm going back on the road with them at the end of this month. I'd love to bike through Europe someday. Ireland in particular."

"Well, I hope you do it. It sounds great. My dream is to go to Italy and learn to cook real Italian food from a local nonna. I want to stay on working farms and move around Italy and learn to cook regional food. My husband promised we would go someday, but you know how that goes."

112

We fell silent for a few moments, comfortable in each other's presence.

"How are you doing these days without Carolyn?" I dared to ask.

"It's different every day, you know?" Dean replied slowly. "Some days I miss her so much I can hardly stand it. Other days, I remember all the irritating things she used to do," he chuckled. "She wasn't happy for a long time. She wanted kids. I encouraged her to adopt, but she chose to spend a fortune on fertility drugs and treatments. That got her nowhere for years and put a real strain on us. She became sad after that. Carolyn wore a happy face, and we enjoyed each other, but behind the smile lived a disappointed woman. I could never change that for her no matter how hard I tried. Then, she got sick," he concluded.

"That's tough," I said. "Life doesn't make sense to me sometimes. The older I get, I think life has gotten more complicated instead of easier."

"You're right," he chuckled again. "We're supposed to have it all figured out by the time we are our age, right?"

"Well, maybe your age…I'm not as old as you are," I corrected him. We both laughed.

The moon was full. Although we didn't need the extra light, Dean turned on his flashlight. He stood it on end, illuminating us even more. I was absorbed in gazing at the stars when I suddenly became acutely aware of his eyes focused on me. He seemed puzzled, and I lifted my eyebrows in inquiry.

"What?" I asked him.

"Remember when I told you that I thought I knew you from somewhere?" he said. "It's the curly hair…New Year's Eve party around 1980." He tried to explain and read my face at the same time. "You were there with some friends and a guy named Charlie. You guys fought, and he left you sitting on the porch steps in the backyard. Was that you?"

My expression changed as I remembered that night. "Yes, I do remember that party. I had huge hair then...I mean big hair," I laughed. "Wait, you weren't that guy who..."

Smiling, he nodded. "Yes, I was," he admitted, grinning from ear to ear.

"You sat down next to me and handed me a beer. You said, "You know, everybody thinks Charlie is a jerk. You can do way better than him. And I said, "Like you for instance? Then you said, "Well, I know you could do a lot worse."

I laughed at the memory. "Small world," I almost whispered.

Dean jumped in, "Then you said something like: "My Gran always said that true love is like seeing a ghost. We all talk about it, but few of us have ever really seen one. Or something like that," he said and laughed.

"That's right, I did," I replied shocked that he remembered. "Gran was not a romantic. You remember me saying that? I can't believe it."

"It was funny; you were funny. You left an impression on me. And you wouldn't give me your number," Dean said.

"Hey, Charlie was a bad experience. I wasn't too sure I wouldn't get more of the same."

"I have a confession to make," he said.

"Oh, what would that be?" I asked.

"I had no idea who Charlie was. I just said that to sit down next to you with that big hair and little short skirt of yours. I overheard your friends call him Charlie," he confessed, grinning.

I shook my head. "I remember you had pretty big hair too."

"Everything was big then. Big hair, big flared pants, big shoes, and big wide collars too. Remember that style? All the guys tried to look like Barry Gibb."

We both laughed out loud.

"Then at midnight, when everyone was shouting "Happy New Year" I leaned over and kissed you."

"Yes, you did," I said, nodding my head, remembering what a great kiss it was.

"And you still didn't give me your number," he said.

"This is so embarrassing," I said as I placed my hands over my face.

"Don't be. It was a long time ago. The last thing I remember, you smiled at me and said, "See you around." For a long time, I wondered about you. It could have been interesting had we bumped into each other again," he said thoughtfully.

"I thought I would see you again," I explained. "I left it to fate. My mother taught me to believe in fate."

"And do you still?" he asked.

"I don't know. You met Carolyn, and I met Edward. We got married. Was that our fate? At least we can say we've been loved by someone good."

Dean nodded. "See, if you hadn't gone natural with your hair, I may have never put it together," he teased me and tugged at my bangs. "Hey, let's get out of here."

I packed up my bag and pulled on my helmet. Less than five minutes later, we were back on the bike and headed toward home. I couldn't help think what a crazy weekend I had with Henry announcing he wanted to be a chef and dating Ben's daughter. My new hairdo. And now discovering that Dean was the New Year's kiss I thought about for a very long time. As Mother would say, "Life can be fascinating."

I sent a text to Henry and Isabella along with the photo of me in front of Dean's Harley: You'll never believe what I did. Went on Harley ride tonight and it was fun. See what a new haircut will do! xoxo, Mom

# Chapter 19.

A few days later, I was back at work. I decided to come in early, before my shift, to talk to Ben about Henry and Samantha. I parked my Mini in my usual place and noticed both Ben and Dean were already at work. The doors opened automatically, and familiar smells came rushing back to me. I took the stairs straight up to Ben's office, on the second floor, with a dozen freshly baked limoncello cupcakes for good measure.

Tami, the office receptionist, wasn't in yet, so I walked through to Ben's office and knocked on the door.

"Hi, Maggie," Ben greeted, quickly standing up as I entered the room. "Welcome back," he said. "You've been missed around here. And you're sporting a new look. I love the curls."

"Thank you, Ben. Glad to be back. Yes, I have naturally curly hair. My daughter insisted on a makeover while she was visiting. Do you have a minute to talk?" I caught myself nervously chattering.

"Always. What's up?"

I removed the napkin from the plate that covered the wrapped cupcakes and placed them on his desk. He looked at the cakes and began to speak when he realized he had seen them before. He stared at the cupcakes for a moment, then looked back at me.

Ben took in a deep breath and said, "You're Henry's mom?"

"Yes. You told me your daughter's name was Grace, so when I met Samantha, I didn't put two and two together until after Henry met you. He reported back to me, and to make a long story short, how small is this world anyway?"

"Wow," he said. "Wow...now that I see your curls and having seen his, the resemblance is unmistakable. Grace is my nickname for her…ballet. I called her Princess Grace once, and it stuck.

You raised a good man, Maggie. I would have been tough on anyone Sam brought home for me to meet. She is my one and only."

"Yeah, I get that. And Samantha is lovely. When Henry announced your last name during our family dinner celebration, iced tea sprayed out of every opening in my head. I was astonished, to say the least."

I could see Ben imagining the scene, as he began to laugh and shake his head. "I can only imagine, Maggie. Shocked were you?"

"This is a crazy coincidence, isn't it? They met in San Diego for heaven sakes; it's a pretty big place, right? They didn't even know we knew each other. Strange, funny strange."

"I know this is a little awkward, but don't worry about it. It's their journey after all. Sam thought you and I should meet, which is ironic. You've done a great job raising Henry. He's bright, has your sense of humor, and seems to care about Sam. And now that the shock is wearing off…these are the best cupcakes I have ever eaten. You willing to share the recipe with our bakery?"

"That might be up for discussion. My grandmother's recipe. I need to get downstairs and clock in. Thanks, Ben. Enjoy the cupcakes and don't forget to share."

I quickened my step around the courtesy booth when I heard Dean's voice call out to me, "Bloom, you have three minutes!"

With my best Irish accent, I hollered, "Top of the morning to you, Phillips!"

As I passed the meat department and waved, I heard whistles and wolf calls, so the least I could do was a 360 for the group. It was a good feeling to be back and part of my work family again.

"Seriously, Bobbie? I haven't even clocked in yet, and rumors are flying around about me. They must have seen me coming from the parking lot. I bet you twenty bucks the source is Melissa in the bakery. You should see her around Ben. And the look on her face when he bought me a bagel last week. If looks could kill."

"Well, apparently you're on a manhunt. I bet you twenty bucks you'll have had a facelift and a boob job before lunch," Bobbie laughed. "Welcome back, Maggie. I did miss you."

I clocked in and asked Dean which register was mine.

"That would be five, Maggie. Hey, have you heard the rumors about you?"

"Apparently, getting a haircut around here means you're looking for a man."

"I better be careful," Dean laughed. "I was planning to get one on my lunch hour."

"Did you hear the rumor about you?" I quipped.

"There's a rumor about me?"

"Yep. Words out you've got it bad for Martha."

"It's a little hard not to notice her. But could you imagine being suffocated by…?"

"Aghh, no visuals, please. I better get to work, or you'll end up on my short list too."

I put in my code and was ready for business on register five.

"Welcome back, Maggie," cheered the morning men's group.

"Thanks, guys. You're the best."

I heard the off-loading of groceries and looked up to find Bruce at my register. Bruce is affectionately known as the Mountain Man. He is nearly seven feet tall and built like a brick wall. Someone you would never want to meet in a dark alley. He has a low booming voice, long black hair, and a gruff manner. The box boys were intimidated by him, but I believed Bruce was misunderstood.

"Aaron, could you please help Bruce unload his groceries, please?" I said.

Aaron gave me a look that I interpreted as "you've got to be kidding."

"Good morning, Bruce," I said.

"Yeah. Hello. You know the way I like my groceries packed, Maggie. Don't let these knuckleheads screw it up, will you?"

"We'll get it done for you Bruce, don't worry."

As I scanned Bruce's groceries, I also organized them in a manner they were to be packed, guiding Aaron along the way. The produce was weighed and then returned to Bruce's care. One tries hard not to judge the service a customer requires, but merely ensures the best service he or she needs.

"Aaron, please double bag all the canned goods and make sure the weight is evenly distributed among the bags," I requested. As I continued to scan Bruce's groceries, I looked up to find Ben and George watching us from above.

I placed the baked goods in plastic bags and added small paper bag hats to cover the exposed portion of the baguettes. I directed Aaron to get another shopping cart for the groceries. It was a well-rehearsed dance for Bruce's peace of mind. The learning curve was a difficult one.

"Bruce, your total for today is $378.92. Let me call a manager for the store charge." The store charge was set up for customers who settled their bill at the end of every month. These were longtime customers of Thomas Warner's. In Bruce's case, his mother had established the credit and extended it to her son.

Dean had entered the checkstand without me realizing it, and as I stepped back, I felt his hand press against the small of my back. His hand remained there, as his other hand reached around me, pushing the necessary keys on the register. It surprised me that I felt discomposed, as his breath brushed against my neck.

I managed to thank Bruce and hand him a copy of his receipt. Dean reminded me it was time to take a well-deserved break.

# Chapter 20.

Henry called to tell me that upon graduation he decided to stay in San Diego. Through catering parties, he had met the owner of a trendy restaurant called Sergio's. Sergio loved Henry's food and offered him a paid internship with his restaurant. It isn't often in life we meet someone who is willing to help us succeed in our dreams. Henry jumped at the chance and was going to dedicate himself to learning everything he could about the food industry.

I've adopted the philosophy that if we expect great things in our lives and maintain a grateful heart, two things happen. One, we are much happier when we focus on what is right in our lives. And second, given the appreciative perspective, we are open to recognizing opportunity when it comes our way. Soon your path will begin to unfold in front of you, one possibility at a time.

Given that perspective and inspired by my son, I decided to apply for the management position that had opened in the bakery. Not only would it be good for me to learn how to run a department, but the bump in salary would also allow me to help Henry realize his food truck dream.

I finished my favorite breakfast of scrambled egg tacos with fresh dill and washed my dish. I hurried into the bathroom to brush my teeth. I wanted to be at work early to make an appointment to see George and Ben. I was hoping to discuss the possibilities for the management position.

When I got to work, I briskly walked the grocery floor looking for George. I found him back in the produce warehouse talking with Russ Gentry, the produce manager.

"This must be where all the cool people hang out," I said as I came through the double doors.

"If by cool, you mean the temperature, then I would say you're in the right place," quipped Russ.

"The smell of those fresh herbs you're snipping is intoxicating."

Russ was one of my favorite people at Bay's. He was sixty-two years old with great hair. Russ took good care of himself and always sported a tan from fishing on his pontoon boat. He spoke kindly of others and had a twinkle in his eye, ready for mischief.

"George, can you spare me a minute?" I asked.

"Hold on to your belt, George," Russ joked. "This one can charm the pants off of you."

"Lucky me. See you around, Russ," George said and turned to me. "You can't be asking for vacation time because you just got back."

"See you later, Russ," I called out.

George Smith was the kind of man that said what he meant and meant what he said. Although he was always good for a joke now and then, he ran a tight ship. George asked for only one thing from employees, and that was a job well done. He strove for excellence and was a tough, albeit fair leader. At the age of seventy-two, he was nowhere near slowing down. I liked George. If he were single, I would introduce him to my mother.

"George, I was wondering if you and Ben could spare me a few minutes this morning? I have a proposition for you," I said.

"Sounds interesting. Give me a minute to run up and see if Ben is free and I'll call you."

"Great. Thanks."

I was reminding myself to expect great things today. I heard

George's booming voice calling my name over the intercom.

Adrenaline coursed through my body, almost forcing me to take the stairs by two. I walked into the receptionist room, and Tami was receiving a call, so she smiled and waved me through to Ben's office. George shared an office with Dean, just left of Tami's desk.

I entered Ben's office with a cheerful, "Good morning."

Ben's smile always stopped me for a split second; my attraction to him unnerved me. He was a tall man with the rugged good looks of T.V. characters Magnum PI and the boyish qualities of Richard Castle.

"Hello, Maggie. How are you this morning?" he asked.

"I'm great, thank you. Thanks for making time for me."

"Always," Ben smiled.

I wasted no time, getting to the point. "The reason I wanted to meet with you was that I'm very interested in the bakery management position. I believe my skill sets are just what the bakery needs."

The two of them looked at each other and then back at me without comment. I trusted this was the moment where I was supposed to prove my point.

"I'm incredibly organized. And although I haven't had any formal training in management, I have spent years organizing and managing volunteers for countless charities. My customer service skills and personality are needed in the department. The bakery seems to be the only department in the store where employees come and go through a revolving door.

That in part is due to our last bakery manager's lack of leadership. But I also believe the bakery has an identity crisis. There is no reason we can't be known as "the best bakery in town." We already have the best bagels. The girls need to be met with individually to assess their strengths and weaknesses. With some organization and leadership, we can build a cohesive unit." I took a deep breath to calm my nerves.

George cleared his throat. "Maggie, I appreciate your interest in improving our store. Your presentation is just another reason why I believe you are not here just punching a clock and getting a paycheck. I wish we had more employees that were as committed to the success of our store as you are. Although I believe that everything you said about yourself and the department is true, there is a matter that needs addressing before we could consider your promotion."

"What kind of matter?" I asked.

"Maggie, I wanted to talk to you about this before you went on your vacation," Ben said, "but I decided to wait and see how things shook out first. I believe there is a reasonable explanation for this problem, but we need your help solving it. Your tills have been coming up short for a few weeks now. Between one and two hundred dollars."

I could see Ben choosing his words carefully. "Before this time, and before I arrived here, your till has always balanced near perfectly."

"Is it my tills only or have there been others?" I questioned.

"There have been others, but your till has been the most consistent. Do you recall any transactions that have been out of the ordinary?" George asked.

"I can't image why this has happened," I scowled. "Can you give me dates and amounts? Maybe there is a pattern here?" I suggested.

The intercom paged for George's assistance. He excused himself, and I turned my attention to Ben.

"I've created a spreadsheet. Come around the desk and take a look. Does anything here ring a bell? We've checked and double checked through accounting, and nothing appears to be out of place there."

I stood on wobbly legs to make my way around to Ben's side of the desk. It took a second to regain my bearings. Nobody had accused me of anything yet.

"Can we compare this with scheduling to see if on the days the tills went short, the same people were working," I said fighting to keep my composure. "There has to be an explanation. I don't see myself handing out the wrong change all of a sudden. What about upper management? Who was here those days?" I asked, trying to keep my voice from shaking.

Ben looked up at me. It was a fair question.

"Well, let's take a look." He compared the schedule to the dates on the spreadsheet and wrote the names of the managers on duty in blue ink. There wasn't a consistent pattern.

"And ownership?" I bravely asked. Ben looked up at me and met my eyes. "I wouldn't steal from you," I asserted firmly. "I wouldn't steal from anyone."

"I know that."

"Have you looked at the security camera tapes?"

"No, not yet. I kept thinking accounting would find the discrepancy."

"What days was Michael closing the store? The word on the grocery floor is he treats when they party."

"I don't see him stealing from his own business. He's a lot of things, and that's why I'm here, but I don't see him stealing from his own family," Ben said defensively.

"What if he's in deep? Look, I don't want to be saying this about Michael. I know we haven't gotten along since he...." I stopped abruptly.

"What happened? Did he come on to you?" Ben questioned,

guessing at the truth.

"Let's say that he's not a fan since I turned him down."

"Damn it, Michael," Ben said under his breath.

"In all fairness Ben, you haven't accused me of stealing, but we are dancing on the edge of it. Please take a look at the security tapes on those dates. I don't think it's too much to ask."

"I don't know if they exist anymore. We reuse the tapes eventually. But yes, of course, I'll check it out. Maggie, I'm not accusing you of anything. I was hoping you had an explanation. Let me call on the tapes. Are you alright?" Ben asked.

"I saw this day going much differently. I'd better get back to work." I turned and walked out of the office. Before I got to the landing, I could hear Ben's voice ordering up security tapes from Tami.

I left the office and clocked in late. As I walked to my register, I began talking to myself and doubting my abilities. What if I'm having a brain fart or something and I've been giving out the wrong change. I am over fifty, and that's when weird shit starts to happen to you. I'm not good at math, but I'm not several hundred dollars bad at math. In fact, I know deep down something isn't right here.

I saw Dean approaching me on his way to the courtesy desk.

"Hey, you up for a ride after work?" I asked him.

"As in Harley."

"Just a short one, through the park maybe. I could go for a ride. My day's not going so well."

"What time are you off?" Dean asked.

"Five, you?"

"I'll pick you up around 6:30....and don't eat," he added.

"Thanks." I looked around to make sure nobody was in earshot.

My day slowly improved and then Martha came through the doors. There are some days the universe does not cooperate or does it?

Martha looked perfect today. Beautiful actually. Things must be going well for her. She wore a leopard baby sling across her chest that contrasted with her black suit. Her heels were nosebleed high but made her already beautiful legs even more shapely. In spite of all the work she continued to do to her body, Martha was beautiful. She had a lovely face with almond-shaped eyes. I wished she could see herself as I did, and leave well enough alone.

As she swept through the store, many a male customer strained their necks to get a better look at her. I decided to stay close to the phone, just in case one of them took out a pickle display.

When Martha finally deposited her grocery items, onto the belt at my register, I caught sight of what she carried in her leopard baby sling. Crushed between Martha's large breasts was a tiny dog.

"Maggie, I would like you to meet Mr. Beasley," she said, in a small baby voice. "Mr. Beasley, this is my terrific friend, Maggie."

"How do you do, Mr. Beasley," I offered. I had no dogs of my own. I didn't have cats. I was not fond of cats. Edward had a dog that I adopted after we were married. He was a handsome white lab named Gary. Gary was delightful, but he had bad hips. Eventually, we had to put him down. We never replaced him.

"Mr. Beasley is smart and potty trained, and sometimes you forget he's even there. He's quiet. Do you like Mr. Beasley, Maggie?"

"He's a fine…dog, Martha. How long have you had him?" I asked uninterestedly.

"I had him flown here, when he was a pup, from North Carolina. He's a little over a year old now. You would like him, Maggie. He is loyal and sweet and does the funniest things," she continued.

"I'm sure he's all of those things. That will be forty-seven, sixty-three, please," I said feeling suspicious of all this dog chatter.

"Oh, I'm sorry. I'm going on and on about the dog and not paying attention."

She handed me a hundred dollar bill and sixty-three cents. I counted back the change, twice, just to be satisfied. As she walked away, two box boys fought over her plastic bags of groceries.

It was time for my lunch break; I decided to eat in the store. Clocking out, I grabbed my handbag and walked over to the deli. The special was a French dip sandwich, with a bag of chips and a drink for five-ninety-nine. I placed my order and waited.

A familiar voice came from behind me and asked if he could join me for lunch.

"Parcey, how are you?" I said. Parcey was tall, slim, and had good posture. His black hair was slicked back and slightly receded. He had a strong square jaw and broad nose. He was short of handsome but carried himself like a movie actor; like Bogart or Lancaster. My mother would have appreciated him.

"I'm fine, Doll. Can I buy you some lunch?" he asked.

"I think my superiors might frown on it, but you could join me on the patio."

"What are you having?" Parcey asked.

"The special; a French dip."

"I'll go with the clam chowder soup," he told Emily behind the counter.

We picked up our orders and headed toward the checkout station. I looked up and saw Ben looking down at me from the office. He didn't seem happy. We paid for our food separately and walked toward the patio. I was going to use this time wisely with Parcey and see what I could find out.

When we sat down, I asked him to tell me about himself. He volunteered that he lived with his father. His father was ninety-one and didn't want to live in a nursing home. Parcey sold his father's house and moved him into his home.

"We take care of our own. We're not like most people these days; dumping our parents off in some home. I have a woman who comes in and helps with a few things, but Pop is doing ok. He still likes doing things for himself," Parcey told me.

He then informed me he had divorced from his wife when Gabriel was a little boy. But, he assured me, he did enjoy a variety of companions now and then.

"That surprises me," I said, "because I worked a night shift, not long ago, when you came in with a tall, dark-haired woman. You were wearing a tux. You looked very dapper, I might add, and I thought you were celebrating an anniversary."

"Oh no, that was my lady friend, Sheila. We had gone to a charity event, and I popped in to pick up a bottle of champagne," he explained.

"Oh, I see. You have a way with the ladies, huh?" I teased.

"How long has it been since your husband died?" he countered, ignoring my question.

"My husband? Did I tell you about my husband?" I asked feeling forgetful.

"I heard about him," he said.

Heard about him? Who would have told him something personal

about me, I thought? "I understand you own a psychic business? How did you get into that line of work?"

"Have we talked about that before?" he asked.

"I've heard about it," I said with a smile.

"Yes," Parcey chuckled, "my family comes from a long line of gypsies. We have that ability, to read the future."

"Can you read my future?" I asked, holding up my palm for him to see.

"Yes," he studied my palm. "I see a rich, tall, dark, handsome older man sweeping you off your feet," Parcey chuckled. "You need to pay a visit to my Aunt Dika. She has a real gift, that one. You should let me take you some time. We can have some dinner first and get to know one another better," he suggested.

"That sounds interesting. I've never had my fortune read. How does it work?" I asked.

"Tea and cards. She's extremely accurate," he assured.

I looked at my watch and saw I was running out of time.

"What does Gabriel do?" I wanted to sneak in a few more questions. "I see him come in, once in a while. It seems you've raised a respectable man."

"Gabriel works with me. He's all right. His mother spoils him too much. But hey, he's my only son. What can I say?" Parcey shrugged.

"Well," I stood to go. "This was nice, Parcey. Thank you. Unfortunately, I must go back to work now," I told him as I picked up my trash.

"It was my pleasure. Hey, how about Friday night? You working?"

"I'm on the late shift. You can pick me up here at eight?" I suggested. "Too late for dinner, but I'll let you buy me some coffee."

"Sounds great, Doll. I'll see you Friday," Parcey winked at me before I turned to walk away.

As I headed back toward my register, Bobbie fell into step next to me.

"Interesting lunch date you had today," she quizzed. "You had some heads turning. Ben is one of them. He tried to be all nonchalant, but I noticed him looking out the window at you about every five seconds."

"What?" I snarled.

"Just sayin'."

I rolled my eyes. As I reached for my closed sign, Ben snatched it up and handed it to me.

"You open? Did you have a nice lunch?" he inquired casually.

I grabbed his sandwich and drink and pulled it through the scanner. "Yes. Unexpected company. I'm just keeping my ears opened."

"You're not going out of your way for what we talked about, are you?"

"Not at all," I assured him.

Ben studied me for a few seconds while I smiled innocently up at him. As he walked away, my gut was telling me Michael had something to do with my tills being short and it was up to me to prove it.

# Chapter 21.

Dean picked me up at six-thirty sharp.

"How is it that you always avoid my security gate? You are
supposed to call me, and I buzz you in. That's how I know you're here.
I've never once buzzed you in, Phillips," I scolded him.

"Bad day, Bloom?"

"I'm sure you would know."

"How's that?"

"You are my boss, aren't you? My register tills ring a bell?"

"Oh yeah, I heard about that. Accounting will figure it out. Don't
worry about it, Bloom. No one is accusing you of anything."

"It bothers me. Things like that don't happen to me."

"They happen to all of us, sometime or another. Hop on."

We left my complex and drove through one of my favorite
neighborhoods, as we made our way to the park. The Bluffs were an
established neighborhood filled with tall trees and well-manicured lawns.
However, no one living here was mowing their front yards. The homes
were traditional, extensive, and the gardens were those featured on the
cover of magazines.

Perfectly trimmed boxwood hedges framed the walkways and
drives. Cascading hydrangeas, ivy and wisteria-draped stone fences and
trellis'. Each home was showing up his neighbor. I loved every inch of
this neighborhood.

We pulled into the park and followed the winding road that led
past the Japanese gardens. We drove toward the back of the park, where
the outdoor amphitheater stood. Adjacent from the theater, benches lined
the walkway that faced the bluffs. Each seat wore a brass plate inscribed

with its donor's name.

Dean parked the Harley near the walkway, and we walked toward the benches. We chose one, that garnered the best view, and sat down with our dinner and drinks.

"Chinese?" I asked, giddily.

"Joy Luck," he announced bouncing his eyebrows up and down.

"A man after my own heart."

We sat and ate in silence, enjoying the shadow effects the sun created as it made its way down.

"Do you have any plans on Saturday?" Dean asked. "The club is going on a road trip to Yosemite for the day. You want to come?"

"I can't go on Saturday. I've already accepted another invitation," I explained, regretfully. "That will be an amazing trip. I don't think I've been to Yosemite since the kids were in middle school," I said.

"That's a shame. We're supposed to have nice weather. Can you reschedule your plans?" Dean asked.

"No, I don't think so. I've put this one off before," I explained with hesitation.

"Bloom, do you have a date Saturday?" Dean asked.

I hung my head down as I confessed. "I do. My sister has been trying to set me up with someone she works with for months now. I've been putting him off, but...I don't know...I guess I'm ready for some companionship. Someone to do things with, you know? Company."

"Huh? Well, I'm good company. If you like this guy, you won't be able to ride with me anymore."

"How would that change anything? Of course, I'll still ride with you. No man is going to tell me I can't ride with you," I said as I waved my index finger in mid-air.

"I know how you women are. You'll want to spend more time with him and yadda, yadda, yadda," he complained.

"I guess you don't know me very well. You sound pathetic, Dean Phillips," I laughed at him. "Are you feeling sorry for yourself?"

"No. It's just if you want someone to hang out with; I can hang out with you. That way you don't have to put yourself through all that uncomfortable, first date bull shit," he clarified.

"It does suck, doesn't it? Well, a crazy thing happens to your friends when your spouse dies. Suddenly, you find yourself without friends. You find out they were your "couple friends." If you are no longer a couple, it changes the dynamic of the group. So you wake up one morning to find that your friends, the ones you have known for years, have all but vanished."

"Or, their wives start hitting on you," Dean added.

"Exactly. Right? Then, you're forced to make new friends. And that's why I should go on this date Saturday. Besides, it would be nice to get out of my uniform once in a while and feel like a girl again," I said thoughtfully.

I sensed Dean felt annoyed as he sat silently looking out onto the bluffs. I welcomed the break. After a while, he stood up and announced it was probably time to head back. I concurred, grabbing empty food containers and tossed them into the trash, as we walked back toward the Harley.

We traced the same route back, enjoying the cool breeze the evening brought with it. I thought about our conversation and was puzzled over Dean's reactions. I had to confess; I felt a strong connection toward him. Whenever he got too close to me, I started to sweat. Whenever he touched me, I felt the electricity. But he kept me off balance and unsure of myself. It felt dangerous, and it was something I intended to avoid. And he was my boss.

As we pulled into my driveway, the security gate gave way to us. Dean slowly rolled up to my front door and turned off the Harley. We both got off the bike, and I took off his jacket and helmet and handed them back to him.

As Dean reached for them, he said, "Maggie, I like you. You're fun and easy to be around. You've understood what I've been through this past year and you don't keep asking me… If I was to ask you out, would you go with me on a date?"

My body tensed and I felt the heat, like a hot flash, consume me. I looked up at him with his sexy mess of dirty-blond hair and swallowed hard. I could handle a friendship with him, but that was where I drew the line. I didn't know myself well enough yet, for anything more.

"First, you are my boss which makes that a messy question. I like spending time with you as a friend. The truth is I'm not ready for someone like you. But, I hope you'll ask me again, another time," I explained.

He smiled at me with understanding in his eyes. He nodded, "OK. See you at work."

"I still get to ride with you, right?" I asked.

"Absolutely," he said. I waved goodbye to Dean and went inside my condo. After closing the door, I leaned up against it, listening to him slowly drive up to the gate. I slid down until my butt touched the floor, as I heard him drive away.

I sent a combined text to both Isabella and Henry saying: Miss you-love you. Mom.

# Chapter 22.

There were over sixty employees who work at Bays Market. In the nearly three years of employment, I've witnessed three marital affairs and one divorce as a result. One of the couples I walked in on inside the milk cooler. I said "sorry" as if I were in the wrong place. I had a hard time making eye contact with either one of them after that.

The box boys were always chatting up the single young ladies on their breaks. Plans for parties or dates were arranged publicly without discretion. The look on their faces the next day was telling of who participated in what. I have, on more than one occasion, been invited to go out and rage. I had no idea what that meant.

My identity at the store was one of mom, counselor, and confidant. The young women shared their broken hearts with me, while the young men kissed and told. Interestingly enough, Michael's name seemed to come up fairly often. According to some of the boys, he apparently had the best s#*! As a mother, I counted my blessings that my children were safe and sound.

People from all walks of life and backgrounds; short, fat, tall, odd, broken, and the beautiful happen into a grocery store on a daily basis. Some are forthcoming. You quickly learn a lot about their lives while others never even mention their names. But the familiar faces come and go on a regular basis. And when you're off of work for a day, you are missed. They hold you accountable the following day. You become a family of sorts.

What makes a grocery store unique from other workplaces, I'm not sure. But I've seen more of life happen here, than anywhere else I've been. I've seen couples outwardly argue about dinner or personal finances, to couples who should literally "get a room." I've had a front-row seat watching lives in progress, over these last few years. Maybe it's the preservatives in our food.

The toughest days on the job are when customers, you have become close to, have experienced a loss. Half of our customers are elderly due to Bays location in an older established neighborhood. Couples who shop together regularly, suddenly, begin to come in alone. You become hesitant to inquire about the Mr. or Mrs. that's absent. Today was that kind of day.

It had been a while since I saw my friends Elizabeth and Joe. Joe kept me apprised of Elizabeth's battle with specialists who were trying to locate the source of her pain. On her last visit, not long ago, Elizabeth didn't seem herself behind her jolly exterior. She shared with me how blessed her life was. She had accomplished all she had dreamed. Elizabeth wished me the same. She said, "It's never too late for dreams to come true and you're never too old to dream them. So dream big, Maggie. You are just the sort of person who will follow through."

One afternoon, I clocked out for my lunch hour without much of an appetite. I wandered over to the deli to view the daily specials. As I approached the salad counter, I spotted Joe looking into the glass case.

I walked up next to him and tapped him on the shoulder. "Hello Joe, how are you today?" I asked.

He slowly looked up at me and said, "Hi Maggie. I'm...I'm just trying to figure out what salads to buy."

"What do you like?" I asked.

It took me a moment to realize something was different about Joe.

"I don't know, Maggie," he mumbled. "Elizabeth always bought the salads."

"Joe, where is Elizabeth?" I asked. I held my breath waiting for his answer.

"She's gone, Maggie. My beautiful bride is gone," he said with slumped shoulders and the appearance of age beyond his years.

I felt a blow to my stomach. "When, Joe? How long has it been?"

"It's been four weeks now. I'm looking at these salads, and I don't know which one to pick."

I wrapped my arms around the small and frail man. "I'm so sorry to hear this, Joe. I had no idea. I am so very sorry for your loss."

Joe's body began to quake in my arms. My tears began to flow freely. We stood in front of the salad case, sobbing in each other's arms. I took him by the shoulders, turned him around, and lead him away from the deli. We found an open table in the dining area. I poured us both a cup of coffee and sat down next to Joe.

"Joe, do you have anyone at home helping you?" I asked.

"My niece, Christy, has been stopping by every day after work."

"Good. That's good, Joe."

The rest of my lunch hour was spent listening to stories about Elizabeth. Joe and I laughed together and cried, then I walked him to his car.

As I walked back to the store, I realized I didn't even know his last name. To me, they were mere "Joe and Elizabeth." The happiest couple I had ever met. My life was touched, changed by someone I hardly knew.

I clocked back into work and made my way back to my station. I was paged to pick up line one. I picked up the phone and found Ben on the other end.

"I noticed you didn't get a chance to eat lunch. Do you need extra time to grab something?"

"No, thank you, Ben. I can't say I'm even the slightest bit hungry."

"Are you alright?"

"Joe and Elizabeth were regular customers. Joe lost Elizabeth a few weeks ago. He just shared the news with me. I hadn't heard she had passed."

"I'm sorry to hear that, Maggie," Ben sounded saddened by the news. "I know they meant something to you. Be sure to take a break whenever you need it."

"Thank you, Ben. It seems that Bay's Market is a family made up of strangers. I'll be fine, but Joe will never be the same."

# Chapter 23.

Friday came quickly. Laying in bed, I wondered what progress, if any, was being made on the security films at work. My gut told me Michael had something to do with the missing money. But why? He didn't hate me enough to set me up, did he? Was his ego that big? I would guess he made a handsome salary. He wouldn't have to skim the till for more. Unless... I thought as I reached over to check the time on my phone which lay charging on the nightstand table.

"Five more minutes?" I whined. The coffee pot in the kitchen came to life. The aroma drifted through the air, summoning me out of bed.

I slipped my feet into my house slippers and padded toward the kitchen. I opened the cupboard door and retrieved my favorite coffee cup, the one shaped like a frog. The kids had given it to me for Mother's Day a long time ago.

Moving toward the hissing pot, I whispered, "Come to Mama." Splashing a bit of almond milk into the bottom of my cup, I left the remainder open for the magical, ebony brew.

I filled my cup, inhaling the aroma of the freshly brewed coffee beans and dreamily took my first sip. Sometimes, it is the simple things in life that can bring us so much joy.

I was up early enough that I had a few minutes to spare. Flipping open my laptop, I logged into Facebook. I had opened an account with the social media network, some time ago, at the insistence of my children. News of my friends was now at my fingertips. Whether I'm working or asleep, I won't miss a thing.

I scrolled down the screen, checking the latest news, hitting the

"Like" button along the way. Did I want to "Share" anything? Not at this time. Did I have anything on my mind to post? Hmmm...

"Hello, Facebook friends. I'm in a constant battle with myself these days. I love to cook, and anyone who knows me knows that I especially love to bake. Cooking is my yoga...Eating is my equivalent to a psychologist. I tell my beautiful cupcake all of my sorrows, and it tells me everything is going to be fine. Here's the problem; the fifteen extra pounds of therapy do not want to come off my backside. I've tried running, dancing, and stretching them away, but they don't want to go! Someone, please tell me that it's menopause and not my therapist! Have a delicious day."

I hit the post button and took another sip of coffee. Was anyone out there listening?

Within the first five minutes of my post, seven of my Facebook friends reached out to me. Six out of the seven comments suggested I find myself a man. The seventh told me it was menopause.

I scrambled up a quick egg and ate it over the sink. I checked on the herbs growing outside my kitchen window. Sighing heavily, I had to admit, I concurred with the conclusion of my six friends.

"It's probably menopause," I reassured myself out loud.

I pulled on my running shoes and jogging clothes and decided a two-mile run wouldn't hurt me. I stretched outside my front door. Twisting at the waist, was for good measure before trotting toward the security gate in my complex.

I stopped to open the pedestrian gate, then continued my slow jog. The repetitive movement of jogging gave me time to think. Tomorrow, I had a blind date. How did I feel about it? I decided I needed a change of pace in my life and a little less baking.

I forgot my iPod, so I focused on the sound of my breathing. Ha, ha, whoooo...ha, ha, whooo. I began to pick up my pace. My stride seemed off this morning, and I felt as if I was running with two left feet. I fought the impulse to turn around and give up.

Making a right at the next block, took me past a community park. As I cut through the park, I noticed this time of the morning brought out the husbands in baseball caps, holding dog leashes in one hand, and a tumbler of coffee in the other.

Continuing the fight, I decided to run the perimeter of the park carefully avoiding dog poop the husbands neglected to pick up. My chest felt heavy as I breathed in and out, keeping time with my stride.

"You're halfway there," I reminded myself.

I didn't want to date strangers. I wanted a companion. Someone who already knew me, so I didn't have to explain myself. If I remembered correctly, the dating process wasn't all that fun. I didn't want to be married again. As much as I loved Edward, marriage was the hardest thing I ever did.

How was it I lost myself in those years? Maybe I didn't know myself as well as I thought.

My body fell into a natural rhythm, while I kept my mind occupied. Favorite movie: Pride and Prejudice. Best line: You have bewitched me body and soul.

Before I knew it, I was back at the security gate. I bent over, securing my hands to the top of my knees, breathing heavily. Slowly, I stood erect and moved at a walking pace to my front door, cooling myself down.

When I walked inside, I heard my phone ringing. I recognized the number; it was the grocery store.

"Hello," I managed to say in between breaths.

"Maggie? Bad time?" Ben asked from the other end.

"No, I was out for a run. Just catching my breath."

"I'm sorry. Would you rather I call back in a few minutes," Ben asked.

"No, I'm good. But it would help if you did all the talking, for the next three to five minutes."

Ben chuckled and said, "I had two checkers call in sick this morning. I was wondering if you could come in early. I can get Bobbie to stay a little later to cover your first shift and Tami used to cashier. She'll fill in somewhere in the middle. Would that work for you?"

"How early were you thinking?" I asked.

"Can you be here within the next hour?"

This change would mean, coming back to the store to meet Parcey. "Yes, sure I can do that, Ben," I said after a moment's thought.

"Thank you, Maggie," Ben sounded relieved. "You've just made my day a little less complicated."

"You're welcome. While I have you on the phone, did anything come of the security tapes yet?"

"The last tape was the only one not recorded over. I'm sorry, but there wasn't anything of significance on it."

"Oh. Thank you for checking."

"We'll figure it out, Maggie. Don't worry."

"See you soon."

If Ben wasn't my boss, I mused, he would make a good companion.

On that note, I clicked on some music and checked for more comments on my Facebook query.

I had nine "Likes" and two more comments that supported menopause. The last comment read, "Cupcakes are my legal drug of choice. Although there is something to say about vodka and one night stands : )" That comment was from Bobbie.

My till balanced all week. That meant either I was more careful, or Michael was. Michael and I were working together on Sunday. It might be telling if anything changed.

There wasn't a way for me to reach Parcey, so I decided to go home after my shift, freshen up and be back at the store by eight o'clock. Ben left the store around six-thirty. I planned to get Parcey on his turf, where he was more likely to be himself. Maybe, I would get the opportunity to work Michael into a conversation.

I spent an uneventful day at work. Some hours later, I waited outside the store for Parcey to pick me up. I spotted a black Cadillac coming my way. I gave him a wave and walked toward his car.

Opening the passenger door, I slipped inside his car. The scent of aftershave lotion immediately assaulted my senses. Parcey suggested we see Aunt Dika first, then go for a drink after.

We made small talk as we crossed one intersection after another. I saw the familiar neon "hand" sign, blinking at us. Above the blinking palm, the words "Fortune Teller" were lit up in green.

Parcey came around to open my door. Feeling a sudden onset of nerves, I managed to smile back at him. Having your fortune read was terrible mojo from where I came.

We followed the sidewalk up to the front door. It jingled as Parcey push it opened, letting Dika know someone had entered the shop. In the dimly lit room, I could see the worn burgundy velvet furniture. The lamps were covered in colorful shawls, adding to the mystic ambiance of the place.

From around the corner trotted a short, stout woman. Had she been able to stand erect, she would be under five feet tall. Standing next to Parcey, she barely cleared his navel. Her gray hair was tightly tied into a bun, exposing her old features and gray eyes.

She clapped her hands at the sight of Parcey, and they exchanged words in a language I didn't understand. Parcey introduced Aunt Dika to me. She looked me over and smiled slightly, nodded approvingly, and motioned me to follow her.

She mumbled something to Parcey, which led him to switch the sign to CLOSED and locked the front door. I felt a chill in the air, and my hands began to sweat. A minute later, I sat across from her at a linen covered table. The bottom cloth was a burgundy flowered pattern, and the top was speckled dark green.

Parcey pulled up another chair to the table and sat down between us. Dika stood up and made her way slowly behind a short wall, a few feet away.

"She's going to brew a cup of tea for us," he explained.

"How many of these storefronts do you own?" I asked.

"Quite a few across the country."

Dika slowly walked back and placed small espresso-like cups in front of us and motioned us to drink. I took a sip of the strong tea and began to choke. I smiled as I tried to suppress my cough.

Drinking the bitter-grassy tea casually, I listened to Parcey and his Aunt exchange pleasantries.

When I finished, she smiled at me and held out her hand. I handed my cup and saucer to her. Dika gazed at me with great interest. She looked above my head and around my frame, causing me to feel as if someone were standing behind me. I casually checked over my shoulder when no one was looking.

"You are a very spiritual woman," she finally said to me. "I see it in the aura around you," moving her old hand, in circles to explain. She rolled the leaves around in my cup and looked inside intently. Her brows furrowed as she studied them and flipped it over onto the saucer.

She nodded her head to herself and then reached for the tarot cards. She shuffled them as she breathed deeply, in and out. She placed the cards in front of her and nodded.

"What do you see, Auntie?" Parcey asked her quietly.

"Not yet."

Parcey looked my way, smiled and winked. That made me feel a little better.

Please don't tell me I'm going to be hit by a bus or something like that, I thought.

Dika took two deep breaths and began to speak. "You have a fascinating reading. Love will tear you. I see two men, perhaps three."

I looked over at Parcey and shrugged my shoulders.

"You have deep sorrow inside your heart. You must let it go before you can know another happiness. I see children...three," she said.

She was wrong on that count, but I wasn't going to mention it.

"You will travel far. There you will find something important to you." As she continued to look, her brows furrowed again. "I see danger coming to you soon. You must be brave and remember you are a strong person."

That didn't sound good.

She smiled slightly and asked for my hand. She compared notes between my hand, the cards, and the leaves. "You will help other people, and you will find good fortune. You will have a very long life. It will be good with deep meaning. You are a person who feels deeply. That is a blessing and a curse," she explained, nodding her head.

So far very vague, but interesting.

"Has someone close to you left you?" she asked me.

Surprised at her question, I nodded my head. Parcey looked over at me with some concern.

"Do you have any questions for me?" Dika asked.

"Is there a way to avoid the danger?"

"No. It is very close. But I am not certain of what I see."

"The three men have me confused," I said.

"Yes. It's tangled. But listen to your heart; it will not deceive you."

Parcey asked, "You see me in there anywhere, Auntie?" and laughed out loud, breaking the tension we felt.

She shook her head and pointed her finger at him, "Be careful." She looked at Parcey sternly. Parcey's smile faded.

"OK. Are we done here? Anything else?" he asked, standing up and pushing his chair away. "This one's on the house, Dika. Maggie is a friend of mine."

She stood with me. I shook her hand and thanked her. She looked at me and smiled. My heart continued to beat quickly, and I was ready to leave this place. I walked to the door and waited for Parcey, who was bidding his aunt a good night. He kissed her on both cheeks, and I overheard Dika tell him she was exhausted.

We walked silently to his car, and I waited for him to open the door for me. I realized I had chills on my arms for such a warm night. Parcey opened his door and slid behind the wheel.

"What kind of loss did you have, Maggie?" Parcey asked with concern.

"Someone I cared about recently died."

"I see."

"Parcey, if you don't mind, could I have a rain check for a drink? My schedule was changed on me this morning, and I had to be at work early. And with the sad news, it's been a very long day."

"Of course. It will give me something to look forward to. I'll drive you back to the store."

"Thank you, Parcey. The evening was interesting."

We filled up the drive with small talk. Parcey told me a story about his Aunt Dika that made me laugh. Apparently, she was quite the disciplinarian when he was young.

"She still pulls me by the ear now and then," Parcey laughed out loud. "Trust what she tells you; she's rarely wrong."

He pulled up next to my car without me pointing it out. I paused for a moment, reflecting on that, and then thanked him for the night. I unlocked my door and slid into my Mini. I started up the engine and waved at Parcey. He drove away. I put my car in gear and trailed slowly behind him. I could see him look at me through his rearview mirror. He pulled ahead toward the curb and made a right turn at the light. I had my blinker set to turn left. I pulled up to the crosswalk after he made his turn. I found myself holding my breath, as I waited for the green light.

Suddenly, I felt exhausted. How much thought should I give Dika? I assured myself her information was general and it would take my imagination to create anything more.

The light turned green, and I sped toward home. I looked into my rearview mirror many times. My gut sensed I was followed. I shook my head fretfully and said out loud, "He already knows where I live."

# Chapter 24.

I couldn't sleep. My fortune read like a paperback novel. A romance triangle, danger, travel...well, at least Dika said I would have a long life. Unless she said it so I wouldn't worry. I was laying in bed, my hands rested on my stomach, while my fingertips tapped.

It was a foolish thing for me to do; getting closer to Parcey. Did I think I would accomplish anything? I hoped he would open up to me. But after the reading, I wanted to get away from him. He intentionally revealed he knew things about my life that I hadn't told him. Why?

Eventually, I got tired of tossing and turning, so I decided to get up. I made some coffee and rummaged through the fridge for a snack. At six, I went for a run. A run always made me feel like I accomplished something.

When I got back home, I went straight for a shower. Feeling the fatigue, I counted my blessings I was off today. There was only one thing I could do about this... see my mommy.

My mother was a colorful person. She made growing up fun. As kids, we hunted for garden fairies, buried treasure, and always roasted marshmallows on the first day of rain.

My mother, Jacquelyn Sofia Simpson-Morgan, had fallen in love with my father, Charles Peter Morgan, as a junior in high school. The Morgan family moved into the neighborhood, the summer before their junior year.

The fall harvest festival was always at the end of September, in the little country town of Avalon, outside the big city of Fresno. Since the age of five, young Jackie and her best friend Marsha never missed going to the harvest festival together. Avalon was a safe town. No one locked their doors or worried that their children weren't safe.

Everyone knew everybody. Little happened in Avalon that the whole community didn't find out. After Jackie and Marsha turned 16, they went to the harvest festival on their own.

As the Morgan family walked the arcade strip at the festival, so did Jackie and Marsha. When the two passed one another, Jackie and Charlie's eyes locked and it was love at first sight. They never left each other's side after that night and were married the week after graduation.

Mother was heart-broken when Dad died. Although she had the opportunity, Mom chose not to marry again. One day, I asked her why she never remarried. She responded that no man could ever live up to Charlie, so why bother?

Mom had her style. Her way of dressing, decorating and looking at life was all Jackie. What you see is what you get, when it came to my mother. I think she embarrasses Elizabeth, but I find her inspiring.

When I got to Mom's, she answered the front door quickly. The door flew open, and she called out, "Darling," rushing out to greet me.

Today, Jackie was wearing hot pink stretch crops, a multi-colored sheer blouse, with a hot pink tank underneath. Her auburn colored hair was pulled back with a pink cotton knit headband. Her sandals sported rhinestones that showed off her colorful pedicure.

"Hi, Mom," I said embracing her.

"I'm so glad you called me, Ellie."

"Me too, Mom. You are my go-to person."

"That I am. You come inside and tell me all about it."

My mother is a lot of beautiful things, but a cook she is not. That's why I came bearing good eats.

"I stopped at Steven's Bakery on my way over and bought a few fresh baked danish, including a Bear Claw just for you," I opened the box, pointing to the delicious pastries inside.

"A daughter after my own heart," she said dramatically, both hands covering her heart. "I made some coffee and also put on a kettle in case you rather have tea. I have fresh honey, I picked up at the Farmer's Market from the honey man, and lemon too. You know that honey man can go on and on about his bees. He could bore me to death but lucky for me he's good-looking." My mother chattered on, bustling around the kitchen.

"Thank you, Mom. The tea sounds great."

"Start talking while I get everything on the table. Haven't you spoken to your sister about any of this? Although she can be over-protective."

"No, you're the first to hear my story. You're my voice of reason. I couldn't possibly tell you why, because it makes more sense that Lizzy should be the voice I hear in my head, but it's you."

With her hand on her hip, she looked at me and said, "You know I love your sister with all my heart, but honestly, sometimes she has a stick up her..."

"Mom!"

"Elizabeth is a very dependable and capable woman. She will always be there for you Ellie. You know that. Let's face it, Ellie, you are your mother's child. Elizabeth never believed there were fairies in our garden. You on the other hand, still do."

"I'm a train wreck, Mother."

"No, you are not! Ellie, the way I see it, you took a little detour at some point in your life. But the wonderful thing about detours is; eventually, they lead you back on the main road again. I loved Edward, rest his soul; he was a fine son. He gave you two beautiful children, and he took care of all of you, the very best he could. But he didn't know how to handle someone as special as you are, Ellie. He loved you with all of his heart, but he didn't know how to love you with his arms open wide. You are a person who needs room to fly. Edward unintentionally clipped your wings. But the good news is it is never too late to soar."

I could feel the tears running down my face as I listened to my mother speak to me. "Mom? Did I love Edward enough? Am I capable of really loving someone? I feel like I can give only so much, and then I close myself off. It makes me wonder if I was ever really in love at all."

"Darling," my mother said, reaching for my hand. "Do you know why I have always been a morning person?" she said. I shook my head. "Because when I open my eyes in the morning, it's a new day to recreate myself. The past is what it is, the past. At the end of every day, you take note of what you learned, and then you let it go. You cherish the good stuff; those are our memories. The things that aren't so pleasant are life's lessons. You learn the lesson and move on. Remember the good stuff with Edward. You did love him the very best you could while he was in your life."

My mother stirred her coffee. "Did you love him enough? Well, what is enough? Enough for you or him? Ellie, you are my sensitive child. You love deeply and wide, but you limit yourself. Why? Because you fear the man will leave you someday as your father left me. Edward affirmed that by dying. But you must know, I had twenty-four earth shaking years with your father. I would have never traded one minute of those years, regardless of how painful it was to lose him. Loving someone is risky business, but if you're gonna do it, jump in with both feet. You need to make peace with Edward, Ellie. He knows you loved him. Learn, cherish your memories, and remember tomorrow is a new day."

We filled ourselves with danishes, as I brought her up to date on my life. I included details about Dean, Ben, and the fortune teller. Mom thought Dika was vague. I didn't mention my worries with Parcey or that Dika saw danger in my near future.

Mom thought the traveling sounded exciting, but what peaked her interest were the three lovers, as she put it.

"Hmmm? Maybe the lovers are Ben, which would be my first choice, Dean, and Edward. After all, you are struggling with moving on. It's alright not to want to be lonely anymore. You have waited a respectable amount of time to start dating again."

"Mother, Ben, and Dean are not my lovers. I do have a blind date tonight."

"They are not your lovers...yet! Admit it, Ellie, you have feelings for these men. Stop holding back. Have some fun. There is nothing wrong with a little companionship. And what blind date?"

"They are my bosses, Mother. How complicated would that be? The store is a fishbowl; everyone would know about it. It's too...close. Anyway, I'm going on a blind date that Elizabeth set up. His name is Paul, and she's been wanting this for awhile. She thinks he would be good for me. Maybe he is the third lover, huh?"

"She thinks he will be good for you? What does that mean? Honestly, I think your sister sometimes forgets you already have a mother. I say you are talented and smart. You can do anything. Find a new job, and then you could easy date either of the two men or both."

I shook my head in disbelief. Then I asked, "Am I out of line, asking how long you waited for, Mom? You know until you dated again?"

"Everyone has their own time, Ellie. You need to find yours."

I nodded, "Fair enough, Mom. I love you. I know why you're my person." I got up and walked over to her chair. I hugged her from behind as she remained sitting. She reached up and patted my arms.

When I left, she reminded me to be careful and to call her any time of the day or night. Except of course, on this particular night because she had a date with a gentleman from her bridge club.

I was grateful I had her in my life. Mom understood me in a way no one else seemed to. I was, after all, my mother's daughter.

On impulse, I decided to take a detour and drive to the cemetery. Edward chose cremation. I had his urn interred so the kids would have a place to come. Dad also rested here. Today, I would visit the both of them.

I turned into the long driveway that wound around the many graves and mausoleums. The cemetery had become a place of comfort to me after my father had died. He was buried up on a hill under a giant pine tree. There was a place next to him reserved for Mom.

I had always been fascinated by the way people chose to remember their loved ones; simple headstones, elaborate statuary, tombs, and the like. The beautifully landscaped cemetery goes back hundreds of years. There is a rose garden near a small wooden church that sits not far from my father's grave. The church was used for services and was always open during the day for prayer.

At one time, the church had been the most central location of the cemetery, but the graves have long since exceeded the original plan. The street names were deliberate in choice and meant to comfort family members. My father's address was between the streets Quiet Hallow and

Serenity Skies.

I parked my car on Quiet Hallow and walked up the hill to say hello to Dad. I had come empty handed today as this was an impulsive visit.

I walked the row of headstones until I came to the one that read "Charles Peter Morgan."

"Hello, Dad."

The grieving process was an interesting one. The voyage takes you through a myriad of emotions that twist and turn until finally, you arrive at a peaceful, reflective destination. I no longer cried for Daddy; time does heal all wounds. Now, I stop in on occasion and bring him up to date on all the news and gossip, as if we were meeting on his front porch.

It was a pretty day, so I decided to walk over to Edward's grave. Along the way, I read headstones and walked in and around the quiet resting places of those long gone. If one wasn't vigilant, it was easy to get turned around in this neighborhood.

I checked the next street sign which was Fountain Way. Headed in the right direction, I continued my journey to Quiet Falls.

The sculpture depicting children at play moved me. They were free now, to play as they wished, I thought. I stopped long enough to calculate ages and mourned for their parent's loss.

I came upon Quiet Falls and knew Edward's grave was to my left. It still caught my breath to read his name on the bronze plate, Edward J. Bloom. It was real; it had happened.

I brushed the tears that fell on their own. I sat on the grass cross-legged and cleaned the debris from the plaque.

"Hello, Edward."

I brought him up to date with the children and told him how proud he would be of them. I sat quietly for a few minutes before I began again.

"Edward. The kids have their own lives, and I find myself alone. I'm ok with being single, but the loneliness can be painful. You were always good at being alone. In fact, I think you preferred it at times. But I don't do it so well.

No one could ever take your place in my heart, Edward. No one. I'm not asking for permission this time. I want your blessing. It's time to make room for the possibility of love."

I sat a while longer remembering his face when he laughed. How he cried when the kids were born and what it felt like when he held me close. Then I kissed my fingertips and pressed them to his name. I rose to my feet, keeping my eyes on his bronze plaque.

"Thank you for a good life," I said breathlessly.

With a steady pace, I made my way across the cemetery toward my car.

"Maggie?"

I swung toward the voice.

"Dean? You startled me! I was in deep thought, apparently," I said as I moved toward him.

"Bad place to sneak up on someone?"

"I guess it is," I chuckled.

"Visiting your husband?" Dean asked.

"Yes, and my dad is right over there on top of that hill. I thought you were headed to Yosemite today."

"Rescheduled. Two of the guys had to drop out last minute."

"Oh. Too bad. I know you were looking forward to it."

"There will be other times."

"It's a beautiful cemetery, isn't it? I didn't know Carolyn was here."

"Right over there. Where are you off to?" Dean asked.

"I'm feeling hungry all of a sudden. I was thinking of grabbing a burger. I need comfort food before my date tonight."

"Oh yeah, that's tonight, isn't it? You want some company?"

"On my date or for a burger?"

"Either. But I was thinking burger."

"You don't do burgers, do you?"

"Depends. Where are you headed?"

"Where they use real potatoes," I teased.

"Done. Which one."

"Natural Habit on Palm Street. Meet you there. Give me five minutes. I have a little walk yet," I called over my shoulder.

"You want a ride?" Dean offered.

"No thanks."

Though I felt solemn, as I passed the baby angel statues, my mood changed when I approached the fiddler playing so happily. Before I knew it, I was back on Quiet Hallow and my car parked on the side of the road. I wound my way out to the main road. With the cemetery in my rearview mirror, I couldn't help feeling I was about to discover a new kind of brave with a less ladened heart.

# Chapter 25.

When I arrived at Natural Habit, Dean was already comfortably seated at a booth. He waved me over. I smiled as I walked toward him.

"Well, this was an interesting coincidence," I said as I sat down.

"Do you usually go out to the cemetery on Saturdays?"

"No, not really. I went to see my mother this morning, and on the way home, I made a detour."

"Oooo, spooky. I was out running errands when I suddenly had the thought to go there."

"It's the Twilight Zone," I teased.

The waitress came over to our table, offered us menus, and took our drink orders.

"So what do you recommend here?" Dean asked.

"I love their veggie burger. The jalapeno turkey burger is pretty good too. The veggie is a homemade patty with pickled zucchini, sprouts, and avocado. And for fifty cents more, you can add fried shoestring onions. Which I do."

"Sounds good."

I looked up from the menu and was surprised to see Ben walking into the restaurant. He looked our direction and made a face. I waved him over to our table.

"Hey, Ben, fancy meeting you here. It's like old home week. Look who I ran into," pointing to Dean. Dean turned to face him and reached out to shake his hand. "Sit down and join us."

"Ok," Ben said. "Thanks."

"Good," I said sliding over toward the window to make room. "We happened to bump into each other at the cemetery, of all places, and decided we were hungry," I explained. Looking at them both, I felt my face flush, replaying the conversation I had this morning with my Mother.

"Ben, are you on lunch or off today?" I managed to ask.

"I went in this morning. On my way home, I remembered how much I used to like this place."

"It's one of my favorite places too," I agreed.

The waitress returned to take our order. I suggested a basket of sweet potato fries with aioli sauce for us to share. Ben and Dean spoke briefly about grocery business.

"So, what are your plans today?" Ben asked.

"I finished up all my business this morning. I don't have any plans for the afternoon," Dean offered. Then, they both looked over at me.

"I have dinner plans later," I said, hesitantly.

"You don't sound very enthusiastic," Ben quipped.

"Bloom has a blind date tonight," Dean smirked.

I looked over at Dean and sneered at him. Then, I politely nodded affirmatively toward Ben.

"Ahhh. I'm not in favor of those," Ben remarked.

"My sister wouldn't let up on me until I agreed. She teaches at the university and apparently, she works with the perfect man for me. He teaches literature," I said.

"I bet he has a great personality too," Dean teased. The men shared a laugh at my expense.

"I love to read, so I'm sure we'll have a lot to talk about," I remarked.

"Favorite book?" Ben asked me.

"Pride and Prejudice. And I've seen the movie a hundred times."

"BBC version or the Hollywood version?"

"I prefer the BBC version. You've seen it?"

"Samantha," was all he had to say.

"A girl after my own heart," I said and smiled.

"Samantha?" Dean asked.

"My daughter," Ben responded.

"She's lovely," I added. Ben looked at me and smiled.

"You know Samantha?" Dean asked me.

"We've met," I said and left it at that.

"And what are your plans this evening?" I asked Ben.

"I've got a gig tonight."

He took both Dean and me by surprise.

"What kind of band are you in?" Dean ask.

"We're a country-rock band. I play all kinds of music. I love blues, jazz. I play some classical piano, but the band is how I blow off steam. I'm also the lead vocals. We're all from San Diego, but since I've been up here a while, we've been taking turns making the drive every other month."

"Wow. I wouldn't have ever guessed you were in a band. Where are you playing tonight?" I asked feeling a little harmless crush. Why is it that musicians are so sexy to females, I thought?

Ben told us where he was playing as our food arrived. He filled us in on all the details as we ate. I was having trouble concentrating on my veggie burger while Bon Jovi's elbow kept brushing up against mine.

After we ate our lunch, we continued to tell stories and laugh. Time seemed to fly by when I suddenly noticed Ben's wrist watch. I grabbed his wrist to get a better look.

"Is that the time? I need to get home and get ready for my date. I'll suggest we go to the club after dinner to hear you play. And if the date happens to end early, I'll come by on my own."

"Good," Ben said meeting my eyes. "I hope you can make it."

Ben stood which allowed me to slide out from the table. As I got near the edge of the bench, he reached for my elbow to help me up the rest of the way. I felt a tingle run through my arm and wondered if he had too.

# Chapter 26.

When I arrived home, I took a long bath and thought about my day. I shaved my legs and gave myself an entire body loofah treatment. I stood up, dried myself off, and slipped my feet into my house slippers. Now to find something to wear. I examined my wardrobe with a critical eye. Choosing something to wear that made me feel feminine, but not too sexy, was a problem. Wearing a uniform to work, that compliments a man's body more than a woman's, left me wanting to look ladylike as often as possible.

Slimming black pants, with the built-in tummy panel, would suffice. For a top I chose a long lavender stretch-cotton-blend tee, that hugged all the right curves. The tee had a large scooped neckline and sleeves that came to the elbows. Accessories were always tricky. I choose some bangles for my wrists and a long summer scarf in colors of lavender, gray, and yellow, to wrap around my neck. I left the ends dangling in front, near my hips. I chose my favorite open toe, high-heeled black pumps, hoping he was a man of stature. I took out the essentials from my large handbag and dropped them into a smaller yellow leather bag. Thank goodness for Isabella and our last shopping spree.

After brushing my teeth, I tried to decide what to do with my hair. I pulled it behind my right ear, for the "evening" look, and sprayed it into place. Last was make-up. I accented my eyes and chose a soft natural lip color.

A full-length mirror was in order. I ran down the hall, to the spare room. Checking the frontal, side, and rear views, I determined I looked date-worthy. My confidence was another story. My heartbeat quicken, as I anticipated the evening. Did I want to do this, I thought? It had been twenty-five years since my last date.

Text to Isabella: Aunt Lizzy set me up on a blind date tonight :0 Thanks to you, I have something to wear : ) Update tomorrow!

I checked the time. With not a minute to spare, I rushed out to my car. Ready or not, I was going. Putting the car into gear, I made my way to Parma's Italian Restaurant where I would meet Paul. If it didn't go well, at least I would have a ride home.

Parma's is one of my favorite restaurants, named after the small Italian village from which they came. It reminded me of Nonna; the region from where she grew up. The décor was light, in colors of blue, white, and yellow. Their food was authentic and the best in town.

As I entered the restaurant, a handsome man with a heavy Italian accent greeted me. To the left of the door was a small bar area, where several men sat. I informed the host, I was there to meet someone. One of the three men seated at the bar, turned in his seat and asked, "Are you, Maggie?"

He was as handsome as Elizabeth had promised. "Yes, I am. Paul?"

We were shown to our table and seated. We both ordered a cocktail and looked at one another.

"So Paul, Elizabeth tells me you are a professor of literature."

"Yes, I am. She tells me you currently work at a grocery store and enjoy gardening," Paul said flashing a smile.

"Yes, yes, I do," I stammered.

I took in a deep breath, hoping we would find a comfortable rhythm to our conversation. To help break the ice, I shared some of my adventures with our more colorful customers at the store. I explained my passion for my garden and its future development. He seemed to appreciate my stories, as he smiled and nodded at all the appropriate places.

"I take it you enjoy the gardening process. Have you considered furthering your education in plant science, or perhaps becoming a Master Gardener?" Paul asked.

"I have a degree in journalism, but I married right out of college, and did very little with it. My interest in gardening is more cathartic than a professional interest. I've learned about plants I'm interested in growing. The Master Gardener program is very cumbersome, given my current employment. It requires a commitment to study and volunteer for projects around the city. I really can't afford the time right now."

"You seem to be a capable person, Maggie. Surely, you could find another job that affords you both."

"Maybe so, but I'm happy where I am for now."

The waiter's timing with our dinner was perfect. He sat a beautiful antipasti platter between us and a lovely, crusty, sliced baguette.

"Saved by the food," I said to myself and ordered another cocktail.

I asked Paul questions about his favorite novels and if he had plans to write. I found if I could keep him talking, it took the pressure off of me to be entertaining. He was knowledgeable and handsome, but I wondered if he had any spontaneity.

"What do you do for fun, Paul?" I asked.

"Astronomy. I live up in the foothills and own a pretty awesome telescope. There is nothing like looking at the universe to put things into perspective."

"Yes, I bet it does. How interesting. Have you always been

interested in astronomy?"

"My father used to take us camping up in the Sierras as kids. I remember laying in our sleeping bags looking up at the stars and asking my dad a million questions. He would call bedtime, just to get me to shut up. I've been captivated ever since."

"You said us. Sisters, brothers?"

"One older brother and a younger sister."

"Ahh, the middle child."

We continued with pleasant small talk throughout dinner. Over coffee, I asked Paul if he would be interested in listening to Ben's band play tonight. He agreed it might be fun. Paul insisted on paying for dinner, so I offered to pick up the tab at the club. Paul touched the small of my back as we exited the restaurant. Hmmm, nothing. I could hear my sister's voice telling me, to give the man a chance.

We agreed to take his car to the club and leave mine behind at the restaurant. We arrived around nine-thirty. I paid the entrance fee, and we both got stamped on our right hands. The club was full and louder than I remembered it from college.

Ben's band Warner & Company sounded great. His vocals were low and sultry. Paul and I made our way through the crowd, to get a better view. There he was, on stage strumming his guitar. He wore tight blue jeans and a dark gray tie-dyed tee shirt. His muscular arms were doing double time, as the girls in the audience swooned to his every word. I understood the attraction.

"Do you dance?" I asked Paul.

"I don't mind the slow ones."

I nodded. My eyes perused the crowd for an empty table. Suddenly, I spotted Bobbie and grabbed Paul's hand to follow me. As we approached Bobbie squealed with delight.

"I didn't know you were coming tonight," she shouted over the music.

"I didn't know he was playing here until this afternoon," I yelled into Bobbie's ear.

"I didn't know either. I come here all the time. Imagine my surprise," Bobbie laughed.

Bobbie motioned us to join her at her table. We rustled up two more chairs and pushed them toward the table. I introduced Paul to Bobbie, and when he wasn't looking, she nodded in approval. After placing an order for two beers with the waitress, we settled into our seats.

As the applause died down, Ben announced they were going to slow it down. He introduced an original tune called I Should Have Known.

As promised, Paul took my hand and led me out to the dance floor. I looked up at Ben and waved; he smiled in recognition. I gave him the thumbs up sign. Paul pulled me closer to him, and I placed my left hand on his shoulder. As we swayed back and forth to the music, I couldn't keep my eyes off Ben.

Ben announced a fifteen-minute break after the song ended. We stood where we were, applauding, while Ben came around to say hello. After introductions, I complimented the band and invited Ben to our table. A young female fan pushed a marker into Ben's hand and asked him to sign her chest. I chuckled inwardly. Ben complied.

Our beers arrived, and I paid the waitress. Ben told her, the next round was on him. The table cheered. As we chatted amongst ourselves, I noticed a familiar face approaching our table. It was Dean.

"I didn't know you were coming tonight," I said elevating my voice slightly.

As I introduced him to Paul, I realized Dean was inebriated. A woman, around thirty, walked over to Dean and wrapped her arm inside of his. He introduced her to the group as Lori. She wore a shirt unbuttoned to her navel and she was pretty in a lot of make-up sort of way. It was a mystery how she got into her tight jeans, but I was pretty sure she knew exactly how to get out of them. Dean lifted his beer bottle up to mine and tapped it.

Dean wore his hair, in his usual messy style. His v-neck tee shirt accented his blue eyes and hugged his form. He was ruggedly handsome and sometimes acted aloof as a cat. I wondered if he was impressed with his date's antics.

The break was over, and the band was back on stage. The next song was a cover of Keith Urban's, Where the Blacktop Ends. It was one of my favorites, so I jumped to my feet and pulled Paul to the dance floor. The room spun briefly from the effects of the drinks I had consumed throughout the evening. My limit was two drinks, and I was well into my fourth drink of the night.

I could see Paul was out of his comfort zone. The crowd moved into the Electric Slide. Paul gave up and watched from the sidelines. With Bobbie at my side, we moved to the rhythm of the song, stepping, sliding, and shaking our hips. When the song was over the crowd cheered, and I heard Ben say, "Let's hear it for the ladies in the front row!" Bobbie and I howled and gave each other a high-five.

Paul excused himself to the men's room. I sat down at our table and slowly sipped my beer. Dean walked around the table and took Paul's seat next to me.

"You look beautiful tonight, Bloom," he said.

"I believe you're seeing me through the bottom of your beer bottle. My name is Edith, and I'm 4'6" and 300 pounds. I have bad skin, bad teeth, and a wart on the tip of my nose."

We both laughed and took another sip of our beers.

"The thing is you're pretty, sexy, and funny, and if you did have a wart on the tip of your nose, it would look good on you," he insisted. "And the best part is you don't even realize it."

"How many beers have you had tonight? The rumor is you don't drink anymore," I said.

"Don't worry. It's my last one of the night and probably the last one for a very long time."

"Good to know. You are not to drive yourself home. Do you understand me?" I scolded.

"Gotcha," he said as he lifted his beer to his lips again.

Paul came back to the table and said he was ready to call it a night. Disappointed, I nodded. I stood up and turned to get my handbag from the back of the chair. Paul reached over to shake Dean's hand to say goodnight. Dean stood up and accepted his handshake, then pulled him in and said something to him.

Suddenly, Paul pushed away from him. The two men began shoving one another, shouting profanities. Ben stopped singing and jumped from the stage, and ran over to our table.

I tried to push my way in between Paul and Dean, while I shouted, "Knock it off" at the top of my lungs. I turned to look at Ben coming toward us when Dean threw a punch at Paul. Paul ducked, and Dean cold-cocked me. My world went black. Apparently, I wasn't out long before I woke up in Ben's arms.

There was a flurry of activity that exploded around me. Ben sat me down in a chair, and security came over to see what happened. Ben advised Paul to go home, and he forced Dean to sit down in a chair away from me. Ben asked the waitress to bring Dean a cup of black coffee and keep it coming.

Paul didn't want to leave without me. Disoriented, I told him I was alright and how sorry I was for the whole mess. Ben assured Paul he would make sure I got home safely, and he should leave before anything else happened.

My cheek exploded with pain, and I felt my eye begin to swell. When I caught sight of Dean, my temper flared. I was confident he provoked Paul and caused the whole scene.

Ben asked the waitress for ice. She promptly returned with ice wrapped in a bar towel. Ben was in control of the chaos, and people responded to him.

He bent down on one knee in front of me and gently placed the towel over my left cheek. "You ok?" he asked.

By this time, the band had stopped playing, and the volume in the bar was decibels lower. The jukebox kicked on, and the party around me continued.

"I think so. I've never been punched in the face before. I can tell you this; I'm a lot soberer than I was ten minutes ago. Although a shot of whiskey might dull this throbbing pain in my face," I babbled.

"Let me see," he said lifting the towel. He pressed against my check bone slightly to measure my response. "How's your vision?"

"One of my eyes sees perfectly."

"I'm wondering if I should run you over to the emergency to make sure you don't have any fractures. Do you feel like you have a bad headache behind your eyes?"

"My entire face hurts. I don't think I need to go to the hospital. How does my eye look?"

"You've looked better," he smiled. "So what happened?"

"I think you'll have to ask Dean. Paul was ready to go, so I turned to get my handbag and then he and Dean began a shoving match. And you know the rest."

"Well, I've got Dean over there drinking coffee in the corner. Will you be all right here while I finish the set? I'll take you home after."

"I can call for a ride. You needn't bother," I protested.

"I'll take you home. I want to make sure you're alright unless you would rather leave now?" Ben asked.

"I'm fine. Go on and finish. I could use some coffee too."

Bobbie came over to see what was going on. "I go to the ladies' room, and I miss everything...what happened?" she asked.

I gave Bobbie the run down.

"Was Dean fighting over you? Hell lady, when you got it – you got it!"

"It's not like that Bobbie," I couldn't help but feel irritable. "Gosh, my face hurts."

"Do you need a ride home?" she asked.

"No, I've got one. But could you please get me a cup of coffee?"

"Yeah. Cowboy, get my friend here some coffee. Would you please?" Bobbie asked the man standing next to her.

"Looks like you're not going home alone," I teased.

"Girlfriends come first. I can get me some of that anytime."

The cowboy brought me coffee while Bobbie held my hand.

"Are you sure you'll be ok without me? Where's that ride of yours anyway?"

175

"I'm ok. My ride's coming. Go and have fun. It will make me happy knowing one of us is getting lucky."

"You are too funny. Take care of that pretty face, and I'll see you later. Call me if you need me in the next forty-five minutes. After that, don't bother me," Bobbie smiled down at me and then turned toward the cowboy waiting for her.

I closed my eyes while I iced my cheek. I should probably call Paul and see if he was alright, I thought. I opened my eyes and found Dean sitting in the chair opposite me.

"I'm furious at you. Are you sure you want to be sitting there right now?" I growled.

"Let me see what I did to you," he said pushing my hand away that held the ice pack. Dean shook his head in disbelief. "I'm sorry, Maggie. You know I didn't mean to punch you."

"No, you meant to punch my date! You shouldn't be punching anyone. What happened?" I asked.

Dean looked down at his bruised hand for a moment and said, "I'm an ass, that's what happened."

"I won't argue with that. What did you say to Paul?" I demanded to know.

Dean paused a minute and said, "You screw with her, and you screw with me, Buddy."

"What was that supposed to mean?" I asked.

"Then he said, don't tell me who I can screw. That made me mad, so I shoved him a few times. He called me an asshole. That's when I punched him," Dean explained.

"No, you punched me, you big jerk. So, you guys had a pissing match? How mature of the two of you."

"I'm sorry, Maggie. I feel awful about punching you. I screwed up your entire evening. I'm sorry," Dean said. "I was way out of line."

I sat upright in the chair and leaned forward, so my face was a few inches from Dean's.

"It's none of your business what I do. I take care of myself. It was one blind date. And I'm pretty sure I won't be seeing Paul again, thanks to you. It's not like my opinion matters on who you date – Lori? Please go away. My face hurts, and I'm woozy."

Dean stood up and walked toward the exit. Ben finished the set and loaded up his gear.

"The band will take care of the rest of this so I can get you home. Are you alright?" Ben asked.

I nodded. I grabbed my handbag and steadied myself toward the bar.

"Thanks for the ice," I told the bartender as I dropped off the towel.

We walked through the bar toward the back door with Ben's arm around my waist, guiding the way. As we passed the women waiting in line to use the restroom, they were unapologetic in offering themselves to him. Ben paid no attention and pushed the door open for me.

"That must happen to you a lot," I said.

"I'm here for the music," Ben replied.

We got into his SUV and buckled in.

"Do we need to make any stops on the way home...hospital, pharmacy?" he questioned.

"Can I pick up my dignity at any of those places?" I asked.

"You don't have any reason to be embarrassed. I think Dean owns this one," Ben said.

I looked over at him. Ben was always in a state of calm. It was comfortable being with him.

"I'm thinking Paul won't be calling for a second date," I said.

"Did you want him to?"

"My sister would."

"You didn't answer my question," Ben said.

"I don't think so. Too soon to tell maybe."

"It's been my experience you know right away, whether someone is a good fit or not. That mutual attraction; the sparks are either there or not."

"I found him attractive, but no sparks," I said thoughtfully.

"You sound disappointed," Ben said.

"Well, I did shave my legs and everything."

Ben laughed out loud.

"By the way, my car is sitting in front of Parma's. You can drop me off there, so I can pick it up," I instructed Ben.

"You plan to drive with one eye and beers in your belly?"

"My head is fuzzy too. Fuzzy and swirly."

"Fuzzy and swirly? I'm taking you home, so I know you're safe. And I'll pick you up sometime tomorrow and drop you off at your car," Ben stated.

"I'm sure you have plans tomorrow. It's your day off. I can get a ride."

"It's officially your day off, too. I'll text Michael that you're taking a sick day. We can't have you scaring away our customers looking like that," Ben teased. "As far as my plans go, I don't have any."

"You're a nice man, Ben Warner. By the way, the band...impressive. And howdy, you can sing. Is there anything that you can't do?" I wondered out loud.

"Now who's being nice? Nice and a little drunk," Ben added.

As we pulled into the driveway of my complex, I reached into my handbag and pressed the button on the gate clicker. After the gate opened, I directed Ben to my door.

"You know what I could eat?

"What's that?"

"Waffles. I love waffles. Would you like to join me? It's the least I can do," I offered.

"You read my mind. The band and I always go out to breakfast after a gig," Ben said.

"Is the band waiting for you? Do you need to go?" I asked.

"You're much better looking, even with one bad eye. I will see you home, make sure you're alright and then ask you nicely to make me waffles."

As I smiled at Ben, a grim reminder I was punched coursed through my face.

"Shoot!" I grimaced. "But you cannot make me laugh or smile the rest of the night."

"Deal," Ben said.

Ben came around and opened the passenger door for me. I showed him in and set my handbag and keys on the mirrored desk that sat in the small entryway.

"I'll give you the grand tour," I offered.

"Nice place, Maggie. These photographs are amazing."

I explained the disrepair I had found the place in when I purchased it. I flipped on lamps and switches as I showed Ben my home. I always left the garden for last. As the grand finale, I flipped on the exterior light which activated the fountain and the fairy lights.

"You did all this? Very impressive. It's magical," Ben said.

"It's a work in progress but yes...I did all this. It's my form of therapy. Gardening helps me center myself and gives me a sense of accomplishment I can measure, much like your music," I said.

"It's beautiful, Maggie, and serene. I like the feel of this place. Do you mind if I freshen up a bit and then I'll help you with those waffles?" Ben asked holding a clean tee shirt.

"Not at all. Let me show you the way," I offered.

I walked him down the short hallway to the guest bathroom. I showed him where he could find an extra towel if he needed one.

"Yikes, Maggie!" Ben blurted out as I turned toward him.

"What?" I said startled.

"Your eye. In this light, it looks much worse."

I turned around to look in the mirror and gasped.

"Sit down on the toilet and let me look," Ben ordered.

He examined my eye as I suddenly began to cry.

"Did that hurt? Did I hurt you?" Ben asked.

"No, you didn't hurt me. My face did."

"Don't cry, you'll make it worse," he said gently cradling my face.

"Ok. But I better get my contact lens out."

"You're wearing contact lens? Shit, Maggie," Ben swore.

"Can you find it in my swollen eye?"

"I'm afraid I'll hurt you."

"You won't."

"Let me wash my hands first. I'm going to pull on the lower lid. Look up so I can find it."

Ben washed his hands thoroughly and dried them.

"Do you see it?" I asked.

"Move your eyeball toward your nose. There it is. Come here, you little sucker." With pride, Ben handed me the contact lens.

"Thanks. I'm going to get the other one out too."

I walked down the hall to my bedroom and entered the master bath. I gently pulled on my lower lid and removed the lens. I surveyed myself in the mirror. My cheek was purple and the bruise extended up along the soft flesh under my eye which caused it to swell.

"Attractive, Maggie. I need some ibuprofen," I said to myself.

Attempting to pull myself together, I brushed my hair and teeth and added lip gloss. There was only so much I could do to look better. I removed my bracelets, the scarf around my neck, and left them on the counter and headed toward the kitchen for a couple of pain relievers. I forwent my glasses due to the tenderness of my cheek.

Not long after I got to the kitchen, Ben came in holding the towel he had used to freshen up. I took it from him and tossed it into the laundry room. From my perspective, he looked good either way.

"Any ache or pressure behind the eyes?" Ben asked.

"No, Doc, just throbbing in my face."

"Do you have a cold pack?"

"I do."

"How about you leave me to the waffles, and you sit down with a cold pack."

"I won't argue with you, on account of I can't see the recipe."

I got Ben situated in the kitchen and went into the living room with a cold pack in hand. I turned on the stereo which was set to the country rock station and took a seat at the breakfast bar so I could watch him in action.

"Country music, waffles, and a pretty girl. Life doesn't get better than this. And not necessarily in that order," he amended with a grin.

I watched him whisk the batter together as I instructed including the secret ingredient which after tonight, I figured he could handle. Ben placed some butter in a skillet for eggs.

"The worst thing about tonight was that I was looking forward to dancing. It's not every day I get all dressed up," I complained.

"Let's not forget about shaving your legs too."

"Don't make me laugh," I scolded.

"The lady wants to dance...dancing she gets," Ben said wiggling his eyebrows. The waffle iron beeped, signaling it was hot. Ben filled it with batter and lowered the lid. He made his way around the breakfast bar to where I was sitting and extended his hand to receive mine. I laughed gingerly and got up to dance with the man.

Randy Houser's song Running Outta Moonlight came on the stereo as Ben twirled me around in my bare feet on the hardwood floor.

"You need to teach me the two-step sometime," I said.

"I can do that. But tonight, let's take it slow," Ben suggested.

He held me close in his arms, twirling me, and smiling. The man was an excellent dancer. The waffle iron began to beep. We stopped.

"Waffles," we both said.

I pointed to the cupboard that housed plates.

"There is only one way to eat waffles," I explained.

"Only one?"

"Well, only one way in my book. Dare to try it?"

"Hell yeah, I'm all in. What's the secret?"

"My grandmother taught me that food tastes best when prepared with love. So, I will lovingly prepare your waffles for you," I explained.

"Ah ha," Ben said. "Then that's the reason these eggs are going to be so tasty," he said as he turned his attention to the eggs in the skillet.

Meanwhile, I took out two waffles, placing one on Ben's plate and one on mine. I topped each with a large dollop of sour cream and then poured real maple syrup on top. I placed the second waffle on top of the first and repeated the process. I looked up to see Ben's expression.

"I promise to withhold judgment until I taste that," he said, staring down at his plate. "Although, I have seen what you can do to a bagel."

"It's a sweet-savory thing, trust me. The secret is to get the proportions just right. Besides, if you hate it, we can make more waffles. But I think you will love this as much as I do," I said.

Ben placed the fried eggs next to the waffle stacks, and I carried the plates to the breakfast bar.

"Bon appetite," I said as we clinked our forks together. "What would you like to drink?" I asked.

"Not now, Maggie, I'm going in."

And he did. And I was guessing by the moaning; he liked it. It was the sweet-savory combination that was a winner every time.

We ate in silence for about a minute when Ben finally managed to say, "I will never again eat waffles any other way."

"It's good with raw honey too. My grandma used raw honey on everything," I said.

"I love your grandma," Ben said.

I smiled. We split another round of waffles and ate until we couldn't breathe. After we cleaned our plates, I placed the dishes in the sink and brewed some coffee. We waddled our way to the living room. I pushed the ottoman to the sofa so that we could rest our feet.

We sat listening to music and talked about traveling until the coffeemaker signaled the brewing cycle was complete. The rich aroma filled the air. I got up to make us both a cup. A slow song came over the speakers. Ben met me in the kitchen. He put our mugs on the counter and took me in his arms for a slow dance. I flushed with anticipation.

"The lady didn't get to dance," he said quietly.

With my belly full of waffles and my arms wrapped around the perfect man, I was a happy woman. I decided I could pretty much die right now and my life would be complete. Well, pretty much. Ben sang along with the song on the stereo.

"Hey pretty girl, can I have this dance, and the next one after that...." we swayed to the song until it was over. He looked down at me and smiled. Then he took my hand and walked over to the freezer, retrieved the cold pack and placed it in my hand. Then pointed to the sofa. He poured us each a cup of coffee and joined me there.

"Thank you," I said looking over at him as he looked at me.

We talked about music, food, and our kids until our eyes grew heavy from all the carbs we had consumed. Apparently, I had nodded off into a beautiful dream where Ben and I were dancing. I was wearing an evening gown, and he looked like James Bond in a tux. We were dancing slowly and looking deeply into each other's eyes. We were inches from each other's lips when I whispered, "Kiss me."

"What?" Ben asked. "What did you say?"

I awakened to the sound of Ben's voice asking me what I had said. Groggy, I mumbled back, "I'm sorry, I think I dozed off. What did you say?"

"I think you said, kiss me," Ben said.

I straightened up on the couch realizing I had talked in my sleep.

"I didn't say kiss me. I was dreaming about stars. I think I said kismet."

I was a liar. But I also had too many embarrassing moments with this man to count. "Yeah, it was kismet. You must have misunderstood me," I insisted.

"Kismet? I'm pretty sure you said kiss me," Ben pushed the issue.

"Why would I say kiss me when I was dreaming about stars?" I said defensively.

Ben shrugged. I wasn't sure if he believed me. "I've been nodding off myself, so I'd better call it a night."

He pushed away from the ottoman so he could get up.

"I had fun tonight, except for the black eye part. Thank you. The waffles were great," Ben said.

"I had fun too. Thanks for dancing with me."

I walked Ben to the front door and unlocked it to let him out.

"Call me when you wake up, and we'll go get your car. The swelling in your eye should be down by then. Maybe ice it one more time before you go to bed," Ben suggested.

"Will do," I replied.

"Ok, sweet dreams."

"You too."

I watched him walk away, and slowly closed the door. I locked the bolt and leaned against the back of the door. I let out a deep sigh.

"What a sweet end to a crazy night," I said out loud.

I turned off the lights and the stereo and walked to my bedroom. I slipped out of my clothes and stood naked in front of the mirror, surveying myself with my good eye. I needed some work. There was only one man that ever saw me naked. How would it feel to be with another man, I wondered? Suddenly feeling vulnerable, I slipped my long tee shirt over my head. I turned off the lights and went to bed.

The possibility of a new relationship felt strange to me; sharing my body with a man other than Edward. I missed being held, made love to, touched. I hugged myself and shuddered with the longing.

I thought about dancing with Ben, his humor, his compliments, and rescuing me. I thought about how it felt when his eyes looked deeply into mine, albeit, for just a moment. Did he feel it too? I liked being close to him. Sparks, I thought. There were definite sparks. Lots and lots of sparkles all over me. I turned onto my "good" side and stared out into the moonlit night. It wasn't long before I faded off to sleep.

# Chapter 27.

I was up before nine and felt a little hung over. It felt more like tired than drunk. Although, four alcoholic beverages did exceed my limit. I checked my bruised face in the mirror. It was a kaleidoscope of red, purples, and greens. My eye still slightly swollen.

I showered and dressed in white capris and a sleeveless yellow and black floral summer shirt. I was still full from the midnight waffle feast, so I opted out of breakfast. Sipping on black coffee, I combed my hair and decided to leave the rest to mother nature. I applied a thicker layer of foundation to the unusual skin tone around my left cheekbone and eye. I added a soft pink color to my lips and pronounced myself ready for the day ahead.

I sat out on the garden patio with my coffee. It was after ten, a reasonable time to call Ben. I looked him up on my phone's contact list and pushed the number displayed there. After three rings, he picked up.

"Good morning, Maggie. How's the eye today?"

"It's better. Thank you for asking. Did I wake you?"

"Nope. My body clock gets me up early, whether I want to or not. You ready to go?"

"I am. I'm finishing up a cup of coffee on the patio," I replied.

"Have any plans today?" Ben asked.

"Not really. I did promise a visit with my mother later on today."

"The Japanese Gardens, inside the park, is opening their tea room today. Apparently, they built an authentic tea house with a deck that extends out onto the water garden. They also have live music and a Geisha performance at noon. It's a beautiful day, would you like to join me?" Ben asked.

"That sounds lovely. Yes, I would." I didn't have to think long about the invitation.

"Is fifteen minutes ok?" Ben asked.

"I'll be ready," I said, disconnecting the call.

My security phone rang, and I buzzed Ben through the gate. While he waited at the door, I grabbed my handbag, sunglasses, and a white hat. I slipped my digital camera into my bag and my feet into my yellow Tom's. My lips curled into a careful smile. My face was still sore.

"Good morning," Ben said, grinning from ear to ear. "You look great, Maggie. How's the cheek?"

"Better. Nothing a lot of make-up can't fix. However, I'll be avoiding laughter for a while," I said lightly touching the side of my face.

Ben was wearing chocolate brown shorts with matching Converse canvas shoes and a white polo shirt. A man with style.

The park was a twenty-minute ride across town. Ben was right; it was a beautiful day. Temperatures were unusually cool for this time of year. We entered the park, turned right, and followed the road to the gardens.

"I haven't been here in years," I admitted. "Isn't it strange that when you live so close to beautiful places, you rarely visit them. Take Yosemite for instance; it's only an hour and a half away. One of the great natural wonders of the world, right in our backyard, and I've only been there a half a dozen times in my life. People come here from all over the world to see the falls. I live here and can't seem to make the time."

"You're right...we get all caught up in our work and don't take time to smell the roses. Well, today we're changing that," Ben said and smiled.

"We certainly should, anyway."

Ben paid the fees, and we entered through large wooden gates into the first garden area. I released a sigh as I looked around. It was more beautiful than I had remembered. The garden had matured.

"I thought you would like this. I'm glad you came," Ben said.

"Me too," I said retrieving my camera from my bag.

We talked about architecture, Ben's travels and agreed on the importance of the landscape to the design of a building. We crossed bridges and ducked under tree branches. I pointed out the plants I knew and the genius in their placement, snapping photos along the way. As we came around a bend, we could see the tea house up the path.

"There it is. Should we stop for tea now or later?" I asked.

"How about now? We can enjoy the water gardens while we wait for the show."

We traveled the path to the tea house. The simple architecture of the tea house was beautiful. I insisted on paying for the tea and cookies.

We found a small table along the back of the deck, up against the railing. We could see the koi fish in the water, as they swam in and out between the pilings. I put on my white hat to shade my face from the sun. I looked over the side of the railing to watch the fish.

"Aren't they beautiful?" I asked Ben.

"Yes, they are."

"We couldn't have timed this more perfectly. Look at the crowd behind us," I said, turning toward the entrance.

I noticed a gentleman wearing dark sunglasses, sitting with a dark-haired woman near the back wall of the tea house. I realized it was Parcey. He tipped his chin up at me in recognition. I smiled back but felt uneasy.

"Is something wrong?" Ben asked.

"Don't look over, but Parcey is sitting across the deck from us."

"Does he bother you?"

"Long story. Will you do me a favor and pretend that we're together?" I asked.

"We are together."

"I mean like you're into me," I clarified.

"Does this have anything to do with your lunch date?"

"Sort of. I'll explain later. I don't want it to ruin this perfect day."

He picked up my hand from the table and placed it in his for Parcey and the world to see. Our tea came on a wooden tray, delivered by a tiny woman dressed as a geisha. She placed it in the center of our table.

"Thank you," I said.

She bowed and poured our tea into our cups. A small nosegay of white flowers sat in a vase in the middle of the tray.

"I love this. It reminds me of the tea house in San Francisco. Have you ever been there?" I asked Ben.

"No, I haven't. I'm glad you're enjoying this."

I pulled out my camera from my bag and snapped a picture of the tabletop. Then casually snapped a few photos of Ben as the breeze played with his wavy dark hair.

"Hobby of yours?" he asked pointing to the camera.

"Yes. I have always loved seeing the world through a camera lens. My mother bought me my first camera when I was nine years old, and I've been taking pictures ever since."

"Were those your photographs in the foyer in your home?" Bed asked.

"Yes, they are."

"Your talents never cease to amaze me. Photographer, baker, and

I can't even talk about the waffles without crying a little."

"Stop. You're teasing me," I said trying not to smile.

"No really. Have you thought about displaying your work? I know a gallery in San Diego that would take a look at your photographs," Ben offered.

"Thank you. I don't know if I'm confident enough for a gallery. I hope to travel to Italy someday and photograph the architecture," I said taking a bite of an almond cookie.

"You would love Italy. I've been a couple of times, and it's worth seeing," Ben said smiling sentimentally.

We finished our tea, just as the show was about to start. Beyond the pond, located directly in front of us, musicians took their places. Tea patrons moved from the tea house to the lawn area for a closer look. We chose to stay where we were.

The music began with eerie longing sounds and the plucking of instruments. In a voice that seemed far away, a geisha sang. Her voice drifted closer, as she approached. Other geishas surrounded her. Their fluid movements were captivating. She sang her forlorn song of lost love.

I pulled off my hat and began snapping photographs as fast as I could. The world I saw through my camera lens left me breathless. The beauty was ever-changing, and I didn't want to miss any of it.

For a photographer, the perspective through the camera lens is an intimate one. Once a photograph is printed, the hope is to share that vision with others; that they might see it, as you did.

I could feel a pair of eyes watching me work the camera. Between songs, I used the camera as a binocular and panned the crowd. I stopped cold at the sight of Parcey's face looking back at me. Immediately, I dropped my camera and looked over at Ben.

"You're in your world behind that lens, aren't you?" Ben observed.

"I'm sorry. Am I rude?" I asked genuinely.

"Not at all. I enjoy watching you. I've been wondering what you see," Ben said thoughtfully.

"If I get a few good ones, I'll share them with you."

When the show was over the crowd began to disperse.

"He's still watching me," I said to Ben. "Let's take a walk. If you promise not to get angry, I'll fill you in on the whole story."

I put the camera and hat in my tote and stood to leave. Ben skimmed over the crowd and placed his hand on the small of my back, allowing me to walk in front of him. After leaving the tea house, Ben laced his fingers through mine, as we walked to the next garden. I couldn't help thinking I wished it were real. The electricity I felt between us was intense. I wondered if it was the same for him too.

"Let's walk out to that grassy area," I said pointing. "We'll have an unobstructed view from those benches."

"Maggie, you're beginning to worry me a little bit," Ben said as he watched me.

We walked out to the open area and chose a place to sit. Ben rested his arm on the back of the bench. With my bag at my feet, we sat close enough together that we appeared to be a couple.

"So, what's this all about?" Ben asked me seriously. "Start at the top and don't leave anything out."

I began with, "You know how you asked me to keep my ears open..." and continued through to the night Dika read my fortune.

"What makes me uncomfortable with Parcey is that he knows things about me I've never told him. The night he dropped me off in the store parking lot, he parked right next to my car. He already knew what kind of car I drove. Now, maybe I'm reading into this, but I have this gut feeling that he's been watching me. I think he might even know where I live," I said. "But I don't have any proof of that."

"Damn it, Maggie. I asked you to keep your ears open, not go all Nancy Drew on me," Ben said raising his voice slightly.

"You promised not to get mad. Besides, so far, Parcey has only been a nice old man making conversation with me. There is a possibility it's all in my imagination," I offered.

"What did the fortune teller reveal about your future?" Ben asked curiously.

I carefully chose my words. "Dika was fairly general. She told me about relationships, travel, finances, that sort of thing. She mentioned I might be in a little bit of danger...oh, and she said I have a good aura."

Ben looked into my eyes. The intensity caused me to look away.

"What kind of danger?" he finally asked.

"She wasn't clear about it. Her mojo was off or something," I said.

"The fortune part sounds promising. What about relationships?" Ben inquired.

"I don't believe in any of that stuff. What I'm concerned with is Parcey."

"Are you avoiding my question?"

"No. I don't think it's important."

Ben was apparently bothered by what I was saying. "This is all my fault. I should have never brought you into it," he said shaking his head.

"It's not your fault. Parcey would have talked to me anyway. The mistake is mine, not yours. I should have stuck to the plan."

"Maggie, don't you see how serious this could be? He's part of the gypsy organized crime. That's serious business," Ben warned.

"Yes, I do see. But Parcey is also a human being. I don't think he would hurt me," I said reassuringly.

"He seems to be keeping an eye on you. That bothers me."

"That could have happened no matter what I did. The lunch was happenstance. Parcey found out things about me before that."

"He's coming up the sidewalk," Ben whispered.

"Well, well. Look at this romantic picture," Parcey said to the dark-haired woman on his arm yet loud enough for us to hear.

"Parcey. Hello. Isn't this a beautiful day? Did you enjoy the tea house?" I asked him casually.

"Doll? What happened to your beautiful face?" Parcey asked.

"Nothing. Just a silly accident I had at my mother's house. I was cleaning out her closet. It looks much worse than it is," I said to him.

Parcey's attention shifted toward Ben. Ben stood up to shake his hand. "Hello, Parcey. And this is…?"

"Where are my manners. This lovely creature is Elena. Elena, these are my friends from Bay's Market. Maggie and Benjamin," he said accenting Ben's name.

"Nice to meet you," Elena said in a Vampira kind of way.

"Pleasure to meet you, Elena," I said, and Ben echoed.

"Let's leave these young people to enjoy their day, shall we?" He announced and then leaned toward me saying, "Is he part of the triangle?" Without waiting for an answer, he put his cigar back into his mouth and leisurely strolled away. Ben and I watched the couple in astonishment.

"What did he mean by that? What triangle?" Ben asked.

I shook my head before explaining that part of the reading to Ben. "It's all a bunch of hooey anyway. You ready to go?" I asked.

Ben looked at me out of the corner of his eye. "Please, promise me to be extra careful with him. He's kinda creepy, and so is El Vira."

That broke the tension between us. I laughed, holding my cheek. As we stood up to leave, Ben put his arm around my shoulders and faked a choke hold.

"I predict that you are going to drive me crazy," Ben said and kissed the top of my head and released me.

"I'm suddenly hungry for Chinese food. How about you?" I asked.

"You're so tiny, where do you pack away all that food you eat?"

"Come on; I'm buying. Then you can drive me back to my car," I suggested.

"Tell me again about this love triangle. Any idea who the men might be?" Ben asked.

"Paul. One of them has to be Paul. I'm not sure I've met the other guys yet," I teased.

# Chapter 28.

The next morning wasn't any different from most mornings. I pressed the remote, and the stereo came to life playing some good ol' rock and roll. Lately, I've been listening to a lot more country music.

As the coffeemaker did its thing, I did mine. Dressed in my long tee shirt in front of the kitchen sink, I began to dirty dance.

It was Monday morning, and I was going back to work tomorrow. My black eye was taking on a greenish hue, and some parts had cleared up substantially. Lucky for me, my face wasn't any closer to Dean's fist.

I called Mom and gave her the short version of my weekend. I hadn't heard from Paul since Saturday, and I didn't expect to. I knew Elizabeth was biting at the bit to learn about our date. Not in the mood for a lecture, I opted to send her a short e-mail instead of calling.

The grinding came to a stop long enough to pour me a cup of coffee. I strutted my stuff across the hardwood floor of my living room, straight out the back, to the patio. I left my imaginary partners in my wake with their tongues hanging out. I took a seat at my bistro table and tried to catch my breath.

It was going to be a warm day. Even this early in the morning, I could already feel the difference from yesterday. I slipped my fingers into the breast pocket of my tee shirt and pulled out my phone. I sent the kids a morning text and sipped my coffee. My phone rang, and I noticed it was Dean.

I rolled my eyes before I picked up. "Good morning, Dean," I said calmly.

"Are you still mad at me?" Dean asked.

I hesitated before answering, "No, I'm not still mad at you."

"Good. How's your eye?"

"Lovely shades of green and purple."

"Well, girls are doing interesting things with make-up these days. What's on your agenda today? I think I owe you a ride or maybe buy you lunch. What do you say? Give this guilty ridden boy a break," Dean begged.

"Feeling bad, are we?"

"Yeah,...still. I've never punched a girl before," he confessed.

"And I've never been punched, until a few days ago."

"Yes, but I'm trying to make it up to you," Dean repeated patiently.

"Well, let's see...it's going to be a warm day."

"The coast?"

"Ahhh...no. I've had a busy weekend. How about sushi? I've been all about Japan lately," I said.

"Sushi is good. Where do you like to go?"

"Sakamoto's. They have beautiful décor and a lovely garden. I haven't been there in years."

"Perfect. Lunch or dinner?" Dean asked.

"How about a late lunch? I have a few things to get done."

"I'll pick you up in my air-conditioned vehicle, say around two? We'll avoid the office crowd."

"How about 1:30?" I suggested.

"You're going to make this difficult for me, aren't you? 1:30 it is."

"See you then," I confirmed.

I disconnected with Dean and thought about how Sakamoto's had been Edward's favorite sushi restaurant. The last time I ate there had been with Edward. Don't be melancholy about it; I scolded myself. I would end up there sooner or later anyway.

I ate a banana, finished my coffee, and decided to go for a short run. I threw on my jogging pants, a tank top, and brushed my teeth. I decided to skip the gym today. Having been hit on twice in one week, I wasn't comfortable going back just yet. It hadn't felt like a compliment to me; they had invaded my personal space.

After my run, I stretched out my muscles on the living room rug.

"I think you've earned a little spa treatment, Maggie," I said out loud.

I turned on the stereo and popped in my meditation CD. The Zen instrumental music immediately relaxed me. Satisfied, I walked into the bathroom and began to fill my tub. I added lavender bath pearls, stripped out of my clothes, and slid into the bath.

My mind wondered as I relaxed, and I found myself sitting on the deck with Ben at the tea house. Harmless crushin', I told myself. I didn't believe he daydreamed about me.

After my bath, I reached into my closet and pulled out a sleeveless, crossover bodice dress with a high waisted drawstring. It was red and purple, so I decided on red polish for my toes.

Moving on to my face, I used extra makeup to conceal the greenish and purple hues on my fair skin. I accented my eyelids in purple shadow to match the bruise. I tried to think of something different I could do with my hair.

Feeling soft and feminine, I pulled the right side of my hair back away from my face with a red clip, exposing my ear. I worked the soft curls around my face and added a natural gloss to my lips. I slipped into my dress and sandals. I switched out my yellow handbag for a natural woven one. Pleased with what I saw in the mirror, I decided I was ready.

I heard a knock at my door. Rolling my eyes, I opened it.

"How do you do that? You bypassed the security again," I said staring up at Dean.

"You look beautiful," was all he said. Then he added, "Ready?"

I immediately was disarmed. "Yes."

The restaurant was close to home, so it took no time to get there. We were shown to our table right away. We had a view of the gardens. Koi swam under our feet through a glass canal that meandered across the restaurant floor.

"I want to live here," I said to Dean.

"And the sushi is good too. Thanks for coming to lunch with me. I hope this means that you've forgiven me?" Dean asked.

"I can't stay mad at you very long. Look at you. Your hair is always messy, and your shirt is hanging out. You've forgotten to shave, again, and you just wouldn't have any friends, if it weren't for me."

"Is this a pity date?" he asked cocking his head to one side.

"It's not a date of any kind," I reminded him.

"Now, you're talking mean," Dean said and smiled.

I took Dean's hand and patted it for effect. I looked up to see Ben entering the restaurant. He had a beautiful blond haired woman at his side. Our eyes locked. He looked at Dean and then back at me. Ben acknowledged me with a nod, and I noticed an expression of disappointment on his face. I placed Dean's hand back on the table. Ugghh.

Ben slid the chair out for his date and took the seat beside her. From my vantage point, I could only see the top of their heads through a screen of bamboo.

"You alright?" Dean asked. "You look like you've seen a ghost."

The waitress came over to take our drink order. We both thought it wise to pass on the saki and went with the tropical iced tea instead.

"I'm fine. I just saw Ben come in with a lady friend. I was just surprised to see him," I said.

"That man seems to show up whenever we're having lunch."

"Do you think he thinks we're dating?" I asked with a fake laugh.

"I guess it's possible. Especially after the unfortunate bar scene," Dean said and grimaced.

"Is it against company policy?" I wondered.

"Probably, but you know what goes on around the store," he said. "Who isn't having an affair?"

"That's true. This place brings back a lot of old memories. Fun times. Sakamoto's used to be one of Edward's favorite haunts," I commented.

"Let's not go there today, if you don't mind," Dean said without looking up from the menu.

At the risk of becoming Debbie Downer, I let it go.

The waitress came back for our order. For the next hour, Dean did most of the talking while I did most of the listening. He told me about his plans to someday relocate to Jackson Hole. The area left an impression on him after a visit there as a boy. Dean was embarking on a cross-country trip, at the end of summer, with his biker buddies. They would travel for two weeks.

The food was delicious. Even better than I remembered. Ben stood to leave the restaurant, and his movement caught my eye. He didn't look my way. He and the blond exited the restaurant together and shortly after, so did we.

Dean brought me home, and I invited him in. I put on the stereo and lowered the room temperature. I went into the kitchen to mix up a pitcher of iced tea lemonade. While the tea brewed, I admitted to myself I was disappointed. Seeing Ben with such a stunning, younger woman, made me feel old. What was I expecting anyway? We've only exchanged some harmless flirtation between us. After all, he was my boss.

With my back toward him, I heard Dean get up from the barstool and walk into the kitchen. He took the knife I was using to slice lemons, out of my hand and set it on the counter. Dean turned me around to face him and slid his arm around my waist. He took my hand in his and began to dance with me.

"I owe you a dance," he explained.

"I don't recall asking you for one."

"If you weren't on a blind date, I would have asked you. Besides, you told me you hoped I would ask again."

"Are we still talking about dancing?" I asked Dean.

"In a manner of speaking," he smiled.

"If my memory serves me right, that wasn't all that long ago."

"I didn't want you to forget that I asked."

"I've hardly had a chance to catch my breath," I replied nervously.

"You talk too much."

My heart began to quicken as his eyes met mine. He released my hand and slid his other arm around my waist. I wrapped both arms around his neck. I rested my good cheek against his. We continued to slow dance through the next song, even though it was a faster tempo.

I tensed, as he pulled himself away to look into my eyes. His blue eyes burrowed through mine, and my body began to warm. The attraction between us was intense, and I was afraid of it.

Then he kissed me. It was the same kiss from a lifetime ago. As the fireworks set off all over my body, I found myself kissing him back. He began to deepen the kiss and then suddenly stopped.

"Maggie?" Dean said breathlessly against my lips.

"What?" I responded.

"I don't want to push too hard and blow this. You have to tell me if you want me to stop."

I was thinking in slow motion. My mind was muddled, and my body was in overdrive. I missed this and was afraid of it at the same time. We continued to dance with our foreheads and noses touching.

"Maybe we should stop," Dean said. "Do you want me to?"

"You ask a lot of questions."

"You're impossible, Bloom."

"Shut up and kiss me again."

# Chapter 29.

My week at work was somewhat uneventful. The store slowed down during the summertime due to temperatures and vacations. Families took turns by the thousands to escape the summer heat. It's not uncommon for people who lived here, to also rent or own a second home on the central coast.

Deciding to take things slow between Dean and me, we made no promises. Dean was the consummate professional when we both worked the same shift.

To keep myself foremost in the bosses' minds regarding the bakery management position, I took my morning break to speak to them. This promotion meant a lot to me. I didn't want this opportunity to slip through my hands.

On my way up the stairs, Dean was headed down. As he passed me, he winked, and I'm pretty sure he grazed my hand on purpose. I shook my head as I entered the office and greeted Tami.

"Hi, Tami. How goes the crazy grocery business?" I asked.

"Hey, Maggie, you tell me. When are we going to the new Nicholas Sparks movie that just came out?" Tami asked.

"I haven't forgotten. I'm feeling swamped. Let's make a definite date for next week."

"That sounds good. We'll compare schedules later in the week?" Tami confirmed.

"Sounds great. Is Ben or George available by chance? I'm on my break."

"Hold on," Tami got up, walked over to Ben's office and poked her head inside. I heard her ask if he could see me.

I heard him say, "Sure." Tami pulled her head out of Ben's office and smiled. She shook her hand and mouthed, "He's so hot." I smiled at her and went in.

"Hi Ben, thanks for seeing me," I said as I took a seat.

He placed his report down and asked, "What can I do for you?"

"I haven't heard anything more from either you or George about my till shortages. And I wanted you both to know that I'm still seriously interested in the bakery management position," I said.

"We haven't forgotten you, but I'm afraid I don't have anything new to report. George interviewed two people last week for the position, but you are still in the running. He'll set up callbacks for next week sometime."

"Ok. Good to know. Thanks for your time." I left Ben's office feeling a sense of loss. Things were different between us.

"See you later, Maggie," Tami called out to me. I waved and hustled over to the time clock to punch myself back in.

When it's slow, Dean had the checkers restocking and facing the end caps on the aisles near our registers. I was lost in thought when I heard someone pssst-ing me. I turned around to find Martha trying to get my attention.

"Hi, Martha, what's up? Were you pssst-ing me?" I asked.

"Yes. I don't want to get you in trouble at work, but I need to talk to you," Martha said, pointing to the large glass office window upstairs.

"That's ok. Stay where you are in the aisle, they can't see you."

"Maggie, I need your help."

"What kind of help?" I asked.

"I've decided to leave Stanley. I'm relocating to the city, but I can't leave my Mr. Beasley with Stanley. He hates him. I'm afraid he might intentionally hurt him when he finds out I'm gone. I have a friend who will let me stay with him until I find a place of my own," Martha explained.

"And this friend doesn't like dogs?"

"They aren't allowed in his apartment building. Oh please, Maggie. I promise it won't be more than a couple of weeks or so. Mr. Beasley loves you."

"Martha! Mr. Beasley doesn't know me. I'm here all day, and he would be stuck all by himself at home. And a couple of weeks? That's a long time," I said.

"You've always asked if there was anything you could do to help me. Well, now you can, and I'm asking. I'll beg if you want," Martha pleaded.

"When are you planning to run away from home?"

"Stanley has an overnight business trip in two weeks on a Tuesday. He always makes me go with him, but I'm going to start coming down with a cold on Sunday. I'll tell him I am way too sick and sneeze in his face a couple of times; he'll hate that. Please, Maggie, can I count on you?" Martha asked.

"Let me think about it for a couple of days. I'll let you know later."

"Oh...I could kiss you, Maggie," she squealed. Then she closed the gap between us, and hugged me with her arms and breasts, keeping her tiny bottom up and away.

"I haven't said yes, yet," I reminded her.

"Thanks for considering it. I had better go. Stanley is waiting for his dinner. I don't want to piss him off prematurely," she said with a wink.

No matter how much I try not to like that woman, I did.

Later at Dean's house, over a couple of containers of Chinese take-out, he warned me about getting involved in Martha's shenanigans.

"If you do this one favor for her, she'll continue to suck you into the middle of her problems. I can tell the woman is nothing but trouble," Dean said.

"I know that. But there's something about Martha I like. I think she needs a new perspective or maybe just a break."

"People like her never learn. She'll continue making the same stupid mistakes the rest of her life," Dean stated.

"Well, that's a pretty pessimistic view. I'd like to think that people can grow and change," I suggested.

"That's because you wear rose-colored glasses."

"Is that how you see me? As this naive woman who has no idea what life's about?" I asked Dean.

"Not exactly. But you do like to see only the best in people."

"I don't see only the best in people. However, I do choose to try to see the best in them. There is a difference," I begged to differ.

"Gosh, you're cute when you're angry," Dean grinned.

"Oh, please," I said and got up to leave the table. I took my plate into the kitchen. I rinsed off my plate and placed it in the dishwasher.

"See what I mean?" Dean said as he came into the kitchen. "We're fighting, and you haven't even helped her yet."

He took the sponge out of my hand and reached under the sink for a handled brush.

"I can take care of that," I said reaching for his plate.

"We've always had a system. I've got it. Make yourself

comfortable," Dean replied.

I cleared off the table and walked into the family room. As Dean cleaned the dishes, I looked around the room. On the opposite side of the sofa, a bookcase took up most of the wall. A flat panel television sat on the center shelf. Framed photos of Carolyn, as well as friends or family, lined the shelves. A large picture of Dean and Carolyn, taken somewhere exotic, sat on an upper shelf. There were random stacks of books on the shelves. By their titles, I guessed they were Carolyn's. Knick-knacks filled the other spaces.

Dean entered the room saying, "You've spent most of your adult life in a sheltered environment, raising your kids. That's all I'm saying," Dean concluded.

I turned to look at him and was silent for a moment before I burst out. "Did you seriously just say that to me? You don't know the first thing about how I lived. For one, you've never asked. Two, have you looked around this place? You're living in some shrine to Carolyn. I bet you haven't moved one thing since she died. Don't talk to me about being sheltered," I was suddenly so furious that my hands began to shake. The man was intolerable.

To my shock, Dean just stood there as I picked up my purse and stormed out the front door. I drove away with tears spilling down my face.

I parked the car in the garage and let myself in through the laundry room door. Walking directly to my bedroom, I threw off my clothes and changed into my long tee shirt. I used the toilet, washed my hands, brushed my teeth, all without looking at myself in the mirror. In bed, I reached over to turn out the light. I caught sight of Edward's photo on the nightstand table and paused. I picked up the photograph, opened the drawer and placed it face down. I begged sleep to come.

"How was it that I could be in the same room with you, and feel lonelier than if I were in it alone? You didn't see me, Edward. Did you ever?" I murmured into the darkness and listened for an answer that never came.

# Chapter 30.

The following Sunday came quickly. With Michael running the store, I was hoping I could discover something about him. I knew he was behind my till problems, and I needed the promotion. But how could I prove it?

As expected, business was slow. Whenever there were significant events in town, the store went quiet. Today, was the all-day jazz festival out at the park. Prominent performers were headliners, and the weather forecast was in the low nineties. We were experiencing a coolish summer so far. I wondered if Ben would be at the festival.

Because I opened the store, I was first for lunch. I clocked out at eleven-thirty and made my way back to the warehouse to get my handbag out of my locker. I was in the mood for something different to eat. I decided to take a shortcut through the receiving dock to get to Margie's Diner. I pushed the heavy doors open slowly, and heard the echoes of two males arguing. It took a moment to recognize, but one of them was Michael. I scanned the dock but saw no one. I squeezed through the smallest opening possible, trying to avoid the usual squeak.

As if the fates were conspiring against me, Frankie from the meat department came around the corner and shouted, "Hey Maggie, wait up! I've got a question for you."

Great, just great, I said to myself. Without warning, Gabriel popped his head around the corner to see what was going on.

Feinting surprise, I exclaimed, "Hey Gabriel, how's it going? I saw your dad at the park last week, he looks good!"

As if on cue, Frankie poked his head in the door, "Howzit goin'?" He turned to me, "Maggie, I gotta ask you somethin'."

"Sure," I opened the door wider and inched my way back. Suddenly, my world broke into chaos. Out of the corner of my eye, I saw Gabriel lunge toward me. Without warning, his hands grabbed my shoulders.

"Get out of here," he growled at Frankie. Gabriel pulled me back toward the dock. I dropped my handbag and twisted in an attempt to get free. What was he doing? Looking over his shoulder, I saw Michael's face full of confusion and fear.

"Gabriel. Easy, what are you doing? What's going on here?" I demanded. Gabriel drug me to the loading dock gates. He jerked me around so that I was facing Michael. Gabriel grabbed me by the neck. My heart pounded as I felt the cold metal from a gun, pressed to my temple.

"Gabriel, what the hell are you doing?" Michael shouted, stepping closer to us.

"No, Michael," he said, cocking the gun. I closed my eyes, unable to breathe. "I'm done being jerked around by you. You go now, and get my forty-two grand or Maggie here gets a bullet in her head," Gabriel demanded.

Michael was shaking his head. "I don't have that kind of money lying around. You know that, Gabriel."

"Call your big brother or your old man, and get it …now!" Gabriel shouted. He tightened his grip around my neck.

Was I dreaming? Was this happening? I decided to try to calm Gabriel down so he wouldn't accidentally blow my brains out.

"Gabriel, look it's going to be all right," I said in a low voice. "Ben will give Michael the money. We don't have to do this. It's going to be all right," I said calmly. "Gabriel put the gun down, and Michael will be back with the money." I tried to keep the panic out of my voice.

Michael was waving his hands and talking frantically. Suddenly, he turned and ran toward the warehouse doors, leaving me alone with Gabriel.

My captor was agitated, talking to himself. He sniffed several times. It occurred to me that he might be high.

"Come on; we're outta here," Gabriel snorted.

I knew if I got into his car, anything might happen. "Gabriel, let's give Michael a minute," I negotiated. "He'll be right back with the money. There is a safe in the store. The money is probably in the safe."

"I don't trust the guy. He's probably already called the cops. Let's go," Gabriel said pushing me.

Gabriel grabbed my arm tightly and pulled me toward his car which was parked just off the dock. The gun remained pointed at my head. My mind raced as I looked around for a way out. The alley was empty.

Gabriel ordered me to open the door and climb into his car through the driver's side. I did as he demanded. I could feel Gabriel on my heels. He turned on the ignition and floored it.

"Don't even think about getting out or making a scene. You're a nice lady, Maggie. My dad likes you, so don't make me hurt you," he warned me.

"Don't worry, Gabriel. I won't try anything," my mind raced as I tried to process what just happened. I felt nauseous and scared. I didn't have my handbag, so I had no cell phone. My kids flashed through my mind. Although I was frightened, I could feel my blood starting to boil. Get mad Maggie, I told myself. It will help you fight for your life.

Gabriel drove us to the south side of town, where the

neighborhoods were old. These homes were built sometime in the fifties. Old men and women sat outside on their porches because it was cooler than inside their homes. Gabriel turned into the driveway of a home that could have belonged to Hansel and Gretel. He got out of the car and ordered me to climb over the driver's seat. I did what he asked.

We walked down the driveway toward the back of the house. Gabriel opened a gate and guided me toward the back door of the house with the muzzle of the gun, pressed in the small of my back.

"Open the door," he grunted.

I did as he instructed and stepped inside the house. He forced me down into a chair at the kitchen table.

"Pop," Gabriel yelled. "Pop, where are you? Come in here!"

"All right, all right," Parcey's voice echoed from another room. "What's all the yelling about....Gabriel, what have you done?" Parcey appeared, and his voice deepened as he caught sight of my face.

"I had it with that grocery boy! He owes me forty-two grand, and he's going to pay it. Now, that I've got her," Gabriel said, congratulating himself and pointing his finger at me.

"Put that gun away, you stupid son of a bitch," Parcey demanded, as he walked up to Gabriel and slapped him across the face. "Do you realize what you've done here? You're gonna put yourself in jail for kidnapping her, you idiot!" Parcey belittled him.

Instinctively, I remained quiet. The tension was high in the room. I glanced around to find another way out. It occurred to me why Dika was confused about the danger. If any of what she said was right, I was going to be alright.

I thought about Ben. Please help me; please help me, Ben. Undoubtedly, Michael would've gotten a hold of him by now.

"Maggie," Parcey began. "This is an unfortunate situation my son has put us in. We'll try to sort this out as soon as possible. Can I offer you something to drink?"

"No, no thank you Parcey," I said barely recognizing my voice. Could I use Parcey's feelings for me to persuade my outcome? I could hear Ben's voice reminding me these guys were the mafia.

I looked around the kitchen and spotted a clock. It had been over an hour since Gabriel kidnapped me from the store. Something must be happening by now.

Parcey took a seat next to me at the kitchen table. He took my hand in his, "You must know by now, I am very fond of you, Maggie. But you must also understand that Gabriel is my only son. I will protect him at all costs."

Gabriel's phone rang. He checked the caller ID, hesitated, then answered it.

"It's about time, Michael. You have my money?" Gabriel said then listened intently. "Don't give me any bullshit, Michael. I know you have a safe full of money at the store...just get it." He said and hung up. "He's gotta go to the bank to withdraw some of the money. He doesn't have that much in the safe," he told Parcey.

"This is what's going to happen, Gabriel. Michael will call you with the cash. I will take Maggie home," Parcey instructed, and Gabriel immediately protested.

"She'll put me in jail for kidnapping, Pop. We can't let her go," Gabriel argued.

"No one's going to jail, Gabriel. But you sure as hell aren't going to murder over forty grand. Put that outta your head," Parcey raised his voice, standing up to face him.

215

Parcey turned to me and spoke sternly. "Maggie, Gabriel is my flesh and blood. Blood is thicker than water. Sorry, that's the way it is. You will not press charges against Gabriel. If you do, you will be looking over your shoulder the rest of your life or as long as I deem that you live. Of course, if you simply walk away from this with no charges against Gabriel, none of that will happen. Consider it a favor to me, and I will be indebted to you," Parcey explained with a casual wave of his hand.

He met my eyes. There would be no negotiations here, no reasoning, and no choices.

I nodded. "I understand, and I won't press any charges against Gabriel," I heard myself agree.

"Good girl," Parcey said to me.

Parcey turned to Gabriel. "That's the deal. You understand me?" He stared into his son's eyes. I could see Gabriel shrinking under his father's gaze.

"You will not touch a hair on this girl's head," Parcey insisted. "She will honor her promise; she's a smart lady."

"Ok, Pop," Gabriel said in a boy's voice. "Yeah sure, I understand."

"And you're getting off the dope! You hear me! No more of this shit or I'll make your life a living hell," Parcey added, cementing his words with another slap to Gabriel's cheek.

Gabriel's phone rang again.

"Michael? Did you get it? OK, this is what you're going to do. You have a pen?" Gabriel opened his wallet and took out a piece of paper. "You're going to deposit it into this account. Ready?" Gabriel read off the numbers to him. "I'll release the girl when it hits my account. I'll be checking it," he warned.

Parcey looked over at me, "I guess you'll be going home soon."

I looked over at the kitchen clock. I'd been here over two hours.

Parcey opened the refrigerator door. He poured a glass of cold water and handed it to me.

"Thank you," I said, and sipped it. I felt the worst was over. Exhaustion began to set into my body. I urged myself to stay strong.

Sometime later, Gabriel walked back into the room carrying an Ipad, "The money's in my account. You can go home now, Doll," he said.

I rose to my feet, feeling weak-kneed. Parcey steadied me. "Let's take you home now," he said, kindly.

"I need to go back to the store. All my things are there," I said, surprisingly calm.

"I'll have to drop you off at the corner just in case the cops are there," he said.

"Not a problem," I answered.

We walked outside toward the curb where Parcey's black Cadillac was parked. He opened the door for me, and I slid into the passenger's seat. I looked back at the house and saw the curtains in the front room move. It was Dika, looking out at me. Did she live here too, I thought? Chills went down my arms in spite of the hundred degrees temperature.

Parcey dropped me off at the corner of the strip mall. I crossed the street, cut through the gas station and walked the length of the mall before I reached the grocery store. Still numb, I walked through the doors and turned directly up the stairs toward the executive offices. I entered the landing and felt nauseous again. Taking a breath, I walked into the receptionist area.

Ben saw me first. "Maggie!" he said as he rushed over to me and took me in his arms.

"Are you alright, are you hurt?" he demanded to know.

Tears fell from my eyes as the shock began to wear off. I pulled away from Ben, struggling to regain my composer.

"I'm fine. I'm alright," I said as I brushed my face with the back of my hand.

Looking past him, I saw two officers waiting outside Ben's office door. Ben took my hand and walked me into his office, bypassing the officers.

"We'll be right back," Ben said before closing the door. He turned to look at me. He paced back and forth in front of me. "I think I've aged ten years in the last couple of hours."

Then he stopped and took my hands in his and said, "Are you sure you're alright? He hasn't hurt you?"

"I'm fine Ben. Shaken, but fine." That's when the dam broke, and the floodgates opened. Tears rolled down my face uncontrollably. "I didn't know what to do. Gabriel scared me, but he didn't hurt me. I had no control over the situation. I was at their mercy."

Ben wrapped his arms around me. "I was at the jazz festival when Michael called and told me what happened. I could have killed him. He came clean about the money and the registers. All I could think about was you. I prayed and thought of you. I was scared you would be hurt," Ben confessed.

My knees went weak, so I sank into the chair closest to me.

"I'm sure the police have some questions for you," Ben said looking down at me.

"I don't have anything to say. I'm not pressing charges."

"What? The son of a bitch held a gun to your head and then took you as a hostage. These are bad guys, Maggie," Ben said.

My heart told me I could trust Ben with the truth. But I was afraid to get him involved. "This was between Michael and Gabriel. Drug money. Do you honestly want the police involved in that? Michael could go to prison," I replied.

"We are talking about you. Putting that idiot Gabriel away because of what he did to you."

"I'm fine...I won't press charges," I said determinedly.

Ben stared at me. "Parcey got to you, didn't he? Did he threaten you not to press charges?" Ben questioned.

I ran my fingers through my hair and leaned back against the chair. "Ben, I want to go home now," I pleaded.

He looked at me, saying nothing. Then he turned, opened the door and walked out of the office. I could hear him talking to the officers, explaining to them about not pressing charges. One of the police officers came into the office.

"We've been after these guys for some time now. We could use your help. If you press charges, we can put one of them away for a while," the officer explained.

I stood up and faced him. "I'm sorry, I can't help you."

"Ms. Bloom. I don't think you know who you're dealing with. They'll have you looking over your shoulder the rest of your life. You don't have to go through that if you help us," the officer said.

Without another word, I walked out of the room and noticed my handbag on Tami's desk. I picked it up on my way to the stairway. Michael was on the landing and headed toward me.

"Maggie, thank goodness you're alright!" Michael said.

Without thought or hesitation, I slapped him. "No thanks to you,

Michael. Isn't it time you grew up? I swear if anything happens to any one of those kids downstairs, it'll be on your head. Do yourself and everyone else a favor, and check yourself into rehab...today!" I screamed at him.

I pushed passed him and made it down the stairs without buckling. I was halfway to my car when I heard Ben call out to me. I stopped in my tracks and slowly turned around.

"I don't think you should be alone, Maggie. I can take you home unless you're going somewhere else."

I looked at him. Tears streamed down my cheeks. I didn't say a word. Then, reaching into my handbag, I pulled out my keys and dropped them into the palm of Ben's hand.

# Chapter 31.

Ben drove me home without conversation. I felt exhausted and oddly enough, hungry. After coming inside, I switched on the AC. It was a hot day.

"You've gone all day without eating. Can I make you something?" Ben offered.

"That would be great, but I'd like to shower first," I replied. "I have homemade tomato soup in the freezer, and a grilled jalapeno cheese sandwich sounds divine... with pickles inside. Oh, but I'm out of bread."

"Not to worry. While you shower, I'll run out and pick up a baguette. Will you be alright while I'm gone?" Ben asked.

"Yes. And thank you," I said and smiled.

"I'll lock up behind me. See you in a few."

I walked down the hall to my bedroom. Not only was I hot and sweaty, I felt violated. What a stupid asshole Gabriel was, I thought. From my dresser I pulled out a pair of capris yoga pants, and a tank top, and headed for the shower.

Stepping into the shower, I let the water wash over me. I wished I could wash the day out of my mind along with the salty sweat off my body. I began to lather up when I noticed my arms. They were both bruised. I had a more significant, deeper bruise on my upper left arm from when Gabriel had grabbed me and pushed me inside the car.

"Stupid, stupid Gabriel," I repeated, this time out loud, and to the universe. I shook with fear and anger.

By the time I had showered and changed my clothes, Ben was back and making dinner. I slipped my feet into my slippers and shuffled into the kitchen.

"It smells delicious in here," I commented.

"Thanks to your soup. I have it on low in the saucepan. I'll start the sandwiches when the soup defrosts."

He started to walk toward me and stopped short when he noticed my arms. "Holy shit, look at your arms. Gabriel, what a son of a bitch. And you said you weren't hurt," He stated.

"It's just bruising from pushing me around. By the way, thank you for the flowers. They're beautiful," I said and smiled.

Ben's expression suddenly shifted and grew dark. "Maggie, I didn't get you flowers," he said solemnly.

"That's not funny, Ben. They're in my bedroom on the side table."

Ben brushed passed me as he walked toward my bedroom. I stood still. My heart sank, and I couldn't move. He came back from around the corner, carrying a vase of yellow roses. He held out the card to me. Warily, I took it from him. I slowly opened it and read the enclosure.

Sorry for today – Sincerely Yours, P.

As the reality hit me, tears began to form. They weren't from fear but outrage. "He's not getting away with this. I won't have it," I growled.

Shaken, I grabbed the flowers from Ben and slipped into my flip-flops at the front door. "Come on Ben; we have a delivery to make."

Ben turned off the soup and followed behind me. I locked my door and power walked to my car. Once inside, I handed the flowers back to Ben.

"What are you thinking, Maggie? You're beginning to scare me," Ben said.

"We're delivering some flowers. I don't know where Parcey lives but I sure as hell remember where Dika does. We're going there. If I let this go...if I let him have the power...I'll never stop looking over my shoulder," I explained.

I sped down the street toward Dika's house. When Gabriel drove us to the house, I paid attention. My Aunt Maggie once lived in the area, so I was familiar with the neighborhood.

Ben didn't say a word. He hung on as I pulled in and out of traffic. We finally came to a stop in front of Dika's house. I saw the black Cadillac under the carport. He was here.

"I'm going with you," Ben said opening the car door.

"No. Please, Ben. I have to do this on my own. I have to prove to him that I'm not afraid. Wait here by the car. If I don't come back in five minutes come in with both guns blazing," I directed.

"Great. How do I do that with no guns?" Ben said.

He leaned up against the outside of my car with his arms folded across his chest. I handed him the keys and walked up the driveway.

I knocked on the back door. After a minute or so, Parcey opened the door with a cigar in hand.

Smiling down at me, he said, "I see you got my flowers."

I moved up to the next step so that I could look at him more squarely in the eye. "The flowers weren't necessary," I sternly said as I pushed the vase into his chest. "We had a deal. I plan to honor it. Do you?"

My heart was beating so hard and fast I could hear it in my ears. I tried to regulate my breathing so I wouldn't passout but kept my eyes fixed on Parcey's.

He took a moment to size me up. "Ok Maggie, you're right. We do have a deal. And yes I will honor it. You've got a lot of spunk for such a little thing," he said and smirked.

My eyes remained fixed on his. I wasn't going to take any bull shit. "I trust I won't have to change my locks. Remember, you owe me now," I reminded him.

I turned on my heels and power walked down the driveway.

"Drive...let's get out of here," I said under my breath when I reached Ben.

He ran around to the driver's side of the car, got in and turned the engine over. I looked back at the front window, and Dika stood behind the edge of the curtain. I was pretty sure she was smiling.

"Yes, Dika," I said to myself, "I am strong."

As we made the next two corners and got out on the main road, I started to laugh uncontrollably. With my head between my knees, I couldn't stop laughing.

"Are you laughing or crying? I can't tell," Ben asked.

I raised my head and managed to say, "I'm laughing."

"Oh, good. What are we laughing about?" Ben nervously asked and giggled.

"I think I shit myself."

"Oh. You did?"

"No. I don't know, maybe. I think I almost did. I can't believe I just did that. I stared the gypsy mafia down. Am I crazy?" I wondered.

I was trying to catch my breath and get control. My adrenaline was still pumping on all cylinders.

"It must be nerves. Or maybe I am crazy," I repeated.

"What happened? What did you say?" Ben demanded.

I took a few deep breaths and settled down. I started by

explaining to Ben what happened earlier as a hostage and the deal I made with Parcey.

"So then, I looked him square in the eye-- without peeing myself-- and said "I trust I won't have to change my locks," which I will anyway. "And remember Parcey, you owe me now." And then I turned and got the hell out of there," I said.

"Geez, Maggie Bloom, you're a bad ass! You stood up to a gypsy mafia gangster. I have to say I'm finding this pretty sexy. You're my hero, Maggie" Ben added.

"I guess I am a bad ass. Parcey will keep his word. I could see it in his eyes. I believe he respects me now. And he might be a lot of things, but honor means something to him." I turned to look at Ben. "I would appreciate it if you stayed the night with me. If I call my mother or sister, they will be worried sick. I'd rather they don't know anything about this. I may be a bad ass, but I'm a scared one. I'll make a call on changing the locks too. The thought of someone in my home, while I was in the shower...chills me. Do you think he's been in there before?" I asked Ben.

He shrugged and shook his head.

"Will you stay with me?" I asked again.

Ben nodded and put his hand on top of mine. "I'll stay with you. Besides, it was my idiot brother who got you into this mess. I'm sorry about all of this. In the meantime, remind me not to piss you off," Ben said and smiled.

As soon as we got home, I put in a call to the first locksmith I came across after googling for one. There was no answer. According to the message on the machine, they were closed, but my call was important to them. So, I left a message.

Ben had put together a tasty meal for us. After we ate, he banned me from the kitchen. I stretched out on the couch with the television on for distraction. My den was a small room just off the entry, by the front door. I could see the front door from where I was sitting. I decided I couldn't relax until I pushed something in front of it. I got up and pushed the chest from the entryway in front of the door. Satisfied, I walked back to the den and stretched back out on the couch.

As Ben came around the corner with drinks in hand, he stopped for a second to make a note of the change in decor.

"I'm not sure how that will work in case of a fire," he mused. "I brought us two cold beers," Ben said handing me one.

"Nice. You sure know your way to a girl's heart. Ply her with food and beer."

"Let me know if it works. The soup was amazing by the way. You have a gift, Maggie," Ben said and settled in next to me.

"What are you watching?" he asked.

"Nothing, channel surfing."

"How are you feeling?" he asked.

"Alright, I guess. I'm feeling a little stiff, probably just tension."

"Let's see...turn around."

I turned in my seat with my back toward Ben. He began to rub my neck. "You have a huge knot in your shoulders, right there," he squeezed, "Close to your neck."

"Ouch," I cried.

"Relax, tough girl. I'm going to get the cold pack, and I'll be right back. Do you have a hot water bottle?" Ben asked.

"Bottom drawer in the guest bathroom," I replied.

After Ben left the room, my phone signaled that I had received a text. It was Dean: I think we should talk.

Long day. Talk tomorrow?

You OK? Was it busy at the store?

You wouldn't believe the day I had! I'll call you tomorrow.

Ok. Get some rest.

I tossed my phone onto the ottoman as Ben came back into the room. He placed the hot water bottle, wrapped in a towel, on the back of my neck. After ten minutes, he massaged my shoulders.

"Crikey...that hurts so good," I complained.

"We'll ice it for 10 minutes. And then repeat the process."

"Thanks, you're awesome," I said to Ben.

We sat side by side with our legs stretched out in front of us on the ottoman, sipping cold beers. I handed the remote over to Ben.

"Here, you can drive," I said.

Before I knew it, I had drifted off to sleep. When I woke up, I was drooling on Ben's shoulder. I sat up wiped my mouth and his tee shirt.

"Hey, Princess. It looks like you got a little nap," Ben said.

"How long was I out?"

"Couple of hours," he replied.

"Really? Sorry, I drooled on you," I said wiping his shirt with my bare hand.

"Did you know that you snore too?" Ben said.

"I do not."

"Uh huh. You even made these cute little puffing sounds," Ben said and tried to replicate them.

"Stop! I did not," I demanded.

"At one point, I thought you swallowed Eeyore," Ben teased.

"No way!" I punched Ben's arm and sat up straight on the sofa while he snickered at me.

"Would you like a cup of tea while we ice your shoulders?" Ben asked.

"You're spoiling me. I'll get it. I need to walk around a little bit anyway. Are you tired? Did you want to go to bed?" I asked.

"Not yet. I can use a cup of tea myself."

We walked into the kitchen, and I put fresh water in the kettle and placed it on the stove.

Ben leaned against the counter, and I noticed his brow furrowed. "While you were asleep, I couldn't help but think about today. You scared the hell out of me. I don't know what I would have done if something had happened to you," Ben said solemnly.

"What do you mean?" I asked.

"Maggie, you drive me crazy."

"I'm not following," I said confused by Ben's choice in words.

"Look. I've pretty much figured out you're seeing Dean. When I saw the two of you at Sakamoto's holding hands, it confirmed it."

"We weren't on a date at Sakamoto's," I explained. "Dean took me to lunch as a peace offering after the black eye."

"You were holding hands."

"I was mocking him, actually," I replied.

"Wasn't the whole bar scene about him being jealous you were on a date?" Ben asked.

"Maybe. It's complicated. We are seeing each other now in a way, but we are taking it slow and have made no promises. In fact, I'm not even looking for a serious relationship. Just company. I'm not good at the relationship stuff," I tried to explain.

"I find that hard to believe," Ben said.

"Which part?"

"That you aren't good at relationships. From the first time I met you, one of the things I recognized immediately was what an incredibly giving person you were. Maybe, you don't give yourself enough credit. People are attracted to you because of your genuine kindness toward them. You're an arms-opened-wide kind of person. It's that whole aura thing. Dika was right; you have a good one," Ben said.

"Huh. My mother said the same thing about me. What about the blond?" I asked.

"The blond?"

"Yes. The beautiful--young--blond you were with at Sakamoto's."

"Diane? She's my insurance broker."

"You're not dating her?"

"Diane?"

"Yes, or whomever."

"I guess I should be flattered, that you think a girl so young would be interested in me," Ben said and smiled.

"Oh please. Have you seen yourself? Well, except for tonight maybe," I teased him.

"I'm currently not dating anyone. I'm transitioning," Ben explained.

"Transitioning?" I said brows furrowed.

"My daughter pointed out to me a few months ago; I tend to get involved with women that lead nowhere," Ben said and slid his hands into his pockets.

"Commitment issues?"

"It's complicated. The point is I'm transitioning. And you have something to do with that too," Ben admitted.

"Me? How so?"

"You don't have any idea how incredible you are?" Ben smiled.

I shook my head and tried to speak, but hesitated. I pursed my lips together before I said, "I was married a long time," I paused to choose my words carefully. "For a long time, I didn't know how to be anything else but Edward's wife and mother to our children. That was my whole identity. After Edward died, I didn't even recognize myself in the mirror anymore. These last few years have been about getting to know me again. What do I want to do with the rest of my life? I don't want just to be someone's wife again. Do I like poached eggs or were they Edward's favorites?" I said shrugging my shoulders. "I don't know if being in another relationship will mean losing myself again before I have a chance to find myself."

Ben stepped closer to me and wrapped his arms around me. I placed my cheek against his chest and hugged him back.

"Why must relationships be so impossible? It seems to me it should be pretty straightforward. Choose to be with someone who compliments you, not complicates you. By the way, what is your favorite kind of eggs these days?" Ben asked.

"I love omelets," I chuckled. "Because you can put anything you want inside and enjoy them any time of the day," I explained.

"You're a fascinating woman. You do realize that Dika's been right on three accounts?" Ben said.

"Has she?" I looked up at him.

Ben pulled away slightly. He played with the curls on top of my head then gently pulled one behind my ear. "You had a perilous day today. You do have a great aura. And it seems you're in the middle of a love triangle. What do you think comes next?" Ben asked teasingly.

"Hmmm. That would be travel or fortune. Since I can't afford to travel, maybe I should start playing the lottery."

"At least some scratchers," Ben said with a slow smile.

# Chapter 32.

I was awakened by the tune on my cell phone, playing at full volume. I raised my head off my pillow, looked around and found Ben sprawled across my bed. We had been up talking most of the night. I scrambled for the phone.

"Hell—hello," I managed clearing my throat.

"Good morning!" a mysterious, cheerful voice greeted me. "Maggie Bloom, please."

"Speaking."

"This is Joe from McGreggor's Locksmith Services returning your call. Your message sounded urgent, so I thought you should be my first call this morning."

I sat up and hung my feet over the side of the bed, scratching my head. "Yes, thank you so much for calling me back. Sorry about the yawning, late night. I'm off today, and I was wondering if you could come over and change out my locks."

"I have a guy out on mobile right now. Where are you located?" Joe asked.

I gave Joe the directions to my condo, and we agreed on twenty minutes. "Thanks so much, Joe. You've made my day," I said before disconnecting.

Ben rolled over to the opposite side of the bed looking dreadful. His clothes were rumpled, and his hair was a mess.

"What time is it?" he mumbled.

"Seven-thirty. Are you working today?"

"I'm the boss, remember? I haven't decided yet," Ben said and yawned.

He stood and stretched like a big cat.

"The locksmith is on the way," I informed him. "You're on coffee duty, and I'm getting in the shower. I have a clean tee shirt for you." I opened my chest of drawers and pulled out one of Edward's tee shirts, and tossed it to him. "You can shower next."

I was ready in fifteen minutes and chose to wear knee-length white shorts and a red cotton mid-sleeve shirt to cover the bruises. I quickly made up my face and walked out to the kitchen with wet hair.

"That coffee smells heavenly. Thank you, thank you, thank you," I said as I entered the kitchen. "The guest bath has Henry's toiletries in the second drawer. There's a new toothbrush in there too. Help yourself."

"Argghhh. I'm taking my coffee with me," Ben said as he disappeared around the corner.

While Ben showered, I called Dean. I wanted to explain what happened yesterday before he found out from someone else.

The phone rang twice before he answered. "Good morning Maggie."

"Hi, Dean. Did I wake you?"

"I just came in from a run. How are you today?"

I briefly told him what happened yesterday. I excluded my agreement with Parcey and Ben's participation in the event.

"Geez, Maggie! Are you alright? I can be there in five minutes," Dean insisted.

"No, don't do that. I've got a locksmith coming, and I have a friend here. I'm fine... Better, anyway," I added after I thought about it.

"Did the store call the police?" Dean questioned.

"Yes. There were two detectives there. I spoke with one of them."

"What are they going to do about it?"

"Nothing. I'm not pressing charges."

"Why not? Maggie, you could have been seriously hurt," Dean said as he raised his voice.

"I know, but I wasn't. It's a long story. I'll tell you later when I see you. For now, I didn't want you to show up to work and get blindsided."

"Michael is such a prick; always has been. He could have gotten you killed," Dean remarked bitterly.

"I don't think Gabriel had any intention of killing me. He's a mama's boy. He wanted Michael's attention and got it. He threw a tantrum like a two-year-old."

"Are you free to talk after work tonight?" Dean asked.

"Let's do it when we're both rested," I said as I heard Ben coming down the hall. "The locksmith will be here any minute; I have to go."

"Maggie, before you hang up," Dean hesitated. "I want you to know you were right about a lot of things. And you're important to me."

"Thanks, Dean," I replied. "That means a lot. My doorbell just rang. Call me when you get home tonight."

"Ok, bye," Dean said before disconnecting.

Ben came down the hall looking refreshed and wearing Edward's tee shirt. It was a bit snug on his frame. If Bobbie were here, she'd say I did it on purpose.

"Perfect timing. Can you help me move this piece of furniture away from the door? The locksmith is here," I said.

I opened the door to Gary, the locksmith. Inviting him inside, I showed him all the locks that needed to be changed. I also requested an extra bolt on the front door and a chain on the back door. A moment later, I added a lock on the door from the garage to the garden and asked him whether we could add something to the French doors. He was happy to oblige me. I stood in the middle of the kitchen with my hands on my hips, surveying my decision. "Too many locks?" I asked Ben.

"As long as I don't have to move furniture in front of the doors, it's fine with me."

"Good. Gary, I'll be here in the kitchen if you need anything," I said to the locksmith.

I whipped up a spinach and mushroom frittata for breakfast and added a fresh fruit salad. Ben read the morning paper while I cooked. I passed him two of everything, freshened our coffee, and then walked around to the breakfast bar.

"Maggie Bloom, you can cook for me anytime. Breakfast smells delicious," Ben said.

"I hope you enjoy it. It makes me happy to cook for someone."

"You know, I was thinking," Ben said after a bite of melon. "We make a good team; we're like crime fighters. I'll be Kato. Maybe next time you'll let me karate chop someone," he grinned bumping me in the arm.

I bumped him back. "I'd be ok with no next time. What's on your agenda today?" I asked.

"Well, after I beat some sense into my brother, I'm hoping to drop him off at rehab. Apparently, Dad has been enabling him for some years. But after yesterday, everything changes today."

He turned in his chair to face me. "Maggie, I can't tell you how sorry I am."

I turned to face him. "Ben, you had no control over Michael. You weren't even living here when he started all of this. If Gabriel had not lost it, who knows where Michael could've ended up? They don't stop until they hit bottom. Let's hope this is Michael's bottom."

"We might have never met if Dad hadn't asked me to come back and help out," Ben said reflectively.

"Not true. Remember, our two amazing kids found each other in San Diego," I smiled. "We would have met eventually. Speaking of them, maybe we shouldn't mention yesterday. Henry would probably move home to keep an eye on me. I can't have that," I said.

"I won't mention it," Ben agreed. "Are you aware I'm invited to Henry's birthday party?"

"I am. Are you going? I asked.

"We could go together since we probably won't know anyone else there," Ben suggested.

"That would be nice. I turned in my vacation request last week. I'm flying down after work on Thursday and spending a few days with Henry. He's showing me the sites. Not sure about Isabella yet; she's supposed to let me know her plans this week. I'm requesting Friday and Saturday because I'm already off on Sunday and Monday," I chirped.

"I'm happy you're looking forward to it," Ben took a sip of his coffee and added. "Where will you stay?"

"I'm not familiar with the area, so Henry or Samantha will find a hotel for me. Henry lives with three other guys, so I'm not going there. I told him I was willing to splurge to stay somewhere close to the beach."

"You should stay at my house," Ben suggested. "We have plenty of room. I have a spare bedroom, and we're about a block from the beach. I won't be there until Saturday, and I'm sure Sam would love the company."

"Well, that's nice of you to offer. I'll consider it," I replied thoughtfully.

Gary worked diligently and was on his last lock. When he completed the job and packed up his things, I drove Ben to the store to pick up his SUV.

"I'm glad you're alright. Will you be ok on your own tonight?" Ben asked.

"I now live in Fort Knox. I couldn't be any safer," I joked nervously.

Ben held my eyes for a brief second before turning to get out of the car.

"Thanks for being there for me, Kato," I said meeting his gaze.

I watched Ben walk to his truck in Edward's tight tee shirt. Then I turned the Mini around and headed home.

# Chapter 33.

Dean and I made plans to go out on Saturday and talk things over. He made reservations at a place called Gilley's Steakhouse, just north of town, up in the hills. The restaurant sat on Kokanee Lake. Dean arrived in a brand new midnight blue truck.

"I love your new ride!" I exclaimed as I walked to the truck. "What made you decided to trade in the Ford?"

"I can haul the Harley in the back. And I wanted something new."

"It matches your bike exactly. At least you'll be well coordinated out on the open road."

"That's the other reason I chose this truck," Dean mocked me. He rubbed my cheek with the back of his hand.

The moon was bright, illuminating the winding road as we traveled up the hill toward the lake. The stars were more brilliant up here than in the city. I looked forward to watching them dance above the water.

At Gilley's we enjoyed a delicious dinner outside on the deck, overlooking the lake. We each had a couple of glasses of wine. After we finished, we pushed our chairs back to take in the view.

"We can go for a walk along the water to work off our meal," I suggested.

"I have another idea," Dean said as he turned toward me. "My buddy has a cabin up here. We can take out his boat and get a better look at the stars."

"Oh, nice. I like that idea," I agreed.

Dean paid our waitress, and we headed toward the cabin. We

climbed the hill in Dean's truck until we came to a series of cottages along the shoreline. Dean slowed down until he found the cabin address he was looking for.

"Is your friend using the cabin?" I asked.

"Not this weekend," he said pulling up into the driveway.

Dean helped me out of the truck and held my hand as we walked through the gate to the backyard. On the back porch was a built-in bar and grill area. Dean used a mini flashlight on his key chain to find the boat key, hidden behind the bar. From the backyard, we passed through another gate and walked out onto a long dock. Dean helped me into the boat and then untied it from the pier. He started it up and gently backed it away and out onto the lake.

Suddenly, Dean cut the engine and said, "I'll be right back." He went inside the cabin. He came back after a few minutes with chilled champagne and two plastic glasses.

"This is beginning to look more like a conspiracy rather than a spontaneous idea," I said.

"No comment," he said with a boyish grin.

We sat next to one another on a built-in bench.

"Would you like some champagne?" Dean asked.

"I'm still feeling the effects of the wine. I'll need to wait a bit," I said holding my palms out.

We stretched out our feet and leaned back against the seat to view the night sky. The stars were out in full glory, and the night was still. It was peaceful out here on the lake.

"Maggie," Dean broke the silence. "I was wrong to have said those things to you last week. I'm sorry. Your comments hit me right between my eyes."

"I'm sorry if I hurt you," I said meeting his eyes. "I don't exactly know why I became so angry."

"No. You were right. You have been there for me every time I've needed you, and what kind of friend have I been to you? I criticized you unjustly. And you were right about my house. It's Carolyn's home. It's time I make it mine or leave it," Dean said.

I sat silently with nothing to say in return.

"Hey," I said changing the direction of the conversation. "Let's go for a midnight swim. I have never gone skinny dipping. I'm a grown woman in my fifties, and I've never gone skinny dipping. That's crazy, right?"

I jumped to my feet before I lost my nerve. The boat swayed in the water. "Turn around or close your eyes," I instructed.

"You're going to do it, aren't you?" Dean watched me, amused.

"Close your eyes!" I demanded.

I pulled my summer dress up over my head and kicked off my shoes. I stepped over the back of the boat onto the platform and jumped into the water in my bra and underwear. The lake was cold, and I came up breathless.

"Yahoooooo! It's cold, but it feels exhilarating," I shouted.

Leaning against the back of the boat, Dean laughed at me. "Bloom, you never cease to amaze me."

I watched as he pulled off his polo shirt and slipped out of his khakis. He stepped out on the platform, as I had done and dived in toward me.

When he surfaced, I squealed like a schoolgirl as he splashed me. Treading water, I splashed him back. We played in the water until we were out of breath. I swam over to the platform and grabbed ahold of it.

"This is so refreshing compared to how hot it's been in the valley," I panted.

"I see a different side of you, Bloom," Dean observed.

I climbed the ladder to the platform and sat down with my knees to my chest. I ran my hands through my hair. Dean followed my lead.

"Dean, this was a great idea. Thanks for planning it. However, you might have to save the champagne for another time. Haven't you learned your lesson with alcohol yet?" I teased him.

"I wasn't going to drink it," he protested. "The plan was to ply you with it."

"You're a bad man. A very, very bad man," I teased.

In the middle of my sentence, Dean leaned over and kissed my mouth as lake water rolled off our faces and dripped down our bodies.

"You're a sexy woman, Maggie."

I fought the attraction I felt for him. I wrapped my arms around my legs as if to keep me warm.

"There's no use fighting it, Bloom. We're hot for each other," Dean said.

I covered my face and laughed. "I'm beginning to think these are shark infested waters."

"You want me; I can tell," Dean insisted.

"I don't know what I'm doing with you," I exclaimed.

"Can't we just have fun and figure it all out later?"

I looked at him without responding. "You scare me a little, I guess," I finally said.

"Because you're feeling things you haven't felt in a while?" Dean pressed.

"Because I feel like somebody else when I'm with you. Are we trying to live out some college fantasy here?" I wondered out loud.

Dean reached over and brushed the wet curls out of my face.

"We're all grown up now. We can do anything we want. Why make this so complicated?" Dean asked.

"Turn around," I said.

"What?"

"Turn around. I'm getting back into the boat," I said.

"You do know I watched you get out of the water, don't you?"

"Do it. Turn around," I insisted while Dean complied with a grin.

"Fine. I'll fantasize about you instead," Dean smirked.

I got back onto the boat, put my dress over my wet underwear and slipped on my sandals.

"You can turn around now," I said.

"Fine. But now you need to turn around. I'm coming aboard too."

On the way home, we put the windows down and let the mountain air rush in around us. We sang along with the radio at the top of our lungs and stopped for ice cream at the bottom of the hill. As we hit the valley floor, the windows went back up again, and the air conditioning came on. We drove back to my place, saying very little along the way. Dean parked in front of my condo and unbuckled his seat belt.

"Tonight was fun. Thank you," I said to Dean.

"You're welcome. Let me see you inside. I'll feel better knowing you're safe."

Dean walked me to the door, and I unlocked the new deadbolt to my fortress. We stepped inside, and I turned on the lights as he looked around. As I walked him back to the front door, Dean stood inches away from my nose. His hands rested on my hips. He kissed the tip of my nose and then my mouth. I raised my hands and held his face in my palms. He tasted of ice cream and lake.

# Chapter 34.

"This to-do list is not watching a dog, Martha. This looks like work. Are you telling me he won't eat dog food? I have to cook his meals?" I stared at the list on the paper she handed me.

Martha's dog, Mr. Beasley came to stay with me after all. I brought him home and showed him around. From the long list of instructions Martha had left me, he was apparently a high maintenance dog. I sat Mr. Beasley in his basket in front of the couch and looked at him. He was tiny. What if I stepped on him? I guessed that he weighed no more than five pounds soaking wet. How much chicken could he eat, I thought?

The security phone rang, and I buzzed Mom through. When she knocked, I walked over to the front door to let her inside. To my surprise, I found it was Ben standing at my door.

"Hey, what are you doing here?" I asked surprised.

"Were you expecting someone else?"

"Yes, my mother. Come on in."

"I'm not interrupting anything, am I?" Ben queried stepping inside.

"No. Mr. Beasley and I were just getting acquainted."

"Who's Mr. Beasley?" Ben asked.

I took Ben's hand and led him to the couch. We both sat down, and I pointed inside of the basket.

"That's Mr. Beasley," I said while he let out a little growl.

"It's a little rat with a bow on its head," Ben said apparently amused by the tiny dog.

I snickered.

"Why do you have it?" Ben asked.

"Do you know Martha from the grocery store?"

"Who doesn't? She's hard to miss," he said while studying the dog.

"Well, she's running away from home and can't take Mr. Beasley with her. She's afraid her husband will take it out on the dog when he finds out."

"Why can't she take it with her?" Ben asked.

"Dogs aren't allowed where she's going."

"All he needs is a shoe. How much trouble can he be?"

I handed him the list that Martha left me.

Ben looked it over before saying, "You're kidding?"

"Nope," I said staring down at Mr. Beasley.

"You're not bringing him to San Diego are you?" Ben asked.

"No, that's why my mother is coming over. I'm introducing them so he won't freak out when I leave him in a few days. What's up with you?" I asked curious about the sudden visit.

Ben studied Mr. Beasley. He attempted to make eye contact with me until the little creature began growling again.

"I had a craving for Java Chip ice cream and wondered if you wanted some too. I would have called first, but it was an uncontrollable craving. I would have asked you at the gate, but you buzzed me right through," Ben explained.

I debated the offer for a moment, "Java Chip is my favorite flavor too."

"I know. You and Bobbie were having a debate about it the other day."

"It's not your favorite flavor is it?" I asked Ben.

"No. Maple walnut is," Ben confessed.

"Crazy! That's my second favorite."

"Really?"

I nodded. The security phone rang, and assuming this was now my mother; I buzzed her in.

"My mother has a crush on you, you know," I said as I walked over to the door, opening it before she knocked. Ben chuckled from the sofa.

"Hi, Mom," I said.

"Hello, Darling," Mother said hugging me. "How's my favorite girl?"

"Good. Mom, you remember Ben, don't you?" I asked as we walked toward the living room.

Ben stood and stepped toward my mother to shake her hand.

"Yes, of course, I do. How are you, Benjamin? Please call me Jackie," she reminded him holding his hand longer than she should.

"Very well, thank you, Jackie."

"Mom, come on over and meet Mr. Beasley," I suggested directing her to the basket.

"Oh, isn't he the cutest thing you have ever seen?" she said reaching inside to pick him up. Mr. Beasley let out a little bark.

I leaned toward Ben and said, "Birds of a feather."

"Hello, Mr. Beasley," Mom cooed nuzzling him. "I think we'll get along famously. Ellie, don't you worry."

"Wait until you see the shopping list. I'll cook for Mr. Beasley, so all you'll have to do is warm it up," I offered. I turned to Ben and explained, "Mother doesn't cook, she prefers to dine out."

"Now Ellie, you'll give Benjamin the wrong idea about me. I cook," she stated.

"If she invites you for a home cooked meal, decline. Or at least make sure your insurance policy with Diane is paid up," I teased my mother.

"Ellie!" Mother scolded while Ben chuckled.

"If you don't cook," Ben asked, "where did Maggie get her extraordinary talent?"

"That would be from my mother. She immigrated here from Italy and was a marvelous cook. When Ellie was young, she just loved following my mother around in the kitchen. Always watching and asking questions."

"I only learned out of necessity," I teased.

"Oh, stop that! Your father was a pretty good cook. I don't have the knack for it," Mom confessed to Ben.

"I'm teasing you. You know you're my person. Come, sit down," I said to her.

"And what are the two of you up to this afternoon?" Mom asked curiously.

"We're getting ice cream. Would you like to join us?" Ben asked.

"Thank you, Benjamin," my mother waved her free hand, "but I will have to pass. I'm on my way to my afternoon bridge game."

"Maybe another time," Ben offered.

"That's sweet, certainly. I hope to see more of you. I better be on my way. Ellie, I'll see Mr. Beasley when I pick you up here for the airport on Thursday."

"Thank you for doing this, Mother. Let me walk you to the door," I offered.

"I'm happy to do it. I think Mr. Beasley will be good company for me. Good-bye, Mr. Beasley," she cooed and placed him back inside the basket.

"Very nice seeing you again, Jackie," Ben said.

"The pleasure is all mine, Benjamin. Come around more often. You're good for Ellie, I can tell," she said and waved.

I opened the door and gave Mother the evil eye while she walked to her car. She turned around and blew me a kiss. She shook her hand and mouthed "very hot," referring to Ben of course. When she was safely in her car, I waved at her and closed the door.

"Ellie?" Ben asked when I returned to the living room.

"My name is Margaret Eleanor. My mother's sister's name was Margaret or sometimes Maggie. I became Ellie, so not to confuse anyone, when we were in the same room together. I'm only Ellie to my mother. Sorry about all that with her, she can be... pushy," I apologized.

"I like your mother. And what about Aunt Margaret?" Ben asked.

"She died. She said my head was always in the sky and filled with nonsense. My curls annoyed her. She called my hair unruly and licked her fingers to push my hair away from my face. Sometimes she fastened my hair back with Bobbie pins." I shook my head remembering.

"Huh? I love your curls. Can't say as much for Aunt Margaret though," Ben said.

"I'm the only one in our family with curly hair. Mother said I was special... Ice cream?" I said.

"Absolutely. What about...Beasley?" Ben asked.

"Oh yeah. Do you think we should take him with us?"

"Does he need a special car seat or a deep pocket... or something?" Ben teased.

"Oh, Martha left some sort of baby strap to carry him around in," I said. "I'll stick him in that," I suggested.

Ben watched me as I struggled with the contraption. "I think you're supposed to wear it across your chest not carry it around like a slingshot."

"Grrrrrrrrrr," Mr. Beasley growled.

I pointed to the dog. "I don't think Mr. Beasley likes you very much, Ben."

"I think he's growling at you," he replied.

# Chapter 35.

Mother and Mr. Beasley dropped me off at the airport to catch my six o'clock flight to San Diego. I was excited about my mini vacation and the chance to spend some time with Henry. Isabella, unfortunately, wasn't going to make this trip. I was disappointed. I had been looking forward to seeing both of them. It's been difficult connecting with Isabella since she became a teenager. I hoped we could build on the momentum from our last successful visit together.

I checked in at the counter, taking my carry on bag with me. After walking the long corridor, I took the escalator up to the second floor. With some time to spare, I bought an iced tea and sat down to enjoy it. I checked for messages on my phone and found I had one from Dean: Don't forget to use sunscreen. Call me when you get home : )

I smiled at the message. I took out my boarding pass and rechecked the time. They should be calling my flight soon, I thought. My phone jingled, alerting me I had a new message. It was from Mom. She sent a selfie of her snuggling with Mr. Beasley. I hated to admit it, but that dog was beginning to grow on me.

An announcement over the P.A. system alerted me it was time to board the plane. I tossed my cup into the trash can and made my way toward gate 22. Aboard the plane, I stashed my carry on in the compartment above me.

Cleared for takeoff, we picked up speed down the runway and eventually were air born. The captain promised us a clear night and a smooth flight of one hour and sixteen minutes.

Before I left home, I had synced my favorite songs from my computer onto my phone. Now, that we were in the air, I fished my earbuds out of my handbag. Closing my eyes, I listened to Keith Urban's Greatest Hits, and before I knew it, we began to descend into San Diego.

As I exited the plane, I thanked the crew and walked down the tube from the aircraft into the airport. I was cheerfully greeted by both Henry and Samantha, as they waved to get my attention. We loaded into Henry's car and headed toward Ben's house.

"I'm happy you decided to stay with us, Mrs. Bloom," Samantha said. "It didn't make sense to pay for a hotel when we have an empty room no one uses."

"Please call me, Maggie," I reminded her. "I appreciate the hospitality and look forward to spending a little more time with you."

We arrived at Ben's condo in La Jolla. The house was beautiful and exceeded my expectations in many ways. Samantha showed me to my room, and Henry deposited my bag onto the floor.

"What a nice room, Samantha," I said as I looked around. "Your home is lovely, and look at the beautiful hydrangeas on the bedside table."

"Henry told me they were one of your favorites. I hope you enjoy them," Samantha said and smiled.

Samantha gave me a tour of the spacious condo. I could imagine Ben living here. It had an extensive open living room and kitchen concept. The exposed beams accentuated the high ceilings and excellent woodwork. The room was decorated in a clean, modern feel, using metal and stainless steel accents. The kitchen was a home cook's dream, outfitted with a glass refrigerator, professional oven, and beautiful quartz countertops. A metal stairway curved from the entry to the second floor. Samantha's suite took up the second level.

"Dad told me you make amazing waffles and to ask you to make some for me while you're here," Samantha said. "Ever since I was young, we've had a contest to see who could come up with the best waffle concoction. He said you have his peanut butter waffle beat."

"Well, I don't know about that," I laughed. "I've never had your dad's peanut butter waffles, but the least I can do is make you my recipe," I offered.

Samantha pulled out a beautiful antipasto tray while Henry made up a batch of margaritas.

"That looks refreshing. Are those herbs inside the drink? I can hardly wait to try it," I said to Henry.

"Yep and I'm right behind you with a baguette, Mom," Henry replied moving toward the dining table.

"Here's to your mini-vacation," Samantha toasted. "Cheers."

We clinked glasses and dug into the food. We laughed and chatted until Henry called it a night at ten o'clock. He had to be up early the next morning.

"Goodnight, Henry. Sweet dreams," I said as I hugged him.

"Thanks, Mom. I'm glad you're here," he said before Samantha walked Henry out.

When Samantha returned, she said, "Maggie, before I forget. Henry's birthday gift came yesterday, and I've already taken care of wrapping it for you."

"Oh good," I said happily. "Thank you, Samantha. I wanted to ask you about it, but there didn't seem to be a right moment with Henry around."

"It was my pleasure. So, Dad mentions you quite a bit lately. Thank you for keeping him company and out of trouble for me," she smiled broadly. Just like her father.

"He hardly seems the type to get into trouble. He's been helpful to me on more than a few occasions. He's a good man, your father. He's very proud of you and loves you very much," I said heartfelt and wondered what Ben might have said about me.

"It's been just the two of us for a long time. Now, that I'm an adult, we don't spend as much time together as we used to. I keep telling him it's time to find a companion. I worry he's always alone," Samantha explained.

"Being alone isn't always a bad thing," I assured her. "Your father will find someone when he's ready. He has the band. I got to hear them play a few weeks ago. They're great. Samantha, forgive me if I'm out of line, but you never seem to mention your mother. Are you very close?" I asked.

I noticed the way she stiffened at the mention of her mother. "No, I don't see her. We're not close at all. She broke Dad's heart when I was young and then left us both. She didn't want to be a mother, so I've given her a free pass," Samantha said.

No wonder he's in transition, I thought. "I don't know what to say. I couldn't imagine feeling that way. I'm sorry," I said.

"Don't be," Samantha shrugged. "I'm used to it. Dad has loved me plenty to make up for it. You know what he's like." Samantha stood.

I smiled and nodded.

"I've got to get up early for work, Maggie, so please excuse me. Sleep in tomorrow, and make yourself at home. I'll leave a key on the counter for you."

"Thank you, Samantha, for inviting me here. I appreciate your kindness. I plan to spend my time at the beach tomorrow." I hugged her before saying goodnight.

The following morning, Samantha did leave early but not before brewing me a fresh pot of coffee. She left me a note on the counter that read: Make yourself at home and enjoy the day at the beach! See you for dinner -Sam. Next to it was a beach towel and a spare key.

Henry had the prep and lunch shift today at the restaurant. He was off at three. I decided I would spend the day exploring and recharge my batteries.

I opened the sliding glass door out to the balcony and took my cup of coffee with me. Ben had a breath-taking view of the ocean. The weather was perfect, and I planned to enjoy every minute of it.

I went back into the kitchen to make a light breakfast. Using my phones "notes," I made a grocery list for tonight's dinner. I carried a bowl of yogurt and granola, as I explored the rest of the condo. Curious to see Ben's bedroom, I peeked in from the hallway. It was tidy, contemporary, and decorated in a nautical theme. I smiled inwardly and walked back into the kitchen.

Ready for the beach, I dressed in my bathing suit, wrap skirt, and hat. Inside my tote, I placed my camera, beach towel, and wallet. After I locked the door behind me, I hooked Ben's keys onto the keychain inside the tote.

Shops and restaurants lined the frontage road in the village. With its old-world charm, shop owners offered a potpourri of products from lotions to fine jewelry and original art. Cafes, bakeries, ice cream shops, and restaurants all provided culinary delights to entice the passersby. I was going to love it here.

I bought a frothy iced drink and made my way toward the sandy white beach. I slipped off my sandals and carried them to the beach shore. It was a perfect morning. I spread my towel out on the sand and secured it with my tote and a hardback mystery novel I borrowed from Ben's bookcase.

The beach was moderately busy. Natives walked their dogs, and tourists played in the sand. I made a note to myself to ask Samantha if she had a bike I could borrow.

I tossed my hat into my tote and unwrapped the skirt from my waist. Putting my feet in the water, I found the ocean was cold but not uninviting. I walked along the shore, knee deep in the sea. I adjusted to the temperature before daring myself to jump in - all the way.

Holding my breath, I plunged into the water. It wasn't as cold as I thought it would be. I could stay in San Diego forever, I thought. I wondered if Ben missed living here.

On my way back to my spot, I intercepted a beach ball and tossed it back to a group of kids. Stretching out onto the dry towel with the sand beneath me, I closed my eyes while the sun slowly dried the ocean from my skin.

The tension from the past few months seemed to melt away as I listened to the waves and absorbed the heat through my skin. Edward hadn't been a big fan of the ocean. He enjoyed hiking and camping in the Sierras. I wasn't sure if Dean had hobbies outside of his Harley. Not having seen Ben without a shirt, I could only imagine how he looked on the beach. I tried to let go of my crazy monkey brain as one thought swung to the next.

Before long, my stomach began to growl with hunger. Outside the doors of cafes, that lined the frontage road, advertised lunch specials on chalkboards had stirred my appetite. Brushing the sand from my skin, I packed up my gear and headed toward the frontage road, wrapping my skirt around me. Passing by a boutique, I spied a beautiful, organic frame in the window. I went inside to check on the price. Retrieving my credit card from its secret compartment, I purchased the frame for Samantha.

I picked a cafe whose menu advertised a delicious veggie wrap special. Filled to the brim with avocado, cucumber salad, eggplant, and fresh Ovolini Motzzarella cheese I ordered it to go. As I headed back up the hill toward Ben's condo, I could hardly wait to eat it.

I unlocked the door and walked straight out to the patio to eat my lunch. I could get used to this, I thought. After lunch, I showered and changed. I relaxed until Henry picked me up to do some shopping.

Our first stop was the photo center. I printed a picture I had taken of Ben for the frame I bought Samantha.

"Mom, this photograph of Mr. Warner is perfect. Samantha will love it," Henry said.

"It is a good shot. The camera loves Ben's face, which makes my job easy."

"Where was this taken?" Henry asked.

"Ben and I went to the Japanese Gardens. They opened a tea house and expanded the water gardens to accommodate it. It was lovely. We should go next time you visit," I offered.

"Do you and Mr. Warner spend a lot of time together?" Henry fished.

"I see him at work," I said. "One night, a group of us went to a bar to hear his band play. A struggle broke out, and I ended up getting punched in the eye. He felt bad, so he invited me to see the gardens the following day."

"You got a black eye? You never told me that. Mom you have to be more careful," Henry scolded.

"It's a long story. Remember the blind date Aunt Lizzy

arranged?"

"Yes, I do," Henry said.

"Same night and no subsequent dates. Samantha seems to be interested in how often I see Ben too. Anything you want to clue me in on?" I said and smiled broadly.

"Nothing," he said as he kissed my cheek.

"Henry?" I gave him a stern look. He smiled and shrugged.

For dinner, Henry grilled steaks, and I made a wedge salad. When Samantha got home, we enjoyed a glass of wine, great conversation, and laughed at childhood memories of my two children. For dessert, I made a carrot cake with cream cheese and walnut frosting. I brewed a small pot of coffee, and we enjoyed dessert on the balcony.

Feeling the repercussions of a mild sunburn and the glass of wine, I suddenly realized how tired I'd become. Excusing myself for the evening, I left the lovebirds on the balcony. After opening the window in my room to the fresh ocean breeze, I got ready for bed. Grabbing the book I had started on the beach, I propped up my pillows and snuggled down in between the sheets. It was a great ending to a perfect day, I thought.

# Chapter 36.

With the window open all night, I slept like a baby. Awake and refreshed, I checked the time and noticed it was only six-thirty. I sat up and stretched. It was a great morning for a run along the beach.

Dressed for running, I picked up my phone and pressed the music icon. I attached the earbuds, not to disturb Sam and was ready for my morning dance warm-up. I slipped the phone into my tee shirt pocket and turned up the volume.

Heading toward the kitchen, I began to feel the groove. Opening the refrigerator door, I reached in for the orange juice, shaking my hips back and forth. I noticed the smell of freshly brewed coffee, so I shimmied down the length of the island toward the coffeemaker. Bless Samantha's heart for setting the timer before she had gone to bed, I thought.

I drank my juice and did the strippers walk toward a coffee mug sitting on the drain board. Mug in hand, I executed the same moves back toward the coffeemaker. Carrying a full cup of coffee to the breakfast bar, I saw something move in my peripheral vision. Startled, I dropped the coffee mug. It shattered across the stone floor releasing hot coffee as it broke into pieces.

At the dining table, Ben sat smiling at me over his reading glasses. His grin measured ear to ear with the newspaper in his hands.

With my heart pounding, I yanked out the earbuds and cried, "What are you doing here? You scared me half to death!"

"Apparently, I am watching you dance," he said and wiggled his eyebrows.

Shaken, I sat down on the step between the kitchen and the

central living space. Head in my hands, I questioned the universe what it had against me. My heart rate gradually slowed.

"I got in late last night," Ben explained. "How did you sleep?"

"Fine. You can stop grinning now. I thought you wouldn't be here until this afternoon."

"I caught up on my work and decided to sleep in my bed last night for a change," he replied calmly.

I asked for a broom and mop to clean up the mess. Ben walked down the hall and returned with both.

"Sorry about the mug," I apologized. "Although it's your fault I dropped it. It wasn't a special one was it?" I asked.

"Nah. Here let me help you," Ben knelt down and picked up the shards.

"How do I always manage to embarrass myself around you?"

"It's a gift. You headed out for a run this morning?" Ben asked.

"I thought I would."

"Care for some company?" he asked.

"Why, is Sam up?" I replied.

"Touche," Ben grinned.

"Alright, you can come with me. But it'll cost you a muffin from the bakery at the bottom of the hill."

"Deal! I'll get my shoes," he said and hurried down the hall.

I pulled my phone out of my pocket and left it on the table. When Ben was ready, we walked to the elevator and rode it down to the main floor.

"Shut-up," I said without looking at him.

"What?" Ben protested.

"Stop that grinning."

"I'm happy to see you, that's all."

We stretched our muscles before heading out the front door and down the hill. When we crossed the frontage road, I picked up my pace. Ben ran alongside me. We ran three miles along beautiful paths, coves, and cliffs. On the way back, Ben detoured and waved me over in his direction. We caught our breath as we walked toward the beach.

"I love the ocean. Don't you miss being here?" I said controlling my breathing.

"After being here, it's always hard to go back to the valley," Ben admitted. "For this view also," he waved his hand toward the surf, "but mostly because of Sam. It probably won't be too much longer before I move back here permanently."

"Really?" I asked. Disappointed I may no longer see him.

"Apparently, Michael is doing well in rehab. He has a ways to go yet, but it's looking promising. Once he's out and feeling stronger, he'll take over the store for Dad. Tami will send me reports via Dropbox to monitor, and hopefully, everything goes back to normal."

"Normal? That means average, you know? It doesn't sound very exciting. You might even miss us," I babbled.

"There certainly isn't anything average about you," Ben chuckled. "I need to move home just to get some rest. Besides, you'll be too busy to notice I'm gone," Ben added.

"What do you mean?"

"I shouldn't tell you this...but you got your promotion. George was planning to tell you when you got back."

"I did?" I said clapping my hands.

"You did," Ben smiled at my reaction.

"Yeah me! Thank you. I'm sure you had something to do with the decision." I wanted to hug him but recanted.

"You deserve it. You work hard, Maggie. Congratulations. Act surprised when George informs you on Tuesday," Ben said.

"I'll practice in the mirror," I grinned. "Hey, I have an idea. We can celebrate with those muffins you owe me," I suggested.

He nodded. We walked toward the frontage road when I stopped him.

"Ben?" I laid my hand on his arm and met his eyes.

"Yeah?"

"That's excellent news about Michael," I said and smiled softly.

"Yes, it is good news."

# Chapter 37.

Henry took me to a beautiful spot near the harbor for lunch.

"You know, Henry, you could have invited Samantha to come with us," I scolded him.

"Actually Mom, I needed to talk to you alone."

"Why, what's up?" I replied concerned by the serious expression on his face.

"I've slowly been going through some of Dad's boxes from his business. I created new files for what was important and shredded what you didn't need. I found a file that seemed unimportant because it only contained handwritten notes. Some of the notations were even on pieces of scratch paper. One caught my eye. It was on the back of a napkin."

"Really? That surprises me. Your father was extremely methodical."

"I know. The napkin had a man's name on it, David Combs. Then under it was written 10K. It was initialed. The napkin had the name Wasabi's printed on the front of it. I called information, and the restaurant is still operating and located in the heart of Silicon Valley. I looked through Dad's customer files to see if there was a match for the name. There wasn't a file for David Combs. So, I went through each customer file and looked up owner/operator names."

"That must have been a process," I said.

"It took time, but I eventually came to a file named Horizon Systems, owners David Combs and Robert Filgate. Do either of those names mean anything to you?" Henry asked.

"No. Their names aren't familiar to me at all. What did you find out about them?" I leaned forward with interest.

"I thought maybe Dad had invested ten thousand dollars with them. Why else would he have kept the napkin?" Henry said and shrugged. "He could have been busy and forgot to get it down on paper. I was able to find a number for Horizon Systems, but the company no longer exists. I googled David Combs and Robert Filgate and came across an article stating their company was bought out by a huge firm, not long ago."

"Wow," I paused to process the information. "So, you're saying you think Dad may have invested ten thousand dollars of our money with this company? That's a lot of money. I think he would have told me about it. Was there any paperwork to support the investment in their file?" I asked.

"If Dad had made this investment, it would have come out of his business account, so, you wouldn't have necessarily known about it. The file he made on Horizon Systems was empty, except for resumes for each of them; where they went to school, their ambitions, a business proposal that sort of thing. It seemed to me Dad may have been a mentor to both David and Robert," Henry said.

"I don't remember your dad ever mentioning them to me," I said.

"I called the firm that bought them, and apparently David Combs has an advisory position with the company. I left David a message, but I haven't heard back from him. I don't know if he even got the message. I just wanted you to know about it. I'll tell you if and when I hear from him."

"It's been well over two years since your Dad passed away. I think if Horizon Systems had some deal with your father, we would have heard something about it by now."

"You're probably right. It would be interesting to talk with the man anyway. I'm curious as to what his relationship was with Dad," Henry said and smiled thoughtfully.

I smiled at Henry and took his hand. "You know, you're more like him then you think. I know you bumped heads sometimes, but that was because of your similarities more than your differences. He's a father you can be proud of, Henry. And one who loved you very, very, much. He would have been as proud of you as I am," I said. Henry's eyes watered. He shrugged and turned away.

Henry gave me a tour of the harbor and the downtown shops. On the way back to La Jolla, he made another stop.

"Sam and I have a surprise for you," Henry said.

He pulled into the circular driveway of a beautifully designed complex, stopping at the front entrance.

"Sam's inside waiting for you," Henry said.

"What is going on, Henry?"

"Spa day for you and Sam. Enjoy Mom, it's on me. By the way, Mr. Warner designed this hotel and spa. Sam will bring you back after. Have fun," He said and smiled.

"Henry, wait. You can't afford to do this," I protested.

"Yes, I can. And I want to. Go."

"But it's your birthday, not mine."

"Go," he demanded and kissed my cheek.

Samantha and I returned to the condo relaxed, buffed, and polished. It was a delightful girly afternoon. I enjoyed every minute of it especially our chats under circles of cucumber resting on our eyelids.

"Did you ladies enjoy your afternoon?" Ben asked from across the room.

"Oh Dad, it was wonderful. Thanks for treating me," Samantha cooed.

Samantha walked across the room and kissed Ben on his forehead.

"You're welcome, Baby. And you, Mrs. Bloom?" Ben said with a grin.

"It was wonderful. I'm all relaxed and ready for a nap before the big party." I said as I passed through the living room to get to my bedroom.

"Stay there, Samantha," I called from my room. "I have something for you."

Opening my suitcase, I retrieved the wrapped gift and carried it back to the living room. I sat beside Samantha on the sofa.

"This is just a little something to say thank you for all you've done to make this a special weekend," I said as I handed the package to her.

"Oh Maggie, you didn't have to," Samantha exclaimed.

She tore the paper from the frame. Her expression said more than words. "Maggie, it's wonderful. Thank you. Is this one of your photographs? Dad, look," she said as she held it up for him to see.

Ben looked surprised as he saw his face within the border of the frame.

"Where were you?" Samantha asked Ben.

"I took Maggie to the Japanese Gardens. It was a nice day," he said reflectively.

"Maggie, you captured him perfectly. And this frame is exquisite," she said as she hugged me. Samantha jumped up from her seat. "I know exactly where it's going," she said leaving the room.

I watched Samantha go up the stairway. "She's lovely Ben," I said to him. "And intelligent, has a great sense of humor, and very beautiful. You didn't find her in a basket on your doorstep, did you?" I teased.

"Very funny. Sam's a chip off the old block, what can I say?"

"You should be proud," I said as I rose from the sofa like a queen leaving her attendants. "I'm taking my nap now," I announced while leaving the room.

Henry's birthday party was at Sergio's. Sam said Sergio was giving us the entire outdoor patio, complete with a karaoke machine and live music for dancing. Evidently, karaoke is "in" again.

"Hey, Sleeping Beauty," Ben called to me as I walked toward my room. "We leave at six-thirty. Sharp."

# Chapter 38.

My phone alarm buzzed, annoyingly. Feeling cozy and relaxed, I didn't want to move. I reached for the phone on the side table and shut off the alarm. A few minutes later, I sat up and stretched like a fat lazy cat. Feeling thirsty after my nap, I padded into the kitchen for a glass of cold water.

"Yikes!" exclaimed Ben.

I stopped dead in my tracks and looked around.

"Dad," Samantha said embarrassed and shook her head.

"What's wrong?" I muttered.

"Nothing a hairbrush couldn't fix," Ben replied.

"Dad, this is why you live alone," Samantha scolded Ben.

Through a thick patch of curly bangs, I could see they were both looking at me, amused. I turned around to find my reflection in the hall mirror. I let out a gasp. I looked like the nutty professor. My hair had a mind of its own. I turned back around and poured myself a cold glass of water from the refrigerator. I drank it down without stopping for air. Turning back toward my room, I said to no one in particular, "I'll be back at six-fifteen."

I took out my new party dress from the closet. Looking it over brought a renewed enthusiasm for the evening ahead. The gown was the maxi length and had a wide modern blue and black stripe running on a diagonal from the waist down. Its etched hardware gathered the straps at the neckline, creating a halter. A smocked empire waistband streamlined the dress. The silhouette was flattering. I also purchased a pair of black high heeled sandals to complete the look. A girl can always use another pair of black shoes, I thought.

After showering, I applied my makeup and styled my hair. Roberto had almost cried when I came in for a follow-up appointment. Reminding me, I was long overdue; he trimmed my hair and applied highlights before I left town. I slipped on my new dress over my silky soft skin and strapped my feet into my new sandals. My toes wiggled to show off my French pedicure. I checked all angles in the mirror before I was satisfied. Feeling pretty, I was ready to celebrate.

It was precisely six-fifteen when I picked up my handbag and walked into the living room, to see if my date was ready.

Ben was standing on the balcony looking out at the ocean when he heard my heels click on the hardwood floor. He turned around to greet me. He studied me with his mouth open. I twirled for effect and then smiled at him.

"You look amazing," he managed to say finally.

"Thank you," I said feeling beautiful.

I enjoyed the way he looked at me. I hadn't felt this way in a long time. Ben wore black slacks, a black sports coat, and a crisp white shirt. I was hoping he couldn't read my mind.

He stared at me a moment longer and then offered me a drink.

"I think I'll wait until we get to the party. My drink minimum is rather low. Did Samantha already leave?" I asked.

"Yes. She left about a half an hour ago. Last minute preparations. Oh, and she told me to tell you, she has your gift to Henry."

"Then I guess we're ready," I said and smiled.

Ben walked over to me and extended his arm. I wrapped my arm around his, and we headed to the elevator.

Sergio's was a fine-dining restaurant, serving Italian food with a modern twist. The decor of the restaurant was minimalist, but I found it comfortably elegant. We were shown out to the patio by a beautiful brunette in a tight black dress.

Samantha immediately greeted us. "Look at the two of you," she said. "Don't move while I take your picture."

Henry came over to say hello and kissed my cheek. "Wow, Mom, you look beautiful tonight. I'm so glad you're here."

"Thank you, Henry. Happy Birthday," I said. "I wish Isabella could have been here too."

Henry took my arm and Ben followed close behind. Henry introduced us to his guests. Ben already knew a few of Samantha's friends and some familiar faces from the office. Sergio came over to meet us. Taking my hand in his, he kissed it saying, "Buona sera. What a pleasure it is to meet you, Mrs. Bloom finally. Your Henry speaks about you often, but has neglected to mention your beauty."

"Oh, thank you, Sergio. Please call me Maggie. I wanted to thank you for all you are doing to help Henry. Learning from you means a lot to him," I said.

"He's a good man, Maggie. He works very hard. Please excuse me; I should attend to some of my other guests."

"It was nice to meet you, Sergio," I said.

"The pleasure, I assure you, is all mine," he said and kissed my hand once more before walking away.

"Let's go before he comes back for round two," Ben interjected.

"Let's ask Samantha where she would like us to sit," I suggested.

Samantha showed us to our seats and reminded Ben to behave.

"She must know a much different side of you than I do," I stated.

"Oh, I'm full of surprises," he said and smiled.

"I bet you are."

"Wait until the band starts. I hope those shoes of yours are comfortable."

"We should do karaoke," I said jokingly.

"What song did you have in mind?" Ben asked with amusement.

"Aah, how about I Can't Get No Satisfaction."

"My daughter would be very proud. But first, I should order up a few drinks," Ben said.

We both laughed at ourselves and so went the rest of the evening. The food was delicious and the party a success.

"So, I have an idea," Ben said leaning in close so that no one else could hear.

"Tell me," I said enthusiastically.

"I think we should slip out unnoticed and go down to a great club that I know. We can listen to some real music. What do you think?"

"Do you think the kids would mind? I asked.

"Naah."

"We should at least say goodnight," I suggested.

Ben drove downtown. He wanted to show me one of his favorite music venues, a refurbished blues club. We were greeted at the door by a man named Charlie, who was an acquaintance of Ben's.

"Benny...where have you been, man. We've missed you down here," Charlie said hugging Ben.

"I've been living with my father on a part-time basis. I'm home for a visit. I'd like you to meet, Maggie. Maggie, this is Charlie, a good friend, and a talented musician," Ben said enthusiastically.

"Very nice to meet you, Maggie. Where have you been hiding this beautiful woman, Benny? Come on in, Louise will be happy to see you. I'll have her set you up with a nice table," Charlie said.

"So she's here tonight? Thanks, Charlie. Good to see you," Ben said and shook his hand.

"Have a nice night, you two."

We stepped into the club, and I looked around the historic space. The architecture beautifully restored made me feel I had stepped back in time.

"What a magnificent place this is," I said into Ben's ear.

I watched as Ben made eye contact with a stunning, beautiful woman from across the room. With a look of surprise, she walked over to us and wrapped her arms around his neck intimately.

"Benjamin, where have you been?" she scolded him playfully.

"How are you, Lou?" he said to her as he gently removed her arms from around his neck.

"Lou, this is Maggie. Maggie, this is Louise."

"Pleasure to meet you, Louise," I said as I extended my hand to shake hers.

I looked into her almond-shaped, beautiful blue-green eyes. Her skin was the color of a creamy cup of coffee. Her black hair was straight and long and pulled away from her delicate face with a turquoise colored scarf. The ends of the scarf dangled freely down her bare back.

"Go say hello to Hank, Benjamin, and I'll show Maggie to your table. We'll be up in the balcony," she told him.

"OK, but don't fill her head with any nonsense about me," He said to her as he winked at me.

I followed Lou up a stairway with a beautifully carved wood railing. The stairs led to the balcony. Lou wore a black, snug fitting dress with a deep V cut in the back. She showed me to a table that overlooked the dance floor below.

"This is a beautiful club, Louise. Do you own this place?" I
asked as she sat studying me from across the table.

"I'm a partner," she replied. "Benjamin restored this place. That's
how we met. He was interested in the building, and one thing led to
another, and now he is family. He used to love this place. He would come
in several times a week after work and play until closing. We haven't
seen much of him this past year," Louise said inferring that I might be the
cause.

"He's been helping his father with the grocery business," I
echoed what Ben had said to Charlie. "That's how we know each other. I
work for the Warner's."

"Do you?" Louise said as she tapped her long nail on the table
top. "They don't make men like Benjamin anymore. He's a true
gentleman and would protect his family at all costs."

"Yes. I know."

"He's never brought a woman in here before. You must be a
special friend. I'll bring the two of you a drink. Is Benjamin's usual
alright with you?"

"Please," I said as I smiled back at her.

I didn't have the slightest idea what Ben's usual was, but I didn't
want her to know that. My instincts said Louise had been his lover. Her
manner was somewhat cold toward me. Like a cat. I've never trusted
cats.

I watched Ben come up the stairs with enthusiasm. I was
surprised to feel the tingle of excitement as he approached our table.

"Sorry about that. I haven't seen these guys in over a year," Ben
explained.

"No need to apologize. I'm enjoying the sight and the sound of this place. I got a chance to chat with Louise too. She said you restored this place. It must have been a labor of love. It's a handsome place, Ben with a lot of character," I said.

"It's a great old building. I have good memories here," He added.

"It's on the house, Benjamin, welcome home," Louise said as she placed our drinks on the table.

"Thank you, Lou," Ben said and smiled up at her.

We sipped our drinks while Ben told me about the history of the club. He spoke fondly of his friends and said that he missed jamming with the musicians. He never mentioned Louise.

"Why is it that you don't have a piano in your home?" I asked.

"It's right up there, on stage," he said and pointed.

"I would love to hear you play sometime."

"Would you?" Ben asked with a curious smile.

I nodded.

"Well, it won't be tonight, but would you settle for dancing with me instead."

"Will you twirl me?"

"Girl, I'll even dip you."

Feeling a little dizzy from the drink, I held on to Ben's hand when he offered it. He led the way and without missing a beat, twirled me to the middle of the dance floor. I threw my head back and laughed, as he gathered me up in his arms. We slow danced most of the night. He made me feel like I was the only girl in the room. It was hard not to feel romantic toward him.

By the time we got back to Ben's home, it was well past midnight. We spotted Samantha's car parked in the lot, so we were careful not to wake her.

"I could sure use a piece of that carrot cake you made yesterday," Ben whispered as he closed the door behind us.

"You put on the coffee, and I'll get the cake out of the fridge. But first, I have got to take off these heels," I said.

"Why do you ladies do that to yourselves?"

"Do what?"

"Wear shoes that hurt your feet?"

"To make our legs look sexy."

"Hmm. That they do," Ben smiled to himself.

Ben had the coffee brewing when I padded back into the kitchen wearing my slippers. I took the cake out of the refrigerator. Feeling a little drunk, I carefully removed the plastic wrap that safeguarded the cut side of the cake. I cut two large pieces and plated them.

"Let's go out to the balcony; we don't have to be as quiet out there," Ben suggested.

We placed our cups and plates on the glass coffee table outside and sat beside each other on the outdoor love seat.

"It's kind of chilly out here," I commented.

"Here, take my coat," Ben offered.

He wrapped it around me, and I pulled my arms through the sleeves. As he adjusted the coat, I had a strong desire to kiss him. Instead, I stood up and walked to the railing. I knew I needed to put a little distance between us and take in some fresh air. Ben came up behind me and joined me at the railing.

"Maggie, from the first day I met you, I thought you were attractive. But tonight, I have to say; you leave me breathless."

"Ben Warner, you are a lovely man," I said as I tried to shift the mood.

"If I don't kiss you right now, I might die," Ben said in a low voice.

The alcohol I had consumed lowered my inhibitions. I turned toward Ben and looked at him. "I certainly couldn't have that on my conscience," I said softly.

"I'm glad to hear you say that," he replied.

Ben stepped closer to me and took my face in the palm of his hands. He looked deep into my eyes before he kissed me. I rose up on my toes to meet him bringing my arms around his neck. As I kissed him back, he lowered his hands to my waist and pulled me closer. My head began to swim. As our lips started to part, I kissed him again, softly. I didn't want this night to end. I gently slid my hands to the sides of his face and looked into his eyes. I could see the passion he was feeling.

With our foreheads together, Ben whispered, "Maggie Bloom, what are you doing to me?"

"I think it's the same thing you're doing to me," I whispered back.

"I sure hope so. But if you must, please let me down easy."

I closed my eyes and inhaled his cologne. What was I doing? "Our coffee is getting cold," I said.

"I can pour you another cup."

I exhaled softly feeling nervous and enchanted at the same time. I took Ben's hand and led him back to the love seat.

We ate our cake in silence and sipped on our coffee, occasionally looking at each other and smiling. When we finished, I rested my head on Ben's shoulder while he slipped his arm around me. It was an excellent ending to a perfect night.

# Chapter 39.

Somewhere in between dreaming and awake, I was afraid to open my eyes and learn that everything had just been a dream. I slowly opened my eyes and looked around the room, right, I'm still here.

I reminded myself that laying here was wasting a beautiful morning on the beach. After pulling on my jogging clothes, I brushed my teeth and went into the kitchen. It was nice to see father and daughter enjoying a cup of coffee together. I smiled.

"Good morning," I said to them both.

"Good morning, Maggie. Sleep well?" Samantha asked.

"Yes, I did. I've had the best sleep of my life since I've been here. I think it's the ocean breeze coming through the bedroom window at night."

Ben stood up to refill his cup. "Coffee?" he asked.

"No, thanks. Just some juice, I'm going for a run. Samantha, the party for Henry, was lovely. You did an amazing job. Did he open his presents last night?"

"Yes, he did. We took them over to his apartment and opened them there. Your gift floored him," Samantha said.

"What did you get him?" Ben asked.

"A set of chef knives," I said proudly.

"Nice...I bet it set you back a little?"

"I accounted for my promotion," I said and smiled.

"So, this is the plan," Sam announced walking over to me. "We are spending the day at Coronado Island. It's beautiful there; you'll want to take your camera. We'll go through the shops and galleries and have a late lunch at the Hotel. How does that sound?"

"Amazing. Do I have time for a run?"

"Henry will be over around eleven this morning. He's a little hung over. But don't tell him I told you. Since it was his birthday, I was the designated driver," Samantha explained.

"It's a good thing he has you to watch out for him," I smiled and touched her arm.

It was almost nine. I had plenty of time for a run.

"Ben, are you running this morning?"

"I was hoping you'd ask," He said grinning.

We watched Ben run to his room for his shoes. Samantha shook her head. "He's such a big kid," she said fondly.

Ben and I immediately fell into a steady rhythm as we set off on our run. Ben took me in the opposite direction of our last race. It was hard not to stop and admire the scenery. I stayed in the moment and took it all in as we ran side by side.

At the bottom of the hill, back where we had begun, we took our time walking toward his condo.

"If we had the time this morning, I would've shown you some amazing caves by those cliffs," Ben said while he caught his breath.

"I would have liked to see them. When are you flying back?" I asked him.

"I'm on the eleven o'clock flight in the morning. You?"

"The same. There aren't many flights to the valley from San Diego," I reminded him. "Good. Henry will only have to make one trip to the airport," I said while I panted.

"Maggie, if it's alright with you, I think I'm going to skip Coronado today," Ben said.

I stopped in the middle of the sidewalk at looked at him. "Why? You'll miss the time with Samantha. She seems excited about her plans."

"She wants you and me to spend time together. Last night's kiss kept me awake most of the night. It confirmed something I've been struggling with," Ben explained.

"I'm sorry. I shouldn't have kissed you back like that."

"Didn't you want to?"

"I did. That's the problem."

"Why was it a problem?" Ben asked.

I looked around me for the right words. "I'm not exclusive with Dean, but I'm uncomfortable with the...triangle. And then the whole boss thing is very awkward, to say the least."

"I've heard that if you fall for two people at the same time, you should choose the second one," Ben replied.

"Why the second?"

"Because if you were really into the first guy, you would have never fallen for the second."

I looked down at my running shoes and smiled. "I see," I said quietly. "Wise person, whoever said that."

"The thing is, I've developed deeper feelings for you than I was willing to admit. After last night, I realized you're my transition. The problem is, I think there's a possibility you could break my heart. I'm not sure I want to go there with you. If you have feelings for Dean, tell me now," Ben said.

"If you're asking me if I'm in love with Dean, the answer is no. I can't define our relationship. Last night, you rocked my world, too. The plan was to find myself, date a little, travel someday, and then see what happens. Developing the feelings I have for you was not part of the plan," I said and shook my head.

"Discover your favorite kind of egg?" Ben asked.

"Exactly. And change my mind as often as I like. Up until now, I've allowed other people to decide things for me. I want to choose for myself from now on. The dilemma is when I'm with you; I feel more like myself than with anyone else. That's screwing up the plan."

"They say if you want to make God laugh, make a plan," Ben said and shrugged.

"I've heard that," I said.

"The thing is, Maggie," Ben continued. "I have no desire to change anything about you. Not one thing. I don't want to get in the way of your life. If this thing between us works, I want to be a part of your life. One of the greatest misconceptions about relationships, in my opinion, is thinking you're going to change the other person into what you want them to be. Why go through the trouble? If they're not already what you want, they will never be. To expect anything else is just settling. And I don't want that for myself, and I'm guessing you don't either."

"See, there you go again, being all perfect and everything," I said and rolled my eyes as if to complain.

"Oh, I'm far from perfect, but if this is working for you, I can go on for hours."

I closed my eyes. I wanted to touch Ben severely, so I did. I wrapped my arms around his body and held him close. With my cheek on his chest, he hugged me back.

"As far as the boss thing goes, we can handle that. I'll be moving back here soon anyway," Ben said.

"About that. How would that work exactly?" I lifted my head to look at him.

"Well, I've accrued a ton of frequent flier mileage. I'll share them with you." Ben smiled down at me. He was irresistible, even after a run.

"Speaking of moving back to San Diego, I have a question for you," I said.

"You have my attention."

"Is Louise still in the picture?"

"You're very perceptive."

"It wasn't hard to miss. Louise made it a point to show me; there was something between the two of you," I said cautiously.

"She'll always be a part of my life," Ben said looking down at me.

I swallowed hard.

"But not in the way that you mean. Louise is Samantha's mother," Ben confessed.

My mouth dropped open. It was the last thing I expected Ben to say. I stood stunned by the realization. The more I recalled Louise, the more similarities I saw in Samantha.

Recognizing my complete surprise, Ben stepped away from me. He put his arm around my shoulder and led me back toward his condo.

"I'll tell you the whole story when we get back from Coronado," he offered.

"Alright," I agreed. "Ben?"

"Yep."

"Can we take this slow while I work out a few things?" I asked.

"Can I still kiss you once in a while?"

"Definitely."

"Well okay then," Ben agreed.

# Chapter 40.

"Now, this is crucial Mom. You need to call David Combs when you get home and make an appointment to speak with him. I printed out the e-mail he sent me this morning, and it has all of his information on it," Henry explained, outside of the terminal, handing me a printed page.

"I think you should consider taking Ben along with you, when you meet, just to be safe," Henry said.

I put my arms around Henry, "Oh, I love you. Don't worry. I'll take care of it, and I let you know what happens. Thank you for this weekend. I had a wonderful time. Happy birthday to you, Henry. Hey, good luck on your finals."

"Thanks for the knives. They're amazing. I still can't believe you did that for me," Henry said.

"You deserve it, Henry. You've been working very hard. I'm proud of you."

As Henry hugged me good-bye, he whispered in my ear. "I think Ben is good for you."

I smiled as I kissed his cheek and let him go. Henry turned to Ben and shook his hand.

"Thanks for everything, Mr. Warner. Especially for inviting Mom to stay with you and Samantha," Henry said.

"You're welcome, Henry. Take care of Samantha while I'm away."

"Yes, Sir. I will."

We made our way to the gate with time to spare.

"How long are you going to make Henry call you sir?" I asked

Ben.

"Forever. Because I'm a man too, and she's my only daughter," He smirked.

"He's a good man, Ben," I said.

"Yes he is, but he's still a man. Should we grab a Starbuck's for the flight?" Ben suggested.

"Good idea, my treat. Let's go."

As we boarded our flight, the attendants seemed to know Ben by name.

"Hello, Ben. Nice to see you again. Welcome aboard."

"Hello, Ben. If you need anything, be sure to let me know."

"You do have a lot of frequent flier miles, don't you?" I teased him.

Our airplane tickets had us sitting separately, but Ben managed to get us reassigned next to each other. We settled into our seats and buckled in.

"I'm going to hold your hand on the flight home, if that's alright?" Ben asked.

"You certainly may, Mr. Warner, Sir," I said.

Ben certainly smelled good. I breathed in his scent as he sat next to me. I'd stick my nose into his neck and stay there the entire flight if it weren't for my self-respect.

"Now, clue me in on the David Combs story," Ben said.

I made a long story short and included my plans to set up an appointment to see him.

"Well, it's certainly your decision, of course. However, my history with you negates any rational thought of you meeting this man on your own," Ben said.

"What are you saying?"

"Just that trouble seems to follow you."

"I'd prefer to look at it as adventure rather than trouble."

"Call it what you'd like, just let me know if I need to get my cape out."

"Well, who wants things easy all the time, anyway?" I joked.

"Apparently not me," Ben said and picked up my hand and kissed it before he leaned his head back on the seat and closed his eyes.

Fighting the desire to kiss him, I looked out the window. Thoughts began to flood my mind. So much happened over the weekend. I was right when I thought my life would never be the same. It was time for a mother-daughter night with lots and lots of wine. I needed love advice.

"Hey," Ben said. "What are you thinking about?"

I turned my head and looked at him. He smiled at me with affection in his eyes.

"There's a lot up there to choose from," I said.

"You still have a crush on me though, right?"

"Yes. I still have a crush on you," I said trying not to smile.

Upon landing, Ben kissed me before debarking the aircraft. The stewardesses said goodbye to him in unison.

Mother and Mr. Beasley were waiting for me in the passenger loading zone, and Mr. Thomas Warner was waiting for Ben.

I called an impromptu meeting with the Morgan women at my house for pasta and wine. Mother promised not to ask any questions until Elizabeth got there.

"Okay, Ellie, start at the top and don't leave anything out," Mother demanded.

"The weekend in San Diego was wonderful. For a big city, it's stunning. Samantha gave Henry a lovely birthday party at the restaurant where Henry works. Samantha's ulterior motive was to make sure Ben and I spent some quality time together. Which we did," I said.

"Well then, my birthday wish came true," Mother gushed.

"Mom, we said no interruptions until the story was over," Elizabeth reminded.

"Certainly, go on," Mother acquiesced.

"Everything was going smoothly until Saturday night after Henry's party. Ben had taken me to a blues club. We had a couple of drinks, danced, and he introduced me to his friends. After we got back to his house, we had dessert out on the balcony. That's when he kissed me, and I kissed him back," I said and blushed.

"I don't see a problem. Where's the problem?" Mother said.

"Mother, let her finish. Go on, Maggie," Elizabeth encouraged.

"Well, you see Ben knows I've been dating Dean."

"What? You are dating both of your bosses. Maggie, are you insane?" ranted Elizabeth. "This is why Paul was so good for you."

"Oh, now look who's interrupting," Mother said rolling her eyes.

"Let me finish the story, and you can judge me later. I didn't plan on feeling how I do about Ben. My feelings for Dean are complicated. But, I know that I'm not in love with him. Apparently, Ben has strong feelings for me. But you see, the plan was for me to date around, find myself, travel, and at some point down the road, maybe fall in love," I explained.

"Well you know what they say if you want to make God laugh, make a plan," interjected Mom. I smiled at the familiar sentiment.

"Yes, I've heard that. Anyway, Saturday night, I met the most beautiful woman I have ever seen. It turns out; she happens to be Ben's ex-wife and Samantha's mother, which is another story. So, my dilemma is, what do I do about these men?"

Elizabeth spoke first. "I can't believe you're dating Dean after the way he treated Paul?"

"Of course she is, Lizzy. Have you seen the man?" Mother said.

"The problem is…ladies, focus." I raised my voice causing Mr. Beasley to bark. I swooped him up and continued to speak. "I have strong feelings for the both of them. And I'm a different person with each of them. Dean makes me nervous and keeps me on edge. It's very intense between us. I'm extremely attracted to Ben, and when I'm with him, I feel like I know myself. He's comfortable to be around. Does that make sense?"

"Why are you pressuring yourself about these relationships?" Elizabeth asked.

"I've never dated two men at the same time. Lizzy, your sister, is this shy of being a ho," I said holding my thumb and index finger an inch apart.

Elizabeth covered her mouth with both hands and started to laugh. "Maggie, you are so naive," she said and laughed.

"So, let me get this right," Mother interrupted. "My little girl is dating two gorgeous men at the same time, and you think there's a problem with that?"

"That hardly makes you a ho," Elizabeth clarified and laughed again.

"It does if I decide to sleep with them both. Look, I've only been with one man my entire life, until now. I couldn't even get a date in high school. Now, two gorgeous, sexy, men want me, and I want them. I don't know what's come over me?" I said and shook my head.

"You're just a late bloomer, Sweetheart. And it goes to show you, that we do get better with age. Besides Ellie, God sees the bigger picture. Give yourself time; it will sort itself out. Don't rush into anything," Mother stated.

"It's called freedom," Elizabeth said. "OK, I'm going to be honest with you both right now, but there will be no judging. Six. I have had six different lovers. I never planned to get married and had no intention of becoming a saint. I don't think any less of myself for it. I was very cautious and took care of myself. We are sexual human beings after all. Maggie, you're fifty-plus years old; it's about time you experimented a little."

"You're feeling guilty because you are falling in love with one of them. If it were all about having fun, you wouldn't be worried about it," Mother said. "You need to be true to yourself, and be with the man who loves you for who you are and who makes you happy," Mother continued.

I got reticent and introspective. "I've never felt this way before. Not even with  Edward," I confessed.

"First of all Maggie, you were young when you met Edward. Please don't be mad at me for saying this. Maybe you chose Edward for a reason other than being in love with him. He made you feel safe. People pick their mates for all kinds of reasons that aren't necessarily wrong," Elizabeth explained.

"Are you saying that I settled?" I asked.

"Does it matter now? You had a good life with Edward. But now, you have an opportunity to choose differently for yourself. You've changed. It only stands to reason that you would want something different for yourself. So, live a little," Elizabeth counseled.

"This may be the only time you ever hear me say this, but I totally agree with your sister," Mom said.

# Chapter 41.

I could hear Mr. Beasley whining from the laundry room until one o'clock in the morning. I tried closing my door and putting a pillow over my head, but I could still hear him whine. I got out of bed and stomped into the kitchen to scold him.

"Mr. Beasley. Go to sleep! I have to be at work tomorrow." Could he be missing my mother? What was wrong with this dog, I thought?

Against everything I thought was holy and right, I picked up the dog out of the basket and put him in bed with me. He instantly stopped crying. Oh no, I thought. Mother let you sleep with her, didn't she?

"Don't get used to this buddy. We'll fix this tomorrow night because I'm off on Wednesday," I said to him.

I never told Lizzy or Mom the whole story about Ben and Louise. That was a private matter for Ben. Since I couldn't sleep anymore, I thought about what he had told me.

When Ben had met Louise, she was young and passionate. She wanted fame. She wanted to be another Ella Fitzgerald. They had a passionate affair that ended with Louise getting pregnant. Louise wanted an abortion. She couldn't see being tied down to anything or anyone. Ben wanted his baby. He wanted them both.

Ben, finally talked Louise into marrying him and having their child. He supported her career the best he could. Tears spilled onto my face as I shuddered to think, a remarkable person like Samantha, may have never been born. Henry may have never fallen in love.

Louise had no desire to be mother or wife. Ben lamented over pressuring her into something she didn't want, but he never regretted

Samantha.

Ben came home from a short business trip to find Louise standing in the middle of their living room. Her suitcases were packed and waiting. Samantha was screaming at the top of her lungs in the next room. Tears welled in Louise's eyes, but she said nothing to him. She quietly picked up her bags and left.

Ben gave Louise her freedom and exchanged the nightclub for his daughter. Over the years, Ben supplied Louise with letters and photographs of Samantha. After a few brief meetings with Louise, Samantha chose not to see her birth mother again. Ben was the only parent she wanted or needed.

"Samantha gave her a free pass," I murmured.

I scratched Mr. Beasley's head as he laid curled up in the small of my back. Ben allowed me inside. He shared something deeply personal with me. Maybe I was in over my head. Until I figured things out, I'd put some distance between us.

# Chapter 42.

Before work, I called the cell number for David Combs that Henry provided me. He was unfortunately out of the country on business and promised to call me when he returned. He seemed happy to hear from me and said he wanted to speak with me in person. It would be at least two weeks before we could meet. I was curious but needed to put it out of my mind, for now.

I had an easy shift of eight-to-five. I would be leaving the store just as the evening shoppers arrived. Dean followed me back to my locker in the warehouse.

"Hey Bloom, how was San Diego?" Dean asked.

"Beautiful. Flew by much too fast."

"Listen, I need to talk to you. Are you available to get together after work?" Dean asked.

"Yes. Would you like to meet after work or come over? If you would rather meet, I have to run home to let Mr. Beasley out first," I explained.

"How much longer are you keeping that thing?" Dean asked.

"Not certain. But Mr. Beasley is starting to grow on me."

"Uh, oh. How about your place around seven?" Dean asked.

"Perfect. I'll make a steak salad for dinner?" I affirmed.

"Nice. By the way, I've missed you," Dean lingered then briefly touched my hand and wink.

I placed my forehead on my locker for a moment and let out a heavy sigh. I have something to talk to you about too, I thought.

My work day was uneventful. George made no announcements to me negating the promise I made to Ben to act surprised. I was hoping he was having a busy day and not that he had changed his mind. Perhaps Thursday, I prayed.

Stanley, Martha's husband, walked into the store right before quitting time. He grabbed a hand basket and walked over to the deli. Stanley stood staring into the window of prepared foods. He wasn't looking very pleased. In the few times I've seen Stanley, he seemed to be happy with only himself.

Stanley placed the basket on the belt of my checkstand and glared at my name badge. I greeted him in my usual manner.

"Good afternoon, how are you today? Did you find everything you were looking for?" I stated.

"You're Maggie?" Stanley asked.

"Yes, I am."

"My wife has mentioned you on occasion."

"Your wife?" I said playing dumb.

"Yes, Martha. She comes here frequently to shop."

"Oh yes, I know Martha. How is she?" I asked.

"Have you seen her lately? Has she been in the store?" Stanley questioned.

"Let me think. No, I don't think I've seen Martha in quite some time," I said pondering his question.

"Can you ask some of the other people who work here if they've seen her?" Stanley said looking peevish.

I turned around to look at Bobbie, and I mouthed no and rolled my eyes.

"Bobbie. Have you seen Martha in the store recently?"

"Martha? Oh, Martha. No, I haven't seen her around here for awhile," Bobbie said and smiled.

"I'm sorry about that. Is Martha missing?" I asked.

"Yes, she is. Did she mention to you anything about taking a trip?" Stanley asked determinedly.

"No. I'm sorry. I don't know her all that well," I said with some truth.

Stanley paid his bill and hesitated for a moment. Keep going, I thought. Lucky for me, there was a customer right behind him. I was a terrible liar, and I was sure it showed.

Mr. Beasley was happy to see me after work. I took him outside for a quick walk.

"I saw your hateful Daddy today, Mr. Beasley. You are safe with me, don't you worry. I'm going to take a quick shower and Auntie will make you a delicious meal," I cooed.

Did I just baby talk to this dog, I thought? Shaking my head, I undressed and stepped into the shower. When I finished, I found Mr. Beasley waiting for me outside of the bathroom door.

I slipped into a sleeveless summer dress and freshened my hair and make-up. Mr. Beasley followed me into the kitchen to learn the subtler points of gourmet cooking. I looked down at him realizing how much I enjoyed his company. If and when Martha decided to take him home, I was going to miss him.

Mr. Beasley was happily enjoying his meal when I started on the humans' dinner. I grilled the seasoned steak on my indoor grill and set it aside to rest. I washed the fresh produce I had picked up from work and began chopping it into a wooden salad bowl. A creamy feta salad dressing was mixed and put it in the refrigerator to stay cold.

Mr. Beasley began to bark at the sound of a knock at my front door. I looked through the peephole to make sure it was Dean.

"Mr. Phillips is a nasty man," I explained to Mr. Beasley. "He doesn't call us on the security phone, does he?" I unlocked and opened the front door. Mr. Beasley went into a barking fit.

"I heard that. And I'm not a nasty man," he said looking down at the dog as he walked inside. Mr. Beasley continued to bark until I picked him up and shushed him. Dean wrapped his arms around my waist and gave me a quick kiss. Regardless of how much I enjoyed his kiss I had to tell him about Ben tonight, I thought.

"Something smells good," Dean said walking through into the kitchen.

"Let's eat first and then we can talk after?" I suggested.

I poured two glasses of wine, and we took our meal out to the patio. The temperature in the evenings began to cool down substantially. It was reassuring to know the hottest part of summer was finally over. We made small talk and ate our salads while my curiosity began to get the best of me.

"So what's up? What did you want to talk to me about?" I asked.

"Well, a lot has happened while you were away," Dean said.

"I was only gone four days."

"But it felt longer... I have a cousin who lives in Jackson Hole. He's been talking to me about a business opportunity over the last couple of months. Well, things have finally come together for him, and he's offered me a partnership," Dean explained.

"Wow. That's big. You've never mentioned it before," I said.

"I wanted to wait to see if it was going to happen. It's a trucking company. My cousin has already secured contracts with a few large companies in the area. It would be a fifty-fifty partnership," Dean said.

I wasn't quite sure what I was feeling. I think it was a

disappointment. Dean had never shared this dream with me.

"I assume that means you'll relocate?" I asked.

"This is the thing, Maggie. I don't have any reason to stay in this area anymore. Carolyn and I stayed here because her family was here. She was very close to them. I don't have any living family here anymore. My parents are gone, and my sister is back east."

"You have a sister?"

"Yes, I do. But we aren't very close."

"I didn't know that."

"I'm ready for a fresh start. I've been thinking," Dean paused and reached for my hand, "you've been trying to figure out what you want to do with your life too. Maybe this could be a fresh start for the both of us."

"Wait, are you asking me to go with you?" I asked surprised.

"Why not? It's beautiful there. Come to Jackson Hole with me. There's as much opportunity there as here. Why not make a fresh start for yourself too?" Dean said.

My mouth fell open as I stared at him for a moment. A myriad of emotions ran through me. Sadness, fear, anger and above all, surprise.

"We don't even know what this is, Dean. You're asking me to leave my family, job, friends, and go with you?"

"You can move in with me, and see where this leads."

"And if it doesn't work?" I said as I wondered if he had given it any thought.

"We're great together. We'll figure it out as we go along," Dean said.

"Life isn't as easy as being on the back of a Harley. Dean, I have kids here and my mother and sister. I can't just move across the country."

"Why not? It's your life, Maggie. You can do anything you want to do. Your kids are adults with lives of their own. They can always visit us," Dean said casually.

"We live in the same state now, and I don't see them as often as I would like. I would never see them if I lived in another state. My life isn't just about me. I can't leave everything on the chance that you and I might work out. Besides, you don't even know my favorite color," I said crossing my arms over my chest.

"It's never come up," Dean insisted. "Besides, we'll have plenty of time to learn things about each other. I gave George my resignation today. I asked him to keep it private for now. He'll, of course, talk to Ben, but I don't want anyone else knowing about this. I've also contacted a real estate agent about selling my house."

"Wow. You're serious about this. I guess you've made your decision. How much notice did you give George?" I asked.

"Two weeks. Think about it, Maggie. It would be an adventure. Please. You could join me whenever you like. It doesn't have to be in two weeks," Dean assured.

"I wish I was as carefree as you. But I don't think I'm a fly-by-the-seat-of-my-pants type of a girl. I need to know certain facts before I could ever pack up and change my life this drastically," I said.

I stood up from the bistro table, placed my hands on my hips, and walked back inside feeling misunderstood. Dean stood up and followed me. He wrapped his arms around me from behind and spoke into my ear.

"You've left your positive mark on me. I know I haven't said it before now, but I do love you, Maggie," Dean said softly.

"No, Dean. There's a difference between loving someone and

being in love. We have an unusual bond; I have to admit. But is it love? I'm very attracted to you, and you're so dear to me. But..."

"Uh, oh. But?" Dean asked.

"I can't change my life for you. I don't want to move to Jackson Hole," I said plainly.

Dean let go of my waist and took a step back. "I didn't imagine you would say no. I thought you would be all in for this," he said disappointedly.

"How could you think that? That's my point. If you knew me, you would know I wouldn't leave my family. You are asking me to change my life, and I can't do that. Not out of any obligation but because I don't want to," I tried to explain.

Dean's face was full of disappointment, and his eyes began to water. I held his face in my hands and looked into his eyes and said, "I won't be able to pass a motorcycle on the road without looking to see if it's you. I cannot begin to explain what you've meant to me these last few months. We have a lot of fun together, but how long would that last? I can't go with you. Carolyn was the love of your life. Eventually, I would want more than what you're capable of giving me. Neither of us should settle."

I kissed him long and hard before I pulled away from him and walked to the front door.

"So that's it? Maggie," Dean said wiping his eyes. "I'll always be here for you. You can call me for any reason at all. I'll make sure you get all my forwarding information. I won't ever forget you. You must know that."

I smiled at him as tears slid down my face. I opened the door and said, "See you at work on Thursday?"

"Yeah," Dean said and looked down. As he approached the door, he stopped and said, "I'll see you on Thursday." He leaned over and kissed my cheek and smiled at me.

As I closed the door behind him, I clutched my chest, feeling a powerful sense of loss. We were survivors. Mr. Beasley looked up at me and whined in sympathy. I picked him up and headed toward the sofa in the living room. I could hear my mother say, "God sees the bigger picture, Ellie."

# Chapter 43.

My promotion was postponed for the next two weeks while George and Ben searched for a new store manager to replace Dean. George no longer had spare time to teach me the ins and outs of the bakery business.

Michael came back to work on a part-time basis. Part of his recovery was to ask for forgiveness from those he had hurt during his addiction. He began by speaking to the kids he had invited to party with him. His example, I hoped, would make an impact on their carefree minds. Eventually, Michael asked me to join him on a coffee break.

"Maggie, you probably can guess why I want to talk to you. I've saved you for last because I don't know how to begin to apologize to you. Aside from my father and brother, I wronged you the most. Had something happened to you in Gabriel's hands, I can't imagine how I could have lived with it.

And it's not only that. I stole from your registers because I was desperate and disguised it as payback. After you turned me down, on several occasions, I treated you disrespectfully and then set you up by stealing. I behaved unconscionably. I was rude and arrogant toward you. You could have sued me for harassment, but you didn't. I'm very sorry for all of it, and I hope that you can forgive me," Michael concluded nervously.

I searched Michael's eyes for sincerity. I believed he was. His eyes were moist, and his manner was humble.

"Michael, I can see you mean what you're saying. Who am I not to forgive you? It takes a lot of courage to confess these things and strength too. I accept your apology, and I do wish you every happiness.

Never give up on yourself, Michael," I said.

Ben came down the stairs as Michael and I concluded our conversation. His face lit up when he saw me, and so did mine. We spoke quietly and tried to act casually.

"You are a sight for sore eyes, Ms. Bloom."

"Crazy last couple of weeks, huh?" I asked.

"To say the least. Can I take you to dinner tonight?" Ben asked.

"I think that would be a great idea."

"Seven?"

"Perfect," I agreed.

After a lovely dinner, we came back to my place for coffee. Mr. Beasley greeted us at the door. Ben scooped him up, while I turned on the radio to the smooth jazz station. With the music playing quietly in the background, we drank our coffee in the living room facing each other on the sectional. Mr. Beasley sat between us.

"Maggie, I'm sorry I haven't seen much of you lately. Between Dean leaving and Michael's recovery I'm not sure if I'm coming or going," Ben said.

"I understand. Don't even worry about it."

"How do you feel about Dean's decision to leave?"

"I think it's a good decision. Dean has not been himself since his wife died, and I think a new start is what he needs," I admitted and looked inside my coffee cup.

"Has he broken your heart?" Ben asked.

"No. Dean did ask me to go with him."

"He did?" Ben looked at me alarmed. "What did you say?"

"I said no, of course. It's hard to explain. We bonded over widowhood. I will always have a special place in my heart for Dean. I was never in love with him nor was he really with me. I think it's easy to get attached after you've experienced loss as we had. You think no one knows how you feel," I said and shook my head. "Maybe for Dean, it was the idea of me. I don't know," I said and shrugged.

"I'm pretty sure it was you. You're irresistible, you know?" Ben said.

"Am I? I don't know about that," I said and laughed.

"I'm sorry you're losing a friend. But, I would be lying if I said that I wasn't relieved."

I studied Ben for a moment. "Enough about Dean," I said to change the subject. "How are you?"

"Michael's recovery has been nothing short of miraculous. He assures me he can handle the business from now on. I've put in place operations and procedures for the business; such as checks and balances. I would like to believe Michael is well, but we'll have to wait and see. I've decided to move home at the end of next week. I'll be in the valley every two weeks to start, and then once a month. George does a great job, and he'll look after things for me here. I made him promise not to retire any time soon." Ben said and shook his head.

I felt overwhelmed. My life seemed to be a roller coaster. "Well, it seems as if things are falling into place for you. That's good," I assured him.

"Do you remember the first day we met?" Ben smiled.

"How could I forget? One of the most embarrassing days of my life. My modus operandi around you; I continue to embarrass myself. Why is that, I wonder? Perhaps your dashing good looks unnerves me," I said as I smiled.

"Yeah, I'm sure that's it. You were coming down the stairs, and I was going toward them. You missed that last step and went sailing into me. Had I not been there, you would have splattered yourself across the floor. You could have seriously injured yourself. You might even say, I saved your life. Your knight in shining armor," Ben teased.

"I think you might be giving yourself too much credit," I teased back.

He laughed and brushed my cheek. "When I helped you upright, our eyes met. That's when I knew my life would never be the same. As crazy as it sounds, Maggie, it was love at first sight for me. Of course I tried to deny it.

I may be moving back to San Diego, but I'm not moving away from you. We can take this as fast or as slow as you'd like. I'll be here every two weeks for now. I can fly you to San Diego anytime you want to come," Ben said to reassure me.

I could feel my heart expand with every word. I picked up Mr. Beasley and moved over to nestle in next to Ben. Mr. Beasley growled as I put him down again. I rested my head on Ben's shoulder and sighed.

"What are you thinking?" Ben asked brushing his mouth across the top of my head.

"Right this very minute, everything is right with the world. I'm not sure how long that might last, so I'm just going to live in the moment," I said and looked up at him.

"Hmmm. Then it's probably a good time for a kiss," Ben said.

"I think you should and for as long as you like."

# Chapter 44.

On Dean's last day of work, he took me on our final Harley ride. We duplicated our very first ride out to the old bridge. After watching the sunset, he maneuvered the Harley back through the country roads to my front door. We fell into our usual routine. I took off his jacket and placed it on his helmet and handed it back to him.

"I want you to keep the jacket. Something to remember me by. Besides, it looks good on you," Dean said and smiled.

"Thanks, I'll wear it proudly."

"Bring it with you when you come and see me. There are beautiful places in Wyoming that I would love to show you from the back of my Harley," Dean offered.

"I'm not sure how Ben would feel about that."

"Oh yeah, ...that. Serves me right for not paying attention. I have a strange feeling that you'll be the one that got away," Dean said as he touched my cheek with the back of his hand.

"I think Miss Right will sneak up on you when you're not looking. Then you'll ride off into the sunset together," I assured him.

He shook his head. "Kind of like you snuck up on me. Don't forget me," Dean said.

"I don't think that's possible," I said as I smiled at him.

I hugged him and held on tightly for a moment. I gave him a quick kiss goodbye and unlocked the front door, shutting it behind me. I smiled, as I listened to his Harley make its way to the security gate and onto the street. That was yesterday.

Today, I was reliving the moment in my mind as I drove my Mini toward San Jose to meet David Combs. Ben wasn't with me. He was finishing up business at the store before heading back to San Diego.

I left Henry a text that I was meeting with David and promised he would hear from me immediately after it was over.

I found Wasabi's and pulled into the parking lot. As I stepped inside, I imagined Edward walking through the same doors, years before. It was eleven-forty-five, and our meeting was at noon. I sent a text to Henry that I had arrived safely. The waitress showed me to a small table that afforded a view of the busy downtown streets of San Jose.

I hadn't been waiting long when a small framed man, with dark thinning hair, stood by my table. He asked if I was Margaret Bloom. I stood up to shake his hand.

"Please call me, Maggie. You must be David."

"I can't tell you how happy it makes me, to finally meet you," David said.

"Please sit," I motioned to the other chair. "I'm sorry to say that it wasn't until recently I heard your name. I'm anxious to hear the connection you had with my late husband, Edward."

"Let me start by saying how sorry I was to hear Edward had passed away," David said with sincerity.

"Thank you."

"Your husband was an integral part of my success. Edward mentored a group of us in the business department over at San Jose State. We had formed an incubator group off campus, and someone knew someone, who knew Edward, and he came down to talk with us one day. He asked us questions about ourselves and our plans for the future, that sort of thing. A buddy of mine named Robert and I were developing a piece of software at the time." David swirled the ice in his water glass as he thought back.

"Edward thought the idea was brilliant. He connected us with some people he knew, who could help us market the product. The amazing thing about Edward was he didn't want anything out of it. Edward was happy to help. He believed in us and our product and wanted to help us succeed," David said and smiled.

I listened to David describe Edward. He was just as David remembered. The man I knew before our lives got messy. Edward was a good man. I saw the same integrity in Henry.

"We couldn't get our hands on enough seed money to get the project off the ground. So without hesitation, Edward gave us ten thousand dollars to start our business," David continued.

"So, he did give you the money after all. We found a napkin with 10K written on the back of it from this restaurant. I honestly would have tossed it into the trash, but my son Henry was curious about it," I said.

"I can't tell you how happy I am that he was curious. Henry has good instincts. We tried several times to get in touch with Edward to finalize a contract between us. When we finally got through, I spoke with a woman by the name of Elizabeth Baxter. She informed us Edward had died. Edward's cell phone was disconnected shortly after."

"That was my sister. She handled a lot of things for me at the time," I interjected.

"Well, let's fast forward to the present," David said. He reached for an envelope that was tucked away in his leather portfolio. He handed me the envelope. I took it and looked at it curiously.

"What is this?" I asked him.

"With the recent purchase of our business, I hoped I could give you this someday. It's a repayment on Edward's investment with us," David explained.

"Oh, thank you. The money will come in handy for tuition," I said. I placed the envelope beside me on the table.

"Maggie, I'd like you to open it," David said as he clasped his hands together while his elbows rested on the table.

I gave David a puzzled look. Curiosity was getting the better of me, so I picked up the envelope and opened it. I reached inside and pulled out a check. I gasped. My hands began to shake. I was looking at a check in my name, for seven point two million dollars and change. My mouth fell open as I stared at the piece of paper. I could not believe my eyes. I tried to speak, but couldn't articulate even a syllable. "How... what?" I stammered. I held one hand to my chest while the other held the check and trembled. "How could this be? David, this has to be a mistake," I finally managed to say.

"Edward's investment paid off in more ways than one. We sold to a major software corporation, and that's his share of his investment. It gives me great pleasure to see his family receive it."

I shook my head. "David, I'm speechless. I don't know what to say. Thank you is so insufficient."

"It is I who owes a debt of gratitude to a selfless man, who believed in a couple of college kids. I would like you to know he spoke of you, Henry, and Izzy a great deal. He loved his family. He showed me pictures of you in his wallet. That's how I recognized you when I came inside the restaurant. Except you had straight hair then, I believe. He received my calls at all hours and met with us as often as we needed him."

I touched my hair while tears cascaded down my face. Joyful, proud, loving tears. Dear, sweet, sentimental Edward.

"Your husband was an honorable man, Maggie."

"As you are, David. This meeting means a great deal more to me than this check. You have restored my faith in the world and the memories of my husband. Thank you for the kind words about him. My heart is... full. Thank you for all of this," I said and touched his arm.

"Any ideas what you'll do with it?" David smiled.

"Well, I think I should find a financial adviser and update my trust for starters. Then, I think I'll be purchasing an airplane ticket," I said thoughtfully.

"Where to?" David asked.

"Italy. I have a promise to fulfill," I declared.

We exchanged contact numbers and wished one another well. I hugged David, and he walked me to my car. Sliding in behind the wheel, I immediately sent a text to Henry: I'm fine. You will never believe what happened. All is well; I'll call you tonight. David is an exceptional man. xoxo mom.

I sped down the freeway toward home. There was only one person I couldn't wait to see. When I got to the valley, I drove directly to the store, hoping I hadn't missed Ben. As I pulled up to the store, I saw Martha getting out of her car. She stumbled and fell. As I slowed, I realized she looked severely beaten. I pulled up next to her and jumped out of the car to help her.

"Martha! What's happened?" I asked frantically.

"Oh Maggie, I didn't know where else to go. I was hoping you were here," Martha managed to say.

I walked her around to the passenger side of my car and helped her in.

"I'm taking you to a hospital. I thought you were in San Francisco?"

"I was until Stanley found me and brought me home."

"Did he do this to you, Martha?" I questioned her.

"Yes," she said and wept.

"Well, we're going to make sure he never does this to you or anyone else again," I promised her as I sped toward the hospital.

# Chapter 45.

After a long wait in the ER, Martha finally was seen by a doctor. The hospital was legally obligated to report the crime, so a police officer came over to take Martha's statement. Hesitant to press charges, I convinced Martha it was the right thing to do, along with obtaining a restraining order. Someone like Stanley should not be allowed his freedoms.

Thankfully, she had no broken bones; the rest would heal in time. I took Martha home and set her up in my spare bedroom. I called my mother to help me bring home Martha's car. I didn't want it left in the parking lot for Stanley to find.

Mother gasped when she met Martha. But Mom has a beautiful way of making people feel comfortable. She talked to Martha about Mr. Beasley and in no time had her smiling. I gave Martha an ice pack and water for the pain medication her doctor had prescribed. I told her not to answer her cell phone, primarily if it was Stanley. We would be right back with her car and in the meantime, she should get some rest.

"You're safe here, Martha. No one knows that you're here. Get some sleep," I said to reassure her.

On our way to the market, Mom asked me what I was planning to do with Martha. "I don't know if she has anyone else except Stanley. I'll have to ask her. In the meantime, she and Mr. Beasley will stay with me."

I parked Martha's car inside the garage next to my car. Martha was sleeping when I checked on her. I poured two glass of wine and took Mom out onto the patio.

"You will never believe what happened to me today," I began.

"Something other than the beaten woman in your spare bedroom?"

"Yes. I was on my way home from a meeting with a man named David Combs."

I explained the story, from the 10K on a napkin to the seven million dollar check. Mom looked at me in disbelief. Her mouth gaped open just like mine did. She asked for another glass of wine. She looked at me as if her eyes were playing a trick on her as she stared at the check.

"I can't believe my eyes, Ellie. Amazing isn't it? Edward did this for you and the children. Any idea what you want to do with it?" Mom asked.

"Well, like I told David, I need to find a financial adviser first and update my trust. I could do some good with this money. I could help a lot of people. Henry could have his food truck, and I'm not sure what I can do for Isabella, yet."

"Ben could help you with the financial adviser part. But what about you, Ellie? Edward would have loved you to do something for yourself," Mom said and smiled.

"He promised me we would go to Italy someday. Maybe now is a good time. You want to come along?" I said and laughed feeling as if I were in a dream.

Mother sat with me a while longer and then decided it was time for her to go home. I called Henry as I promised. I knew he would be waiting anxiously.

"Mom? I've been thinking about you all day. What happened with David?" Henry asked.

"You are never going to believe what I'm about to say to you," I said into the phone.

I shared with him the entire conversation I had with David. I
wanted him to see how proud he should be of his father.

"He was a good man, Henry, and he loved us all very much. The
money is real. But let's keep it between us for now."

After disconnecting with Henry, I checked on Martha. I could
hear her crying as I approached the bedroom door. I gently knocked
before I came in. As I sat down on the edge of the bed, I gave her a tissue
from the box on the night table.

"Maggie, what am I going to do?" Martha cried.

I brushed her bleached blond hair away from her face and
scratched Mr. Beasley's head.

"The first thing you need to do is come into the kitchen and have
a bite to eat. My grandmother used to say life always looks better after a
bowl of good soup."

I helped her up and walked her over to the breakfast bar. I
motioned her to sit, as I filled a bowl with chicken noodle soup I had
prepared especially for her.

"This looks wonderful, Maggie. Thank you."

"Your welcome. Martha, do you have any family you can call?"

"Not anyone who would want to hear from me."

I looked at her briefly. "Well, you have me. You can stay here as
long as you need to. I don't want you to worry."

"Thanks for taking such good care of Mr. Beasley. He looks
happy," Martha said and tried to smile.

"He's grown on me."

"I knew you'd like him."

"Would you like to talk about what happened," I asked her.

"Not really. I don't know what I'm going to do on my own. I'll need to get a job. But who's going to hire me? I don't have much work experience other than a waitress, but that was a long time ago. My husbands never wanted me working. All I've ever been is a trophy. Now, look at me," Martha mumbled.

"You are more than a pretty face, Martha. I can tell you're smart, you have a big heart, and you love animals. We'll figure it out another day. Today, you need to soak in a nice warm tub and get some rest. I promise you won't have to do this alone. I'll help you. We'll figure it out together."

"Maggie, why are you so nice to me? You hardly know me," Martha asked shyly.

"I know you well enough. Besides, I like you," I said to her.


The next day over breakfast while still in our pajamas, I asked Martha to dream a little. "While I'm out shopping for you, I want you to make a list of possibilities."

"What do you mean, possibilities?"

"What is it you would like to do with your life? Or learn to do? Take a few days and dream big, Martha. There's no wrong answer, and the sky is the limit. Can you do that for me?" I asked.

# Chapter 46.

"Hi, Maggie. It's good to hear your voice," Ben said. "I called Henry when I didn't hear from you. He told me you were alright. How did your meeting go with the mystery man?"

"It went well. I'm sorry I didn't call you, but you won't believe what happened."

"Maggie, we have a history. I've been in a constant state of disbelief since I've met you. Are you safe?"

"Yes. I'm safe. But I need to see you. Are you here or San Diego?" I asked Ben.

"I'm in San Diego."

"I was on my way to the store from my meeting in San Jose, hoping that you were still there. When I pulled into the parking lot, I found Martha badly beaten," I explained.

"What? Was she attacked?" Ben asked.

"Yes, you can say that. By Martha's idiot husband. I guess she was right to get away from him after all," I said.

"You're kidding me?" Ben was incredulous. "That's too bad. She was probably right about the dog too."

"That's why I never made it inside the store to talk to you. I took Martha to the hospital and then to my house. She filed a police report," I said.

"Should I be worried you're involved?" Ben asked. "Do you know anything about her husband?"

"She pressed charges and filed for a restraining order. He has no idea that she's at my house."

"Let's keep it that way," Ben said calmly.

"I'm on my way to see George. I'm going to resign, Ben," I said.

"Resign?"

"That's why I need to see you in person. I have some news, and I need your advice. Can I come and see you?" I asked.

"Of course, Maggie. Just let me know when to pick you up at the airport," Ben offered.

"It will depend on my conversation with George and if my mother is willing to stay with Martha for a few days. I don't want Martha to do anything stupid while I'm away."

"Ok, sure. Just let me know. I'm always here for you," Ben replied.

"Thanks. We'll talk soon," I said before disconnecting with Ben.

I deposited my check and met with George. I told him my time at Bay's Market had come to an end. Grateful for the opportunity, I confessed my experiences at the market would stay with me forever.

"I need time off due to a family emergency. At this point, I don't know when I'd be back. Therefore, I thought it best to resign," I explained to George.

"I'm very sorry to hear that, Maggie. You're an exemplary employee. I wish we had more like you in this store. Go ahead and turn in your apron, key card, and badge. But if you decide you would like to return at any time, just let me know. I'm sure I speak for Ben and Michael too. I wish you well and hope everything turns out for the best," George said and shook my hand.

I thanked him and turned in the items he requested. It seemed as though it was just yesterday that Dean had first handed me a badge. I remembered how much it had meant to me.

After picking up some items for Martha and Chinese food to go for dinner, I headed home. I called Mom and explained my trip to San Diego. She suggested that Mr. Beasley and Martha come to stay at her house. Over Chinese food, I said to Martha I was leaving for a few days, and I felt better knowing she wasn't alone.

"I can't believe your kindness, Maggie. No one's ever cared two straws about me," Martha said.

"Well, I do. And my mother does. To tell you the truth, you're doing me a favor. I need someone to keep an eye on her. I wonder what she's up to," I said and smiled.

On my laptop, I checked the flights to San Diego. I booked a six o'clock flight for the following day. I texted Ben the information and added: P.S. Can I stay with you and Sam?

Ben: Your room's available, and I wouldn't have it any other way. Can't wait to see you.

Me too, sweet dreams.

I opened my closet and pulled down a small suitcase. I placed it on the bed and unzipped it. In the top drawer of my dresser, under all my garments, was a large envelope I had almost forgotten. I removed it and held it to my chest. My name was on the front. I sat on the edge of my bed and opened it. Inside the envelope, was a letter addressed to me and another envelope that was sealed. On the outside of the sealed envelope was the name of someone unfamiliar to me and an address written in Italian. I unfolded my letter and read it.

My Dearest Maggie,

You have been such a blessing in my life. I have treasured our moments together since you were a baby. You are now grown up and a

319

lovely woman. I have watched you with your children, and you are a beautiful, loving mother.

I have left this letter in your care because I know you are the only one I trust. I am asking you to promise me that someday you will deliver this letter in person. When you were a little girl, you would ask me about my home in Italy. Nonna, you would say, take me to Parma. And I said, Maggie, I cannot go, but I know that you will someday. Please, take this letter to Parma for me, my little Nipote.

We are the same you and I. When I look at you, I see my own heart. Go to Parma when you can. I will have to believe it will not be too late. Be happy, my Tesora. Choose wisely. Listen to your voice and follow your heart.

Con amore di,

Nonna


I folded the letter and put it back and placed both envelopes inside the larger one. I packed what I needed for my trip, including the letters. I was ready for San Diego.

I joined Martha and Mr. Beasley in the den to watch television. We decided on an old classic with Cary Grant. When it was over, I got ready for bed. Ben reminded me of Cary Grant.

I couldn't wait to see Ben tomorrow and dream of him tonight. But instead of dreaming about Ben, I saw my grandmother. She was telling me to hurry. There was an urgency in her voice. Before it's too late, she urged. Fulfill the promise. Awaking from a deep sleep, I heard myself say, I'm leaving Nonna. I'm on my way soon.

# Chapter 47.

My palms began to sweat in anticipation of seeing Ben. He was waiting for me as I got off the plane in San Diego. I threw my arms around his neck and hugged him tightly. He reciprocated with a quick kiss.

"Hello, beautiful," Ben said.

"Hi, handsome.

"What do you say we blow this nightclub and go somewhere we can be alone?"

"Sounds like a plan to me," I said and smiled.

Ben unlocked the front door to his condo and carried my suitcase to the guest room. I freshened up while he made sandwiches.

"Is Samantha home?" I asked.

"Nope, she's out with Henry. We have the place all to ourselves. When are you planning to tell me what this visit is all about?" Ben asked.

"After I eat this delicious sandwich you made for me. I'm hungry. What kind of pickles are those?" I asked.

"Homestyle. You know how to keep a guy in suspense, don't you?" He teased.

After dinner, we sat on the sofa with hot cups of tea. I had Nonna's letters waiting on the coffee table. My story began with the meeting in San Jose and the check David had given me. When I finished, Ben sat staring at me.

"He gave you a check for seven million dollars?" he asked.

"Yes. Seven million and some change," I said smiling.

"And it was real?"

"Yes. But I didn't know what to do with it, so I deposited it into my savings account," I said.

"So you're telling me that my hot girlfriend is also a millionaire?" Ben asked.

"Well, multi-millionaire. I need a financial adviser, a new trust and whatever else you think I should have and I need it soon. That's why I'm here."

"Ok. I know people," Ben said still processing the information. He looked at me and nodded.

I slid closer to him on the sofa and snuggled up to him. "I knew you would know people. There's something else," I said.

"Why does that scare me. What else?" Ben said as he inhaled deeply.

I reached over to the coffee table and picked up Nonna's envelope. I opened it and showed him the sealed envelope and my letter.

"My grandmother died a little over fifteen years ago. She gave me this envelope right before she died and had me promise I would hand deliver it as soon as I could. I haven't kept my promise to her until now. I want to leave for Italy as soon as possible. But I need to know all my affairs are in order first. And I want to ask you another favor. If something should happen to me, would you please, help Henry and Isabella in the execution of the trust?" I asked Ben.

Ben sat quietly for a moment. "I'll do anything you ask me to," he said as he reached for my hand. He ran his thumb over the top of my hand. "When are you planning to leave for Italy and how long would you stay?"

"It depends on how soon we can set up appointments with an adviser and a lawyer. Once we get everything in order, I would like us to meet with Henry and Isabella, so they are aware of everything before I leave. I don't know what's in the letter. So, I don't know what to expect when I get there. I don't even know if this person is still alive," I said.

"It sounds like another Maggie Bloom adventure," Ben said and smiled.

"So, what are you thinking, Ben?"

"A lot is going on in your life. You've had a hell of a year. I know how much I'm going to miss you," Ben said as he bit his lip. Ben brought me in closer to him. He lifted my chin to look into my eyes.

"Maggie, nothing better happen to you. It's taken me a long time to find you. Are you going alone? Maybe you should take someone with you," Ben asked.

"Nothing's going to happen to me. That would be too cruel to us both. I thought about taking my mother. It is, after all, her mother's letter," I said.

"About the letter. Maybe you should leave a photocopy of it with me. I lived in Italy for a while. I read and speak Italian fairly well. Should you need it translated, I could probably do that for you. I promise you I wouldn't read it unless you asked me to. I'll shred it if you don't," Ben offered.

"Hmmm. That might not be a bad idea. Let me think about that. How soon do you think I can get an appointment with your people?"

"I'll make some calls in the morning."

"Good. I feel anxiety about all this money sitting in my former small bank account. The sooner this business gets taken care of, the better I'll feel."

"Of course, you'll have to stay here until I can make the necessary appointments," Ben said as he lifted his brows.

"I see where you're going with this."

"By the way," Ben said. "I got an e-mail from George. I guess you no longer work for us?"

"No, I do not. George was wonderful. Although, I wish I could see Melissa's face when she finds out we're dating," I said and laughed. "Melissa has it bad for you. Every time she saw us talking, she shot daggers out of her eyes at me," I said.

"Then it's official. Since you are no longer an employee, you can be my girlfriend," Ben said and smiled.

"Does that mean we're going steady?" I asked.

"Yep. You want to make-out until Sam gets home?" Ben asked.

"Yep."

# Chapter 48.

Martha was now a proud student enrolled in Cosmetology School. Eventually, Martha's customers will benefit from her life experiences after she received her diploma.

"I can't believe you've done this for me, Maggie. You've paid for my education, my clothes, food, and given me a roof over my head. You've inspired me. I'm going to pay it forward. After I graduate, I'm going to volunteer in battered women shelters and help them feel beautiful about themselves. Free services for women needing a fresh start," Martha explained.

"I think that's great. I believe in you, Martha. I think your idea is an excellent one. It's the reason we exist; to help others. Whether it's a stranger or a friend we've known a lifetime. These past few years, I've learned that nothing we gain on earth is ours--it belongs to those we give it to. It doesn't have to be money; a kind word or a good deed can change someone's life.

As far as the roof over your head, it's yours until I get back from Italy. Then, we might renegotiate," I said teasingly. Then I picked up Mr. Beasley and held him to my face. "Besides, Mr. Beasley loves the garden."

I convinced Mom to travel to Italy with me. She's never liked airplanes, so I baited her with first class tickets and cocktails. Martha and her pup dropped us off at the airport in Mom's car. The luggage wouldn't fit in my Mini and Martha was ordered to return her car to her ex-husband.

"Remember Martha, take the Mini out on the freeway while I'm gone. The girl likes to stretch her legs every once in a while."

"Will do Maggie. I'm sure going to miss you. Have a great trip." I gave them both a hug and told them to take care of each other.

Our first stop was LAX. Mom and I checked in and headed toward the gate. After a two hour layover, we would fly nonstop to Parma, Italy.

We settled in with a cup of coffee and snacks. I was purchasing magazines when my phone buzzed with a text message.

Ben: Hi beautiful. I'm here at the airport. Where are you?

I paid for my magazines and rushed over to where Mom was sitting.

"Mother. Ben is here at the airport!" I exclaimed.

"He is? Well, you have to go and find him," she said calmly.

"I don't know where he is. If I leave, I'll have to go through security again."

"Go, find him," Mom insisted. "I'm perfectly happy right here. You should see him before we leave."

I texted: Tell me where you are, I'm coming down.

After dodging hurried people and a few escalators, I spotted Ben through the glass. I waved at him enthusiastically. When I got through the gate, I jumped into his arms, and he spun me around.

"Why didn't you tell me you were coming?" I scolded.

"I wanted to surprise you. I couldn't let you leave the country without seeing your beautiful face," Ben said holding me tight.

"Call me should anything come up, and I'll check my e-mails regularly," I said.

"Text me when you've arrived and settled. So, I don't worry. I hope this village you're staying in has Internet," Ben said.

"The brochure says it does," I placated.

"Don't fall in love with any tall, dark, and handsome Italian men. They can be very persuasive," Ben said.

"I've learned I can handle only one handsome man at a time," I replied.

"Good. Keep your head down, Maggie. If you need me, for anything at all, I'll be on the next flight out," Ben promised.

"I'm pretty sure my luck is changing. I better start making my way back," I said regretfully.

Wrapping my arms around his neck, I gave Ben a long, hard kiss. He brushed the curls away from my eyes and studied my face. I was going to miss him.

After I got through security, I turned and waved goodbye to Ben. He was standing on the other side of the gates. He was waving his arms in the air and shouting something to me.

"Maggie," he shouted. "Sposami!"

Thank you for joining me on the first *Maggie Bloom* adventure with **Paper or Plastic**. If you enjoyed this novel, please go to Amazon and leave a rating and comment. These ratings are very important to authors. Your ratings help us with visibility and growth and getting our books into the hands of those readers interested in our stories.

**FULFILL A PROMISE** is the second book in the *Maggie Bloom* series. I hope you will join Maggie as she travels to Italy to fulfill a promise she made to her dying grandmother. She has quite a few adventures and heart tugging revelations. I think you'll enjoy the trip.

**In Full Bloom** is the third *Maggie Bloom* novel in the series. You can find more information on its release at: veralinton.com.

For more novels from Vera Linton visit: veralinton.com

*Buona per ora.*
*(Goodbye for now.)*

Made in the USA
Coppell, TX
28 January 2021